THE DURHAM DECEPTION

Recent Titles from Philip Gooden

The Cathedral Murder Mysteries

THE SALISBURY MANUSCRIPT
THE DURHAM DECEPTION ★

The Shakespearean Murder Mysteries

THAT SLEEP OF DEATH
DEATH OF KINGS
THE PALE COMPANION
ALMS FOR OBLIVION
MASK OF NIGHT
AN HONOURABLE MURDER

★available from Severn House

THE DURHAM DECEPTION

Philip Gooden

This first world edition published 2011
in Great Britain and the USA by
SEVERN HOUSE PUBLISHERS LTD of
9–15 High Street, Sutton, Surrey, England, SM1 1DF.
Trade paperback edition first published
in Great Britain and the USA 2011 by
SEVERN HOUSE PUBLISHERS LTD.

British Library Cataloguing in Publication Data

Gooden, Philip.
  The Durham deception.
  1. Newlyweds – Fiction. 2. Lawyers – Fiction. 3. Mediums –
  Fiction. 4. Magicians – Fiction. 5. Murder –
  Investigation – Fiction. 6. Durham (England) – Social
  conditions – 19th century – Fiction. 7. Detective and
  mystery stories.
  I. Title
  823.9'14–dc22

ISBN-13: 978-0-7278-6995-1   (cased)
ISBN-13: 978-1-84751-332-8   (trade paper)

All Severn House titles are printed on acid-free paper.

Severn House Publishers support The Forest Stewardship Council [FSC],
the leading international forest certification organisation. All our titles that
are printed on Greenpeace-approved FSC-certified paper carry the FSC logo.

MIX
Paper from
responsible sources
FSC
www.fsc.org   FSC® C018575

Typeset by Palimpsest Book Production Ltd
Falkirk, Stirlingshire, Scotland.
Printed and bound in Great Britain by the
MPG Books Group, Bodmin, Cornwall.

For Eleanor

Act One

The curtain rises and the first reaction of the audience is puzzlement. They have been expecting something eastern, exotic. But there is no painted backdrop depicting snow-capped mountains and plunging ravines. There are no rocks or trees which might conceal apes and serpents. There is nothing at all, in fact, except a tent-like structure surrounded by patterned fabric on three sides and open to the audience on the fourth. In the centre of this space sits a three-legged table not much larger than one which would be used in a card game. The table is bare, without a cloth of any kind.

Then on to the stage strides Major Sebastian Marmont. He is a short man with the soldier's swagger and a complexion long burnished by foreign suns. He wears a tropical suit and a solar topi. He is greeted by applause. Those who have not yet seen him and his Hindoo troupe are familiar with his reputation and, despite that unpromising card-table, they give him the benefit of the doubt. Major Marmont raises one hand to quieten the audience. He steps towards the footlights.

'Ladies and gentlemen, I appear before you tonight as a soldier – as a traveller – and most of all as a tireless seeker into those strange realms which lie tantalizingly beyond our reach – the realms of mist and mystery. It is well known that the source of everything which is truly wondrous and magical in our world lies to the east. Yet, through my endeavours, I am able to bring to all of you assembled here tonight an experience from the fabulous Orient such as has hitherto been vouchsafed only to the privileged few even in those antique lands.'

The Major pauses to let this sink in. He turns slightly and claps his hands, once. On staggers one of his servant boys. The boy is cradling a black travelling case like a small hat box. The Major wags a finger at him to indicate that he must handle the case with particular care. The boy passes the case to the Major who accepts the burden in an almost reverential spirit before dismissing the boy with a nod of the head. Major Marmont places the case in the centre of the table. He stands back. He says, 'Ladies and gentlemen, behold the Sage of Katmandu.'

Major Marmont moves forward again to the case on the table and unfastens the lid, which is hinged. He folds the lid back so that the interior is revealed. It contains a human head. It is the head of a holy man set within folds of red silk. The head has flowing white hair and a seraphic expression. Its eyes are closed. The audience gasps. A few of them start to look at the Major with suspicion and alarm. (There has recently been a celebrated murder involving a head, a torso, two suitcases and the left-luggage department of a railway station. The murder filled the more sensational papers for weeks.) But this object, realistic as it seems, is surely made of wax.

In the meantime the Major has shifted to the side of the stage. He too is gazing at the disembodied head as if he had never seen such a thing in his life before. He is tugging at his moustaches. Now he claps his hands once more, not in the commanding style he used to summon the boy but in a way that is gentle, almost deferential. He says softly, 'Sage, awake.'

The eyes of the head flick open and move from side to side, then up and down, as if the head is ascertaining exactly where it finds itself. There are more gasps from the audience. Then the head of the Sage of Katmandu smiles, as if it is pleased to be here, in this very theatre on this very evening. The smile is not ghoulish or disturbing, it is actually quite benign.

'Sage,' says the Major, 'you have enjoyed a long rest, I hope, in your voyage across the continents of the world.'

The head moves slightly up and down. It is nodding in agreement. Some of the wiser heads in the audience are nodding too. They can see how this trick is worked. It's easy when you know. This is a head made out of wax or a similar substance, somehow operated by pumps or cords or other machinery, although the space beneath the table is absolutely bare. The head will open its eyes and smile. It will nod in agreement and even shake in denial but it will not be capable of speech.

Yet the mouth does open! The head does speak! It says, 'I am content.'

The voice is a curious strangulated sing-song. Is this how people speak in India? Perhaps it is.

The Major, still standing to one side so as to give the audience a clear view of the white-haired head within the box on the table, says, 'Sage, are you prepared to answer questions from these good folk assembled here tonight? They are eager to hear your pearls of wisdom.'

'They are welcome.'

The Major looks round the audience. He shades his eyes with his hand and gazes across the stalls and up into the galleries. 'Your questions, ladies and gentlemen? Ask anything you like.'

No one wants to be the first to speak out. Then comes a screech from the gods: 'Ask 'im where my 'usband is, the bastard! 'E walked out three weeks ago.'

There is some guffawing from the upper reaches of the theatre, as well as plenty of tutting and shushing sounds from the more expensive seats down below. Major Marmont pretends not to understand the question. The Sage of Katmandu blinks slowly as if a response to that kind of query is beneath him. Soon a more sensible demand comes from a gentleman in the stalls (three shillings, reserved). The question is: 'What is the secret of the universe?'

The Major turns towards the head in the box. The head nods and the wide brow furrows slightly.

'The secret of the universe?' it muses. 'The answer lies all around us. But you will not find it by searching for it. You must wait for it to reveal itself . . .'

The head continues in this vein for some time. The same individuals who thought they had the head worked out – it's a waxwork animated by compressed air – now check to see whether Major Marmont is throwing his voice. He's a ventriloquist. That must be the solution. But no, it cannot be, because Major Marmont is wiping his brow with a handkerchief and then drinking from a tumbler of water brought out by one of his boys. He is pretending to be hot and thirsty but, of course, he is really demonstrating that it is almost impossible for him to throw his voice several yards across the stage and simultaneously to be draining the tumbler to its dregs. Nor is there any change in the voice of the Sage of Katmandu as he continues to unravel the secret of the universe.

A couple of other questions are thrown at the Sage ('Where is happiness to be found?' 'Above our heads, below our feet, within our grasp.') before the Major brings proceedings to an end when he asks the disembodied head to show its esteem for the British nation by reciting from their greatest writer. So the Sage reels off most of the 'To be or not to be' speech from Hamlet in a voice that is not so strong as formerly. Since its powers seem to be fading, Marmont thanks the head, wishes it a peaceful sleep and closes up the lid of the case.

The Major lifts the case from the table and bears it towards the footlights. Once again he unlatches the lid and displays the interior to the audience. Cries of surprise. The case no longer contains the Sage's head nor even the silk which had surrounded it. Instead there is a mound of reddish dust or ash.

'Do not trouble yourselves, ladies and gentlemen,' says Major Marmont. 'The Sage of Katmandu has the ability to dissolve and recreate himself time after time. It is a power beyond our understanding; it is the magic and the mystery of the East. The Sage of Katmandu will return in his own good time, with more wisdom from the Orient.'

The Major tips a little of the red dust on to the stage floor in demonstration. Then he closes up the case for a final time and hands it to a boy who carries it offstage. There is a small pause while the audience struggle to take in what they have just seen, a talking head which could answer questions and recite from Shakespeare and which has now been reduced to a heap of dust. Then someone begins to clap, and then half a dozen more and, within seconds, the theatre is filled with volleying applause and wild cheering. The building seems to shake with the noise.

Major Marmont bows to every quarter of the house before striding off with the same manly soldier's gait. For an instant the little table is left in its alcove illuminated by the lights, so that everyone can see that's all it is – just a bare three-legged table – and then the curtain comes down.

67, Tullis Street

'Are you nervous?' said Tom.

'Why do you ask?' said Helen.

'Because your arm through mine feels awkward, and you haven't said very much for the last few minutes.'

'I've been picking my way along the street with care,' said Helen, 'and I am holding on to you for support. It's wet and slippery underfoot.'

It was an early Sunday evening in May but still overcast after the rain which had left a greasy deposit on the pavement. Church bells were ringing and couples were strolling to evensong or just taking the air after being shut up all day. Helen was right, you needed to be careful as you walked. But Tom thought that was just an excuse. She *was* nervous.

'And you, Tom? Are you nervous?'

'Me? No, more curious.'

'Liar.'

'Apprehensive then.'

'I will settle for that,' said Helen, tugging Tom so that he was closer to her. 'Let's be apprehensive together. It's an adventure though, isn't it.'

'And good material for you.'

'We'll see.'

Tom and Helen Ansell were walking arm in arm along Tullis Street which lies to the north of the British Museum. They had taken a cab as far as Maple's in the Tottenham Court Road and got down there because Tom said he wanted to walk the last few hundred yards, even though Helen complained her skirts would pick up the mud. Really Tom wanted to delay the moment before they reached number 67. Not for the first time he was regretting that he had said yes to Helen when she suggested this little outing. This adventure.

Tullis Street was rather dreary in the present weather, perhaps in any weather. The houses were flat and dun-coloured. The windows on the ground floor were smeary with the recent rain. Tom wondered what Mr Smight's callers thought when they came to visit. The man was supposed to have had a distinguished list of clients once: a peer of the realm, Lady such-and-such, as well as a couple of MPs and a manufacturer or two. But perhaps his visitors weren't concerned with appearances or even reassured by a plain style.

They arrived at number 67. Tom noticed a man and woman loitering on the other side of the street. The man looked at him curiously. Tom turned his head away. There were railed steps which led up to a peeling front door. Tom went ahead of Helen and knocked. A housemaid opened the door almost immediately as if she had been waiting on the other side.

'Mr and Mrs Thomas Ansell,' said Tom. It gave him pleasure to say 'Mr and Mrs Thomas Ansell'. He went out of his way to say the words. They were like the ingredients in a pleasing recipe. Helen and he had been married at the beginning of the year.

'You're the first,' said the maid in a familiar manner. She was a girl with pinched cheeks and dark rings under her eyes. She stood to one side of the narrow passage to allow them to enter and then shut the front door before taking Tom's hat and his furled umbrella. She almost hurled the umbrella into the stand where it landed with a clatter. She took their coats and hung them up. Then she indicated the front room.

'You're to wait in there . . . if you please . . . sir and madam. That's the waiting room.'

Tom and Helen went into the front parlour. In the centre was an oval table surrounded by half a dozen dining chairs, only one of them with arms. A large gilt-edged bible was set, unopened but prominent, on a lectern near the door. On the other side was a cottage-piano. Whether because of the bible or because of the musty smell of the room, Tom was reminded of the interior of a church on a wet afternoon. The furniture was heavy and the walls cluttered with pictures. Gaslights were burning low on either side of the fireplace but the lamps were dirty, and the gloom of the room was scarcely relieved by the evening light that filtered through the lace curtains.

Tom and Helen stood uncertainly in the dimness. They could see themselves in a large mirror which was set over the mantelpiece and seemed to be hanging at a dangerous angle. There was no one to overhear – the maid had shut the door firmly on them – but nevertheless Helen whispered into Tom's ear, 'It's more dowdy than I expected.'

'It's very dowdy,' said Tom. But he was pleased at the dowdiness. A bright and cheerful room would not have felt right. Helen paced about, manoeuvring between the furniture as silently and inquisitively as a cat. Tom was content to watch her. Eventually she went across to the oval table and lifted the green baize cloth which covered it. The cloth was too large for the table and its fringes lapped at the legs of the chairs. Helen stooped, peered underneath and then dropped the cloth back with a satisfied 'hmm'.

'What is it?'

'Have a look beneath.'

Tom did so but saw nothing unusual although it was hard to make out much, given the shadows underneath and the general gloom of the front room.

'Well?' said his wife.

'I don't know. It's just a table.'

'Dear Tom. Although it's got these dining chairs around, it's not really a dining table, it's too small. And it is resting on a single central column which means there's much more give in it than there would be with a regular four-legged dining table. More play.'

To demonstrate, Helen pressed her hand a couple of times on an imaginary surface.

'Easier for table-rapping and table-turning, you mean?' said Tom.

Helen nodded and went on, her voice rising as she was caught up by the certainty of what she was saying, 'If we were allowed to examine the underneath of that table properly and in a good light we'd probably find all sorts of things. Compartments and hidden drawers and sliding panels. And you see the glass over the mantel?'

'I see you in the glass.'

'Then look at how this chair is placed at the table. It's the only carver out of the set so it's probably where *he* sits.'

'He?'

'The gentleman we are here to see.'

'Well? What's the link between chair and table?' said Tom. He had already guessed but he asked for the pleasure of hearing Helen make her deductions.

'He can keep an eye on everyone else round the table by glancing up at the reflections in the glass. It hangs at a slant so it would be easy to see from the chair. While the sitters are all eyes on him, he's watching them back, front and sides.'

'You're a suspicious person, Helen.'

'I'd prefer to be called sceptical.'

'A sceptical and imaginative person then.'

'That's better.'

As Tom was kissing Helen on the cheek, the door opened behind them. They swung round, slightly guilty. A large and alarming-looking woman swept in. She was dressed in black. Her complexion was strawberry-coloured and her hair stuck out from beneath a beaded cap surmounted by a single curled green feather.

'Have I the pleasure of addressing Mr and Mrs Ansell?' she said and then proceeded before Tom or Helen had the chance to nod agreement. 'But of course I have. Even if the girl had not told me of your arrival I would have known *you*, my dear. You are Mrs Helen Ansell, née Miss Helen Scott.'

She stretched out her heavily ringed hands and took one of Helen's between them. Seized rather than took. Tom saw his wife's delicate fingers and palm disappear into the clasp of hands which were as red and chapped as if their owner washed her own laundry. But Helen kept her self-possession and did not try to snatch her hand back.

'I'm afraid you have the advantage of us,' she said. 'I am not sure I have ever had the pleasure of meeting you before, madam.'

'Nor I you, though I knew who you were straightaway,' said the woman. 'I am Miss Smight, Miss Ethel Smight. Oh but I can see the likeness in you.'

'Likeness?'

'To Julia Howlett. Your aunt.'

'Aunt Julia. I have not seen her for many years. How do you know my aunt?'

'You are the very image of her,' said the woman, finally letting go of Helen's hand but not answering the question. 'The image of her when she was younger, much younger of course.'

'But how do you know her?' persisted Helen. 'And how do you know we are connected? I was never a Howlett but a Scott and I have another name now.'

She brushed her hand against Tom's sleeve. Tom thought she was enjoying herself. The woman, presumably a sister to Mr Smight, pushed some of her straggling hair back beneath her cap before replying.

'I knew your aunt well at one time. I knew your mother when she married Mr Scott. I am also a devoted reader of the marriage announcements in the newspaper. People of my age are sometimes said to prefer the death column, but I am all for life, yes all for life! When I saw at the end of last year that a Miss Helen Georgina Scott of Highbury was to marry a gentleman called Mr Thomas Edward Ansell, I said to myself that she must be the niece to my old friend, Julia Howlett. Said it over the breakfast table not only to myself but also to my brother Mr Smight. So when our maid told me that a Mr and Mrs Ansell had arrived, I put two and two together. I wonder what brought your feet to our door?'

'Destiny?' said Helen. Tom could tell she was speaking lightly, if not flippantly, but the woman treated the answer with seriousness. Miss Smight peered through the gloom at Helen.

'Is it destiny? If you are able to say such a thing, then perhaps you have the gift.'

Helen looked sideways at Tom, who said, as a way of getting himself into the conversation, 'What gift is that, Miss Smight?'

'There is only one gift that matters,' said the woman, leaving them not much the wiser. 'You have favourable features, Mrs Ansell. Helen, if I may call you that. Blue eyes and fair hair are particularly conducive.'

'That's what my husband always says,' said Helen, looking sideways again. Tom thought she was trying to stifle a giggle.

'He is a wise man then,' said Miss Smight, looking full at Tom for the first time. 'A wise man, sir, to appreciate the value of blue eyes and fair hair. And a wise man altogether to judge by the shape of your head. If you will permit me . . .'

Miss Smight put out her podgy red hands and gently pressed the fingers into the sides of Tom's head. As when she'd seized Helen's hand, she acted as if it were her right to do so.

'It's a pity we have no time for the callipers; in order to take the exact dimensions of the skull, you know.'

'I can do without the callipers,' said Tom, as Ethel Smight continued to palp the sides of his head. She reached round the back of Tom's head and then ran her hand over the top of it. Tom had almost had enough when she lowered her hands and stood back. She cocked her head and the attitude made Tom think of a great bird.

'Ho hum,' went Miss Smight, sounding like a doctor. 'The organs of Conscientiousness and Hope are well developed in you, Mr Ansell. They are next to each other, you know. Secretiveness is quite prominent in you too. That property lies on either side of the head just above and behind the ears. Would you say you were a secretive man?'

'What if I refuse to answer?'

'Hah, good. But the most developed organ or bump is one which also happens to be unique. It is the site of Amativeness and it is the only organ in the skull which stands by itself. It has no mirror in the other hemisphere. As a newly married man, you are an individual with a well-developed organ of Amativeness. An amative husband.'

Helen, still standing near Tom, was gripped by a sudden fit of coughing and had to get out a handkerchief to cover her mouth. It was as well, perhaps, that the maid knocked on the door at this point to announce the next visitors.

'Mr Seldon and Mrs Briggs.'

A man and woman were ushered into the front room. Tom thought he recognized them as the couple who had been hanging about on the other side of Tullis Street when Helen and he arrived at number 67. Their connection was quickly explained: they were engaged to be married. The man was slight with pointed facial features. Mrs Briggs, presumably a widow rather than divorced, was larger than her fiancé and had a dull bovine stare. They looked awkward and uncomfortable at being here, but then, Tom reflected, that wasn't so surprising. Perhaps they had been waiting on the street for others to arrive first before summoning up the nerve to come in themselves. Tom, too, felt uncomfortable, particularly after his skull inspection at the hands of Miss Ethel Smight.

She might have been about to try her technique on the newcomers but was prevented by the arrival of two more visitors in quick succession. Both of these women seemed to be known to Miss Smight and were not announced. There was a young, rather attractive one with a mass of lustrous dark hair, and a severe-looking one in middle age. The young woman was referred to by Miss Smight as Rosalind – if she was given a last name Tom didn't hear what it was – while the older was plain Mrs Miles.

After brief introductions had been made, Miss Smight directed them to take their places at the oval table. She said that it would have been better to alternate the sexes but with two men and four women that was obviously not possible. Tom and Helen sat next to each other with Mr Seldon and Mrs Briggs facing them, and the two single women towards the narrower end. As Helen had predicted, the dining chair with arms, the one facing the mirror, was left empty.

Miss Smight went across to a sideboard, opened a drawer and brought back a collection of small objects, cradled in her arms. She placed them on the baize tablecloth apparently at random. They included a little handbell and a tambourine. Then she left the room.

'It's always a tambourine, isn't it?' said Tom to Helen in a half-whisper. He had never been to one of these events before but thought he should say something, should say anything, to show he wasn't going to be easily taken in.

'They use it because it's small and it makes a noise when it flies about,' whispered Helen.

The two women, Rosalind and Mrs Miles, looked vaguely disapproving at this while the engaged couple gazed straight ahead. The silence was broken by the opening of the door and the appearance of Mr Ernest Smight. He stood there for a moment as if he were making a stage entrance and ready to acknowledge any applause. He inclined his head with a slight smile at his guests. Behind him loomed Miss Smight.

The medium was an imposing man with pale, clear-cut features and a neat moustache. He wore a cravat which was the same green as the feather in his sister's cap. He sat down at the head of the table while Ethel fussed over him, brushing a speck of dust now from one shoulder, now from the other. At first sight there didn't seem any likeness between brother and sister. But the light was not good and it grew poorer still when Miss Smight went to draw the curtains and turn down the already dim gas lamps on either side of the fireplace. The room became sepulchral. Ethel Smight retreated to sit on an armchair in the corner.

'My friends,' said Ernest after a long pause. He steepled his hands like a man in ostentatious prayer. His voice was an actor's voice, resonant and cultured. It was too big for the room. Tom's suspicions were beginning to be confirmed. 'We should join hands for a moment.'

Tom regretted that Helen was sitting between him and Mr Smight. But she put out her right hand willingly enough for the medium to take while she slipped her left into Tom's, who gave it a squeeze. With his own left he clasped Mrs Miles's right hand and wished it had been the dark-haired Rosalind's. Mrs Miles's hand was cool and dry. They all sat like that, in a hand-in-hand ring round the oval table. Ernest bowed his head for a few seconds. Then he looked up in the direction of his sister.

'I require vibrations. Give me a verse please.'

His sister stood, edged her way round the room to the little upright piano, drew out a stool, sat down again and plinked out a few bars. The piano needed tuning. Tom thought he recognized the opening of *Jesu, Thou art all our Hope*. As the music started to play, Ernest nodded as if to show he was receiving the vibrations he wanted. The music stopped abruptly. Ethel sat back on the piano stool. There was another prolonged pause.

Tom was starting to wonder what, if anything, was due to happen next when his ear was caught by a chinking sound. It was coming from the surface of the table. In the very centre had been positioned the tambourine. Tom couldn't be sure but the simple instrument seemed to be regularly rising and falling a few inches up and down above the baize cloth, giving itself a brisk shake each time it did so. He couldn't be sure because the light in the room had grown even dimmer and his eyes seemed to be watering. Yet the tambourine was surely moving a few inches, now up, now down. Then it was time for a contribution from the handbell which made a few dinging noises although without moving.

All this while they sat hand in hand round the table. As the tambourine moved and the bell sounded, Tom felt Helen's hand tighten in his own sweating grasp. Mrs Miles's by contrast stayed cool and unmoving. She'd probably seen it all before. Holding hands was a guarantee that no one could be manipulating the objects on the table – yet the trick might be done with devices involving wires or extending tongs. And where was Ethel Smight? What was she doing? Still at the piano? Tom thought so but the room now seemed so hazy that it was hard to make out.

The noises stopped. Ernest Smight, who had been sitting with his chin sunk on his chest, suddenly looked up in the direction of Mrs Miles. When he spoke, his voice was different, not so resonant, more familiar.

'There is a spirit appearing behind you, dear. A short gentleman with a tanned complexion. He is young but with lines on his face as if he was accustomed to spending a long time in the open.'

Mrs Miles shook her head in a sign that she didn't recognize the description.

'And his clothes are wet,' continued Ernest. 'He is holding something in his hand which I cannot quite discern. A piece of rock, perhaps.'

'He is my brother, Robert,' said the dark-haired Rosalind, speaking for the first time.

'Ah, I see how he moves towards *you* now,' said the medium. 'He has visited us before. I did not remember him at first. There are so many spirits pressing in on me.'

'Robert died three years ago in an accident in California,' said Rosalind, partly to herself, partly to the others round the table. 'He was prospecting for gold. He suffered an accident with a hydraulic sluice. Has he a message for me?'

She spoke in a matter-of-fact way as if she was describing a trip her brother had made to the shops. Tom noticed that she didn't turn round to look behind her. He could see nothing there. Nevertheless he felt a tightness in his chest.

'Yes, your brother Robert has a message for you,' said Ernest. 'He says that you are to follow your heart. Does that make sense? To follow your heart.'

'Oh yes,' said Rosalind with more animation now. She didn't elaborate.

'He is smiling and nodding with pleasure. He is pleased that you understand. Now he can depart.'

Mr Smight nodded with satisfaction himself. He let go of the hands on either side of him, Helen's and Mrs Briggs's, and rubbed his temples. Then he glanced round the table. His eyes fixed on Tom for an instant before darting behind the lawyer's shoulder.

'I can sense a presence behind you, sir.'

'Me?'

Tom's instinct was to turn round but he managed to conquer it. All the same, he felt cold air on the back of his neck as if someone were blowing on it.

'Another young man, of about your own age I should say. And he is a soldier, to judge by his uniform.'

'A soldier?' said Tom, his voice sounding strained to his own ears. 'But I don't know any solders.'

'This gentleman is wearing a blue uniform. He is smiling fondly down at you. This time I am not mistaken. It *is* you he is looking at.'

'Oh God,' said Tom. His head and body were rigid with struggle. Half of him wanted to turn round, the other half wanted to stay staring frontwards. As if sensing his discomfort, the medium said, 'Keep still, sir. *You* would not be able to detect anyone. But from your response I take it that you know to whom I am referring.'

'Possibly. I am not sure. Can you say more about . . . what you can see?'

'It is a peculiar coincidence but this gentleman also is wet, as if he had been immersed in water. Yet his blue uniform is fresh and shining for all that. Are you acquainted with anyone who has drowned, my friend?'

'No,' said Tom. He was reluctant to say more but suddenly the words tumbled out of him. 'I don't know anyone who drowned. But my father was buried at sea many years ago. I hardly knew him. He was on his way to fight in the Russian War. He died on board ship before he could arrive and was buried near the Dardanelles. I was quite young.'

To Tom it seemed as if someone else was speaking these words, yet he recognized the voice for his own. He had heard the details of the death and sea-burial only recently from a former comrade of his father.

'He has a message for you,' said Ernest.

'I did not know him,' said Tom.

'But he knew you, sir, and he continues to know you – from the other side of the veil which separates all that is mortal and perishable from that which endures for ever. Your father is proud of you and what you have accomplished. He has a warning though. His message is that you are to be careful. He sees danger ahead for you and your good lady.'

Tom had almost forgotten Helen's presence beside him. Her hand still rested in his.

'There is danger by some woods, danger near a stretch of water. That is why he has come in this guise, soaking wet in his blue uniform. There is danger, too, from an individual who is not what he seems to be.'

'I can't make sense of this,' said Tom.

'I am merely the conduit, the medium of the spirit world,' said Ernest Smight. 'I do not claim to understand all. Now he fades away, his blue uniform absorbed into the shadows.'

There was a pause. Tom realized he was soaked in sweat. What had he just witnessed? Was it real? Not really real, but really the spirit of his father?

If Tom had turned round in his chair, could he have seen the man he had last glimpsed when he was a child? No, he would not have been able to detect anyone. Only Ernest Smight could do that. *If*, indeed, the medium was being truthful. Part of Tom wanted to believe but the other part, the larger one perhaps, was highly sceptical.

Meanwhile attention had shifted round the table to the couple on the side opposite from Tom and Helen. Arthur Seldon, the individual with sharp features, had placed a coin on the table. It was a half-sovereign, its gold gleaming dully in the gloom. Ernest seemed to start back from it but Tom observed how his eyes fastened on the money. Seldon added a second half-sovereign. The medium's hand hovered then stretched out to shift the coins closer to him.

'Accept them as a love-offering,' said the man. 'They are yours whether you are able to help us or not.'

'I will help you if I can.'

'It's not for me but for her,' said Seldon curtly. The bovine woman nodded. When she spoke, her voice had a surprising sweetness of tone.

'It's my husband, my first husband I should say. He was run down by an omnibus. Can I be put through to him?'

'Where did the accident occur?'

'In the Fulham Road.'

'I am not receiving any impressions,' said Ernest Smight after perhaps half a minute. He rubbed his temples again. 'Wait, I seem to have the sense of a name beginning with the letter E . . . Edward is it? Edmund maybe. Or even Ernest.'

'That's not it, none of them,' said Mrs Briggs. 'Does the name of Angus bring him to you?'

'Angus?' said the medium. 'Possibly. It is hard to tell. There are figures in a mist, all clamouring for attention. However one is coming to the fore. Yes. A tall man, would you say?'

'Why yes, you might say so,' said Mrs Briggs. 'Angus was large, unusually large.'

'He wants to know why he has been summoned back to this mortal vale.'

'I need his advice,' said the woman. 'I am about to be married to Mr Seldon here, and I want to know whether my previous husband – Mr Briggs – is content with that.'

Tom, still feeling the shock of apparently hearing from his father, wondered how the medium was going to answer this woman in the presence of her fiancé. But Ernest Smight was all tact.

'Not everything is revealed to us but, if it is Angus whom I can glimpse in the shadows, he is nodding his head. Your happiness is what matters to him. If you are content then so is he.'

'*I* have a question for him,' said Arthur Seldon. 'Her late husband, the one who was run over by an omnibus, he kept some savings in a cash box in the house. My question is, will we find the box? We have failed to find it so far. Should we keep looking?'

'My dear sir,' said Ernest Smight, 'that is such a material question and you must know the spirits want nothing to do with earthly, material things. They have moved beyond that. What use is coin if one is fed and clothed by the ethereal powers? Nevertheless, Mr Angus Briggs – if indeed it is he – is again nodding his head in a way that I can only interpret as encouragement. Yes, you should keep searching for the cash box.'

There was a sudden stir from behind Tom and Helen. The gaslights flared and the room was illuminated more brightly than before. It was Ethel Smight who'd turned up the lamps. Tom had thought she was still at the piano but at some point in the proceedings she must have got up and moved round the room. Had she been responsible for that cold draught on the back of his neck?

The medium's sister said, 'We should stop this now, Ernest. Say nothing more. I do not trust these two.'

She was referring to Mr Seldon and Mrs Briggs. Her warning came too late. Seldon reached inside his jacket and produced an official-looking badge.

'Despite my civilian clothes I am a policeman, Mr Smight.'

'All are welcome at our table, whether they come in disguise or in plain honesty.'

The medium was doing his best to put on a brave front but, by the brighter light, his face had gone pale and pasty while his voice lost all its confidence. He was older than Tom had first taken him for. Miss Smight's face, by contrast, was bright red. She stood glaring in outrage at Arthur Seldon.

'A complaint has been laid against you . . .'

'A complaint? Has it? By whom?'

'I am not at liberty to say,' continued Seldon.

Ernest Smight sighed and seemed to shrink in his chair. 'What have I done?'

'Money has changed hands.'

'It has not changed hands,' said Ethel Smight. 'It hasn't, has it?'

She was appealing to the others, to Tom and Helen, to Mrs Miles and Rosalind. The single women looked baffled and slightly frightened. All four gazed at the two half-sovereigns, lying golden on the green baize.

'You seemed to accept the coins, Mr Smight,' said Tom, though even as he spoke the words he wondered why he was getting involved. This was no business of his. Yet he persisted. 'I am familiar with the law and you seemed to accept them.'

'In return for services about to be rendered,' said the disguised policeman Arthur Seldon, nodding at Tom as if grateful for this confirmation. 'Services were duly rendered. You have told fortunes and you have predicted the future. You have predicted that I will find money but I can assure you there is no cash box left by Mr

Briggs. If there had been, *she* would've have laid her hands on it straight away.'

'I predicted that your fiancée would be happy with you,' said the miserable medium. 'Surely you do not hold the prediction of happiness against me?'

'I do not,' said the policeman although his tone suggested he resented the idea of happiness. He smiled for the first time that evening, and Tom was reminded of a sharp-toothed rodent. 'But you see, sir, this lady who is assisting me in my enquiries is not my fiancée. She cannot be my fiancée for the simple reason that she is already my wife.'

'Yes, I am now Mrs Seldon although my first husband *was* called Briggs,' said the woman.

'Angus, I suppose,' said Ernest hopelessly.

'Ha, no. I once had a cat called Angus. Several of the facts I provided were correct. Angus the cat *was* large and he *was* run over by an omnibus, a misfortune which occurred in the Fulham Road.'

'My wife, Lizzie, she did not lie, you see,' said Seldon. He reached over and took up the two half-sovereigns from where they lay on the table in front of the medium, who turned his head away. 'These coins are not mine but will be returned to the police station. I will make a full report on this and I would be surprised if you do not find yourself up before the magistrates, Mr Smight. This is not the first time you have been caught out. Do not expect leniency.'

Seldon paused to let that sink in. He was thoroughly enjoying himself. He produced a notebook and pencil as he gazed at the other sitters round the table. 'And as for you, ladies and gentleman, any or all of you may be called upon as witnesses to what occurred here this evening. To wit, how this person told my and my wife's fortunes in return for a cash payment. Your names and addresses if you please.'

A kind of official frost settled over the room while Arthur Seldon noted down four names and three addresses. Mrs Miles lived in Bayswater. Miss Rosalind Minton lived in Camberwell but added that she worked in a shop on Oxford Street. Helen gave her and Tom's names and their address in Kentish Town. The policeman wrote all this down in a small hand while his wife looking on approvingly. When he'd finished he snapped the notepad shut and said, 'Your details I do not need, Mr and Miss Smight. You two are already in our files.'

'It's not fair,' said Ethel Smight. 'It's not fair.' She was divided between anger and tears.

'I don't make the law,' said Seldon. 'I merely enforce it.'

With that he and his wife got up from the table and walked from the room. Moments later they heard the front door slam. There was silence round the table. Ernest Smight looked like a man who has been hollowed out while his sister, with her red face surmounted by the green-feathered cap, had the appearance of an angry and exotic bird. Mrs Miles looked as bland as before but Rosalind was dabbing at her eyes with a lace handkerchief. Helen's hand was still within Tom's.

Abercrombie Road

'I don't see what's so wrong with it,' said Helen. 'If that disguised policeman was right about the law then any fortune-teller at the funfair ought to be brought before the magistrate. But that doesn't happen, does it? You can be sure that quite a few policemen and even a magistrate or two go to have their palms read at the fair. And pay for it.'

Tom and Helen Ansell were walking home. It was still light and the earlier overcast skies had partially cleared to show the setting sun. The air was clearer than on a weekday because the factories were closed. Evensong had long finished but quite a few people were still strolling about in their Sunday best. Tom and Helen wanted fresh air after being confined in a front parlour which was somehow both chill and stuffy. They wanted time to talk about what they'd just seen, to talk out in the open and not shut up inside an omnibus or a hansom cab clattering its way towards north London.

The séance had broken up as soon as Arthur Seldon and Mrs Briggs – or rather Mrs Seldon – departed. Rosalind Minton and Mrs Miles were sympathetic to the Smights, telling them that *their* testimony would hardly be much use in court because they could not be sure of what they had seen. Besides, they knew Mr Smight and his sister for honest people. They said this, glancing defiantly towards Tom and Helen. Perhaps they would have said more if Tom had not been identified with the authorities in some way.

Tom was unable to make the same half-promise about any testimony. He was pretty sure that, in law, the medium had accepted money for services to be rendered. He felt sorry for the brother and sister but at the same time he was impatient with them and impatient to be away from this place. The slightly better light in the parlour revealed how worn and shabby was the furniture, and hinted at why Ernest Smight had fastened on the half-sovereigns.

Surprisingly it was Helen who was more distressed by what they'd seen. She had been the one looking for evidence of fraud under the table before Miss Smight's arrival. She'd speculated on how the fakery might be done and talked about tambourines, but now on the way home she sounded indignant rather than justified.

'There's nothing wrong with fortune-tellers at funfairs,' said Tom. 'They'll never be prosecuted. But Seldon was right, all the same. The law won't hold back. Smight won't get leniency if he's been hauled up in front of the bench before.'

'I don't understand.'

'The law was never meant to apply to a palm-reader at a fair. It's been dormant for years until it was brought back for individuals like Ernest Smight. Mediums can be prosecuted under the Vagrancy Act of eighteen-something-or-other, which was originally intended to deal with vagabonds and gypsies and such. People like that weren't supposed to make money by pretending to foretell the future. They weren't supposed to make a nuisance of themselves at all.'

'But this is different, it is nothing to do with gypsies. It is getting in touch with the dead and hearing their messages. In fact, all their messages were reassuring. Did you notice, Tom? Everything was all right, everything was going to be all right.'

'I thought you didn't believe, Helen. You're the sceptic. You're convinced none of it is true.'

'I am still a sceptic. It will take more than this evening to unconvince me. But Tom, you have heard from the spirit of your father!'

'My father? I don't know. How could it have been? A man in a blue uniform. It might have been a lucky guess by the medium.'

'But the person he saw was soaked to the skin – and your father was buried at sea.'

'Twenty years ago. He should have got out of those clothes by now. He'll catch his death.'

'You are making jokes about it but I can tell were affected by what Mr Smight saw. What he *said* he saw. Your hand was in mine, remember. You were sweating and tense.'

'Let's be rational about it. How many people know some details of my father's death? Quite a few. Others could find out. It's probably written down in some army record. And there's your mother! She knows of course. And it was your mother who told us about Ernest Smight. She suggested we went to consult him.

Probably she mentioned something about my father's death to him or to his sister. And there's another connection. Miss Smight used to know your aunt.'

'But Miss Smight did not seem to have any warning we were coming.'

'She's a good actress.'

'Besides I don't think my mother has communicated at all with the Smights even though she might have known them once. Mother is not well disposed towards mediums and the spirit world. Why should she have said anything to a man she distrusts?'

'Then why did she ask us to go and see him?' said Tom.

'You know why,' said Helen. 'Because of what she has asked me to do. She wants me to have some knowledge of the world I am entering.'

'Like Daniel going into the lions' den.'

'I hope not. Anyway, you'll be with me,' said Helen. 'What will happen to him?'

'Him? Oh, Ernest Smight. He'll be lucky if he is only fined. He could get a month or two in gaol, perhaps with hard labour.'

'Hard labour? But that might kill him. He did not look strong.'

'He'll only get that if he comes up before a magistrate who doesn't like mediums.'

'What if we are called on to give testimony? That policeman took down all our details.'

'He was doing it for effect, to show his authority.'

'We could always say that we saw no money change hands. I would not like to be responsible for sending a man to prison. I didn't care for Mr Smight or his sister very much but they seemed harmless enough.'

'I doubt if we'll have to testify. The word of the policeman and his wife will probably be enough, especially if Smight has performed these tricks before.'

'I agree with Miss Smight. It still does not seem fair. Tom, I have had enough of walking.'

They hailed an omnibus which was going towards Kentish Town. They might have taken a hansom but two journeys by cab in one day seemed an extravagance. Tom, by himself, would have climbed to the roof of the bus but the exposed seating was not really suitable for ladies even if Helen had made a point of doing it a couple of times in fine weather. So the Ansells sat in the cramped interior which was oddly like the Smights' front room, stuffy and cold at the same time. It was like the Smights' too because there were half a dozen other people inside the compartment, strangers pushed up against each other.

The Ansells got out of the bus at the near end of Kentish Town Road. They walked the short distance to their terraced house in Abercrombie Road. Number 24, which they had taken on a three-year lease, was newer and in better condition than the houses in Tullis Street. This spot on the edge of town was about right for Tom and Helen. It was affordable, although they had to be careful with their money (saving on hansom cab journeys, for example). The air was good, or at any rate less dirty and smoky than the air in the centre. There was quite a bit of building going on as the suburbs spread north, and there was a sort of bustle associated with the whole area. The people moving into their street and the neighbouring ones were, by and large, professionals like Tom.

Tom and Helen employed a maid-of-all-work – an amiable, youngish and plain woman called Hetty – who helped with the cooking. They'd contemplated doing without anyone but it didn't seem right somehow. Tom was glad there was company in the house for Helen while he was at work. The place would do for a couple of years until they needed somewhere bigger when the children arrived, or until Tom increased his salary at the law firm of Scott, Lye & Mackenzie in Furnival Street.

Helen was born a Scott, as Miss Smight had accurately remembered from the marriage announcement. Her father, one of the original founders of Scott & Lye, had been dead these several years, and while Mr Alexander Lye occasionally shuffled into the office, his chief activity was to scrawl his signature on correspondence placed in front of him. That left David Mackenzie as the principal partner. Tom had hopes of becoming a partner in due course but he wanted to do it on his own merits and not because of his marriage.

Helen was not content merely to sit at home, presiding over a house which was much smaller than her family home in Highbury while she waited for the almost inevitable children to appear. Instead, she was writing a 'sensation' novel, a three-decker along the lines of those penned by Mary Braddon. Helen's novel involved an heiress who had been cheated out of her property and abandoned by her fiancé because of the actions of a villain. The heroine, whose name was Louise Acton, was compelled to go to extreme lengths to regain her place in the world. Tom hadn't been allowed to see any of this unfinished book, although he did hear from time to time that his wife had enjoyed 'quite a good day' at her desk or that she was reaching an awkward corner in the plot.

Recently, Helen had a short story published in *Tinsley's Magazine*. It was her first appearance in print. William Tinsley himself wrote a gracious note to accompany the cheque for five pounds. The story was called 'Treasure' and Tom read it with admiration and a touch of amazement, hardly able to link the words on the page with the person who was sitting on the other side of the fireplace and pretending to read a book while covertly watching for his response.

Once inside number 24, they settled to a cold supper which Hetty had left for them. As she usually did on Sunday evenings, the maid was out visiting her sister who lived a few streets away. Tom and Helen's mood was subdued, mostly because of what they had seen and heard at Tullis Street. More than once, Helen mentioned Mr Smight's likely fate of a term in prison. After supper Tom tried to cheer her up. He mentioned Ethel Smight's attempts at phrenology, the science of reading character by feeling the bumps on the skull. Helen reminded him that his bumps of Conscientiousness and Hope were well developed.

'And Secretiveness,' said Tom.

'A useful trait in a lawyer.'

'And don't forget my bump of Amativeness. It is unique, according to Ethel Smight. You may feel it. Feel my bump of Amativeness.'

'Where is mine, I wonder?' said Helen.

Tom ran his fingers through Helen's fair curls and one thing began to lead to another. They were suddenly disturbed by the sound of the key in the door and the return of Hetty from her sister's. They giggled like children.

'Later, oh amative husband,' said Helen.

The Mission

Tom and Helen Ansell had gone to visit Mr Smight at the suggestion of Helen's mother. A week before the séance the couple
had been having tea with Mrs Scott at the Highbury house, an
occasional Sunday ritual. Although Tom no longer regarded his
mother-in-law as a dragon-lady, which was his view of her before
the marriage, and although he had even caused her to break into
a smile once or twice, he didn't enjoy these occasions much. Mrs
Scott would quiz him about Scott, Lye & Mackenzie, in which
she still felt a proprietorial interest, or she'd comment on Helen's
appetite – which was either too feeble or too eager – as a round-
about way of establishing whether there might soon be a happy
announcement.

This time, though, it was obvious that there was something
more on her mind than the law or babies. They'd hardly made
a start on the anchovy toast and the ham sandwiches before Mrs
Scott said, 'Helen, do you remember your Aunt Julia?'

'Of course I do.'

'You were always her favourite when you were little.'

'It is many years since I saw her.'

'She particularly mentioned you in her last letter. She hopes that
married life suits you. She never married, you know, although
she was the oldest of us.'

As Mrs Scott talked about her family, with an uneaten ham
sandwich in her hand, she was looking not at her daughter but
at Tom, who asked himself where this conversation was heading.
Helen sometimes mentioned her aunt Julia Howlett in a fond
but distant way.

'Married life suits us very well, mother,' said Helen.

'Your aunt will be glad to hear it when I next write to her.
She was wondering when she might see the happy couple.'

'Aunt Julia lives in Durham, doesn't she?'

'Yes. They have a fine cathedral there, I believe.'

'I don't think we have any plans to travel so far north at the moment,' said Tom, sensing that Mrs Scott had an axe to grind and that it would shortly emerge from its hiding place.

As a sign of her seriousness Mrs Scott replaced the ham sandwich, untouched, on the plate. She said, 'To be honest, my dears, I was wondering whether you *could* make plans to travel so far north. There is a railway line from London. I don't think the city of Durham is inside the polar regions.'

There was a pause. Tom was still recovering from Mrs Scott's attempt at making a joke when Helen said, 'Mother, why don't you tell us what's on your mind? It has been plain ever since you mentioned Aunt Julia that there's something bothering you.'

'Why yes, there is.'

'What is it?'

'I do not know whether it is because your aunt is unmarried but she never seems to have acquired – how shall I put this? – she has never acquired an inoculation against men.'

'What do you mean?'

'I mean that poor Julia never learned to close her ears to half – no, to three quarters – of what men are saying. Their stuff and nonsense if you'll forgive me, Thomas. The poor thing has always had an open heart. An open heart and an open purse.'

Ah, thought Tom, here it comes. Money has been mentioned.

'There was a missionary preacher a few years ago who was raising subscriptions for the unfortunate natives in some part of Africa, and your Aunt Julia was more than generous in giving him money,' said Mrs Scott. 'The fellow was no more a preacher than I am. He had one wife in Bradford and a second one in Newcastle, and probably other wives elsewhere. Certainly he had no intention of sending the money to Africa. He went to prison eventually, I am glad to say. It was reported in the papers. But Julia never saw her money again.'

'And now another preacher has appeared?'

'Not exactly. This time it is one of those spiritualists who claim to be in touch with the departed. A gentleman called Eustace Flask. Apparently he is making a name for himself in Yorkshire and Durham. And your aunt has fallen under his spell.'

'You make him sound like a magician,' said Tom.

'I wish he were,' said Mrs Scott. 'At least magicians are honest. They make a virtue of their trickery.'

'Where is the harm in Aunt Julia consulting a medium?' said Helen. 'Plenty of people visit mediums.'

'No doubt; but they aren't usually told to hand over their fortunes.'

Yes, here comes the money, thought Tom, helping himself to another piece of anchovy toast. Helen said, 'I knew Aunt Julia was well-off but I didn't know she had a fortune.'

'I may exaggerate but not much. Julia has always been lucky with money even though she knows nothing about it. Indeed, I sometimes think she is lucky precisely *because* she is ignorant. Our father left each of us girls a small but adequate sum when he died but only Julia managed to make it grow by investing it in – oh I don't know what – in the railways and mining stock and the like. And I believe she did no more than put a pin in a list in the newspaper! She puts her good fortune down to Providence. The result is that she is thoroughly comfortable and never has to lift a finger and I am glad for her because there is nothing worse than a crabbed old spinster living in poverty. But I almost wish she were poor because then she would not be preyed on by these tricksters!'

Mrs Scott took up the ham sandwich again and tore into it with as much vigour as if she were savaging the leg of a trickster. Helen glanced at Tom. Her glance said, this is serious. When her mother had swallowed the sandwich and regained a bit of control, she went on, 'Now this Eustace Flask person has persuaded your Aunt Julia that he is in touch with the spirit of our late father, and that *he* is instructing Julia to treat Flask like a son. The son she might have had if she were married! The spirit says that Flask is to be provided with a very generous allowance. She has already given him a handful of small cheques. It is an outrage!'

'Have some more tea, mother,' said Helen and she fussed over the pot and strainer and milk jug so as to give Mrs Scott time to calm down.

Eventually, Mrs Scott said, 'I am sorry, my dears, but I am very indignant over this. It is not so much that Julia is throwing away her money on a charlatan. It is that this wretched Flask person is invoking father in order to trick her. Helen, you can scarcely remember your Howlett grandfather, I suppose?'

'Not much, I'm afraid. An upright gentleman with tickly whiskers.'

'Yes, that will do. An upright gentleman. He would have had no time for these mediums and spiritualists if they had existed in his day. He would have called them humbugs. I can hear him saying the word now. So it is especially insulting that this wretch should invoke my father and pretend to be receiving instructions from him over on the other side. Thomas, would you mind bringing me that box?'

Tom went to a sideboard and brought back a little box which Mrs Scott unfolded on her lap to reveal a portable writing-block. Inside there was a flat baize-covered surface and holders for pens and an inkpot. Mrs Scott opened a compartment beneath the green baize and took out an envelope. From it she extracted a photograph which she passed to Helen who, after examining the picture for a few moments, handed it to Tom.

It was a small version of a studio portrait. A man sat in an armchair which was turned at a slight angle from the camera. He had a narrow face. Tom had the impression of very pale skin although that might have been the result of the studio lighting. It was difficult to get much of a sense of what he looked like because something had gone wrong with the exposure of the picture and everything appeared bleached. Nevertheless the man was smiling in welcome, as if to say: 'Here I am. What is it that you require of me?' His hands, resting limply on the arms of the chair, were long and the fingers adorned with rings.

'That is Mr Eustace Flask,' said Mrs Scott. 'You can see how besotted my sister is by the way she describes him in the letter which came with that photograph. She talks about his delicate complexion and his noble brow and piercing stare. She talks of the face of an angel in human guise. I can't see any of it myself.'

'Why did she send you the picture?' said Tom.

'She is like a young girl who has fallen in love for the first time and wishes all the world to see her sweetheart. Yet she is in her seventies!'

'What can we do?' said Helen.

'It is no good my writing to Julia to object to what she's doing. Whatever I said she would only take it as more proof that she is right. Tom, you're a lawyer. Is there any way this man could be stopped? Could he be prosecuted?'

Tom – who was always Tom and not Thomas to Mrs Scott

when her guard was down – thought for a while. He said, 'I don't think so. As long as your sister Julia is in her right mind and provided she is not under any kind of duress, well, she is free to dispose of her property and goods as she wants. Do you know how much she has given him already?'

'Not so much, I believe. This Flask individual seems to be very clever in his approach. He turns down the money for a first time and then a second time before accepting it, with reluctance, only when Julia tells him it is a contribution for the cause. The cause of spiritualism. He pretends to deny himself. She feels sorry for him as if he really were her son. She tells him he must take care of himself and wrap up warmly and eat properly, he is so thin and careworn. He may be thin but he does not look careworn to me in that photograph. It is sickening, I tell you, to see how she is being duped. In her last letter she said that she was considering making Flask an allowance because her father had indicated that was an appropriate course of action. Her father, *our* father, speaking through Mr Flask!'

'Perhaps Aunt Julia will see the light,' said Helen. 'Perhaps she'll suddenly see this man Flask for what he is.'

'Julia is too trusting. She still believes that the last one, the preacher with several wives, was essentially a good man tempted by Jezebels. I fear there is worse to come in this crisis. Her most recent letter, the one in which she enclosed the photograph so that I might admire her *angelic* medium, talked about her own failing health. She hinted she was not much longer for this vale of tears. If Julia is really in a weakened condition – although I must say that her handwriting was quite firm – then there's no saying what mischief Flask might wreak.'

'You mean he might prevail on her to change the terms of her will.'

'That is exactly what I mean, Thomas. It is bad enough her giving out a few hundred pounds here and there but to think of her whole estate falling into this trickster's hands . . . well, that is too terrible to contemplate. The shame for the family, not to mention Julia herself. No, there is only one hope . . .'

'What is that, mother?'

'I would like you and dear Thomas here to undertake a mission for me. Will you travel up to Durham and see your Aunt Julia for yourselves? You were always her favourite, Helen, as I said. She would listen to you where she would turn a deaf ear to me. And Thomas, with his knowledge of the law, might be able to do something. Perhaps he could confront this dreadful Flask. Threaten him.'

The very vagueness of what Mrs Scott was suggesting showed her desperation. Tom was not very enthusiastic, not so much because he didn't sympathize with his mother-in-law – though he didn't, greatly – but because he thought any intervention might well make things worse. Fortunately Helen said, 'I do not know how easily Tom could free himself from work. I could go by myself, I suppose?'

'On no account, Helen,' said her mother. 'For all I know, Eustace Flask has a gang of ruffians and minions under his command despite his *angelic* countenance. No, you need a man with you.'

Normally this would have been the kind of remark to get Helen packing her bags and catching the first train north but she seemed curiously prepared to accept her mother's ban. It seemed that something had to be done, however, so Tom and Helen eventually agreed to consider a Durham visit. They might, said Mrs Scott, make a bit of a holiday out of it. In any case, Aunt Julia would be delighted to see her niece after so many years. And her new husband, of course.

Mrs Scott's mood brightened. She started on the cakes and urged the others to tuck in. She explained that she'd been thinking it might be good for Tom and Helen to get the measure of the enemy – those were the words she used, 'the enemy' – by attending a séance here in London before they travelled north. Tom noticed how what had been a possibility was now a fact: they were going to visit Durham. He listened as Helen's mother talked about a medium who lived in Tullis Street, whose sister she and Julia had known many years ago. She had discovered that the man, Ernest Smight, held regular sessions every Sunday evening. Perhaps Tom and dear Helen might just look in on Tullis Street next week?

This was how it came about that Tom received a message from his long-dead father and how an equally dead cat, run over in the Fulham Road, was resurrected as the spirit of Mrs Seldon's first husband. And soon after that other things occurred which made the Durham visit even more of a certainty.

Death by Water

It was a few days after the Sunday séance that Mr Ashley the senior clerk at Scott, Lye & Mackenzie told Tom that Mr David Mackenzie wished to see him. Ashley, the clerk, had been with the firm longer than anyone. As a mark of his status, he had a separate office which no one would have dreamed of entering without knocking first. Tom was told to go and see Ashley by another of the juniors, a pleasant chap called William Evers. This was how it worked at the firm. Someone told you to go and see Ashley, who in turn told you what you had to do next.

Tom duly knocked and walked in without waiting for permission. By now he was on quite good terms with Ashley. Marrying the daughter of one of the founding partners had, perhaps surprisingly, not counted against him. Tom sensed that Ashley didn't actively disapprove of him, which was probably as enthusiastic an endorsement as he was going to get.

The senior clerk looked up from a pile of papers and folders. Gifted with a prodigious memory, he had a high forehead which was permanently creased. Tom thought of the interior of his head as an orderly storehouse with details from different years, different decades even, filed away on each level.

'Mr Mackenzie wishes to see you at your earliest convenience, Mr Ansell. Which we may translate as straightaway.'

'Do you know why?'

There was a time when Tom wouldn't have asked such a question and Ashley wouldn't have deigned to answer it. Now he said, 'I do know why. A strange affair. Come and have a word with me when you're finished if you like.'

Tom went along the passage to Mackenzie's chamber. He knocked and this time waited to be told to enter. As usual, it was hard to make out much of the interior because of the pipe smoke. Mackenzie waved away a cloud or two and, his teeth gripping the pipe stem, gestured at Tom to sit down on the other side of his desk. With his tonsure of white hair and wide, benevolent face, Mackenzie looked like a monk or a universal uncle. But he was quick and canny.

'How are you, Thomas? Married life suiting you, ha?'

Odd how often that question came up. Tom used his wife's answer: 'It suits us well.'

'Good, good. Time will tell, you know. It usually does.'

Having dispersed a few more parcels of smoke, David Mackenzie got down to business. At least Tom assumed it was business despite the oddness of his next question.

'Know any magicians?'

'*Magicians*? No, I don't know any magicians, sir. I've seen Dr Pepper's Ghost and the Corsican Trapdoor in the theatre.'

'The Trapdoor was Boucicault's idea,' said Mackenzie, showing an unexpected familiarity with stage magic. 'So you have never seen Major Sebastian Marmont?'

'Nor heard of him, I'm afraid.'

'He has a touring show during which he displays some magic feats he learned in the orient.'

'What they call "the mysterious east",' said Tom.

'In the Major's case his learning is as genuine as his rank. He is not like Stodare who was never in the army but still styled himself a Colonel. No, Marmont is the real thing. He served in India for many years. There was always something of the showman in him and when he quit the army he became a magician.'

'It sounds as though you know him, Mr Mackenzie,' said Tom, more and more surprised at Mackenzie's knowledge of the world of magic.

'Like his father before him, Major Marmont is one of the clients of Scott, Lye & Mackenzie. I've met Marmont on quite a few occasions. A most entertaining fellow, full of tales. You will enjoy your encounter with him.'

Well, it would make a change from dealing with codicils, probates and leaseholds. Tom waited for David Mackenzie to tell him more. But the lawyer seemed curiously uncomfortable. He fiddled with his pipe so that, when it was going again, he was almost obscured behind a cloud of smoke. Perhaps, Tom thought, he's about to perform a vanishing trick himself. Eventually, when Mackenzie spoke, his tone was somewhere between the apologetic and the persuasive.

'Tom, I don't know why I should turn to you when the firm has an odd task to undertake. And this is odder than most, like something out of Wilkie Collins. But perhaps I am looking to you because of the way you conducted that business in Salisbury last year. Perhaps it is because I trust your shrewdness and judgement. You showed those qualities most of all by choosing Helen Scott for your wife . . .'

He paused and Tom wondered what alarming or delicate errand was in prospect.

'I would like you to visit Major Marmont and take an affidavit from him. He possesses an unusual item; an ornamental or ceremonial dagger which has, he says, a curious value. The handle is carved with figures. It was the gift of some prince or maharaja out east. But a rumour to the effect that he might have come by it, ah, illicitly is doing the rounds. Marmont wishes to make a statement under oath as to how he acquired the dagger. It should be an interesting story.'

'But it could be no more than that – just a story. Straight out of Wilkie Collins, as you say.'

'Sebastian Marmont is an honest fellow if I'm any judge. He is an officer and an English gentleman.'

'As well as being a magician,' said Tom, still not quite crediting this bizarre combination.

'It's an odd thing but I believe magicians in general are honest folk. At least they make no bones about tricking you, which takes a kind of honesty.'

'Will he be believed though?' said Tom, thinking it was peculiar that Mackenzie's words were an echo of what Helen's mother had said about magicians. 'Will Major Marmont be believed even if he swears an affidavit?'

'Those who want to think ill of Major Marmont will continue to do so but others may be swayed by knowing he has made such a statement.'

'Where is this gentleman magician playing at the moment? In London?'

'Why no, he is touring in the north of the country for the summer. You can catch up with him in York or Durham.'

'In Durham?'

'Yes, a very fine city.'

'Forgive me for asking, Mr Mackenzie, but has Mrs Scott been in touch with you? Helen's mother?'

'She has spoken to me, I'm prepared to admit. I understand that there is some family problem which she wishes Helen to deal with in Durham. But my request to you is separate from that, quite separate, although you will be able to kill two birds with a single stone, as it were. Of course you should accompany your wife on her journey north. As I say, it should make an interesting trip. You can listen to old Marmont's tales of the orient.'

David Mackenzie paused to fiddle with his pipe. He squinted at Tom through the fug, as if the other might raise some objection. But Tom couldn't think of anything to say. It was an odd task, going to see a retired army man about a ceremonial dagger, but not so very odd perhaps. Lawyers were sometimes expected to do out-of-the-way things. The coincidence was that Durham had been mentioned as a destination a couple of times in as many weeks. He suspected collusion between Mrs Scott and Mr Mackenzie, especially because they seemed to have the same opinion of magicians. He'd discuss it with Helen when he got home.

But before that Tom dropped in on Ashley, the senior clerk.

'A strange affair as you said, Mr Ashley. This business of the dagger and so on.'

'Ah, the Dagger of Lucknow,' said Ashley.

'Lucknow?'

'In northern India. Consult your atlas, Mr Ansell.'

'It is quicker to consult you, Mr Ashley. Next you'll be telling me the dagger is cursed, I suppose.'

Tom meant it as a joke and was surprised to see Ashley's forehead grow even more corrugated.

'It may not be cursed exactly but there is a story attached to it. During the siege of Lucknow . . . you *have* heard of that, Mr Ansell?'

'The siege in the Mutiny?'

'Yes, the Indian Mutiny. A historic event within your lifetime and well within mine. It seems that our client, Major Sebastian Marmont, acquired the dagger while undertaking a dangerous mission. He was a junior officer at the time. It appears he was given the dagger as a gift by his Indian companion.'

'You say "seems" and "appears", Mr Ashley.'

'I have been working at this firm since . . . well, for a long time, Mr Ansell. I am cautious when I venture an opinion or report a story. I do know for a fact, however, that there was some question about the provenance of the Lucknow Dagger. A few years ago Major Marmont got wind of some tittle-tattle which was to appear in one of the London papers and he instructed us to send a letter, a shot across the bows if you like. Nothing was published.'

'But now the rumours have started again.'

'So it seems.'

'This Major Marmont is really a magician? I could hardly believe it when Mr Mackenzie said so.'

'Oh yes. Mr Mackenzie has a soft spot for magicians. He – that is, Mr Mackenzie – used to do conjuring tricks for his children at Christmas.'

'I did not even know that the Mackenzies had children,' said Tom, forgetting the magic tricks and remembering instead the tall and bony Mrs Mackenzie.

'Well, Mr Ansell, we have an office life and a home life, you know. Some of us like to keep them separate.'

This unexpected remark naturally made Tom speculate about Mr Ashley's home life, something he'd never done before. It occurred to him he did not even know Mr Ashley's first name. Now was not the moment to ask. Instead he thanked the senior clerk.

When Tom got home that evening he found Helen in a distracted, almost distressed state. He'd been looking forward to telling her about the Lucknow Dagger and planning for their journey to Durham. But first she had something to show him. It was an item from a two-day-old copy of *The Register*. Helen had been about to put aside the newspaper so that Hetty could use it for lining shelves when a heading caught her eye. The heading was *Another Waterloo Suicide?* As Tom read the news item, he felt himself grow cold.

A body recovered yesterday from the Thames has been identified by the authorities as that of Mr Ernest Smight of 67 Tullis Street near the British Museum. It is believed that Mr Smight fell or jumped to his death from Waterloo Bridge. The toll-keeper, Mr Lind, recalls a person of Mr Smight's description crossing the bridge from the north bank on Monday evening at around 10 o'clock. Mr Lind says, 'The gentleman was well dressed for a mild summer evening. I particularly remarked upon his thick clothing. He also neglected to take the change of five pennies from the sixpence which he tendered. Five whole pennies! I had to call him back to my booth and he did not thank me for it. I am certain this was the individual later recovered from the river.'

Mr Smight, believed to be in his early sixties, was a well-known medium who had practised his trade for many years in the purlieus of Tottenham Court Road. According to the authorities his establishment in Tullis Street had recently been visited by members of the police force who were acting on information received. His sister Miss Ethel Smight, who used to assist Mr Smight in his sittings, said that her brother was deeply upset by the intrusion of the police into affairs that were confidential and 'of a delicate nature'. She went so far as to talk of 'persecution'. Although she was too overwrought to speculate as to why her brother might have taken his own life, if that is what has occurred, we understood that the unfortunate demise of this individual may be connected with the possibility of a forthcoming legal action. A coroner's jury will shortly pronounce on the death of Mr Ernest Smight.

'Oh God,' said Tom.

'Yes,' said Helen. 'I have had the whole day to think this over. I've read the story again and again. I couldn't help thinking that the medium warned about the danger to us, the danger near water, and now he is drowned.'

'I am sorry for it,' said Tom, though he wasn't sure whether he was saying sorry to Helen or expressing regret about the whole Smight business. One advantage, the only one, was that there could now be no court case and so no need for witnesses.

'Why was he dressed in those thick clothes?' said Helen, breaking into his thoughts.

'I don't know. Probably because he thought they'd drag him down more quickly.'

'Ugh. Horrid thought. That's if it was a suicide.'

'What else can it have been? It would be hard to fall off Waterloo Bridge by accident. Besides, we know some of the circumstances that led up to it.'

'We do know the circumstances, but I can't help feeling we have a hand in this, somehow.'

'We didn't unmask Mr Smight, Helen. That policeman, Seldon, did it. Smight was an impostor.'

'An impostor who had a glimpse of your late father.'

Tom had forgotten this or rather had done his best to forget it. Now he said, 'I'm sure the medium got the information from somewhere. He no more saw my father than I did.'

'You weren't looking in the right direction.'

It wasn't worth arguing about. Helen now seemed inclined to give the medium the benefit of the doubt even while Tom's own doubts had hardened. But the news story about the drowning of Ernest Smight wasn't the only thing to unsettle Helen. She told Tom how Hetty had been at the shops that afternoon and had discovered that someone had been asking questions about them.

'About us?'

'You know Hetty always goes to Covins for the vegetables? Well, it appears that someone was in the shop earlier today asking about the neighbourhood, saying how it was coming up in the world and so on, and how he'd heard that lawyers and such people were moving out to Kentish Town. He wanted to know whether it would be a good place to start a business or open a shop.'

'Sounds innocent enough,' said Tom.

'Wait a moment. According to Hetty, Mr Covins said that if the fellow asking the questions was a would-be shopkeeper then he was a Chinaman. Mr Covins was a Chinaman, that is.'

'I still don't see what it's got to with us.'

'He mentioned Abercrombie Road by name, he talked about lawyers and notaries coming from the City.'

'Coincidence,' said Tom.

'And that is not all,' said Helen more urgently as Tom was dismissing her words. 'There was a man standing on the other side of the street this afternoon. I watched him from the upstairs window for a good ten minutes. Loitering, I would have said, and casting his eyes across the houses on this side.'

'What did he look like?'

'Small and slight. Dressed in labouring clothes. But when I opened the front door to go and have a word with him he'd gone.'

'It's probably nothing,' said Tom. But nevertheless he felt uneasy. The mysterious figure might have been a 'crow', as they were known, someone deputed to scout a district for potential break-ins. He reminded himself to make certain that all the doors and windows were well fastened that night. On the other hand, the whole thing might be a case of Helen letting her imagination loose. She made up stories, after all, and might see patterns and plots where someone else – Tom, for example – could see nothing at all. But he didn't say this. Instead he changed the subject.

He told Helen about his instructions from David Mackenzie and outlined what he knew of the Major and his dagger, which wasn't much. Her blue eyes opened wider. Now he too had an official reason to travel to Durham. Helen also believed that there'd probably been some collaboration between her mother and Mr Mackenzie. It could hardly have been prearranged though. Just a coincidence – yet another coincidence! – and a fortunate one from the point of view of Mrs Scott, who did not wish her daughter to go on her mission unaccompanied.

So while his wife would be doing her best to persuade her aunt Julia Howlett away from her devotion to Eustace Flask, Tom would take a statement from a Major-turned-touring-magician who wanted to let the world know that he had come honestly by the item known as the Lucknow Dagger.

It was all very odd.

Penharbour Lane

At about the same time as Tom and Helen Ansell were discussing Ernest Smight's suicide, a man in working clothes turned off Lower Thames Street in the area immediately to the east of London Bridge. He walked down Penharbour Lane, which was little more than an alley between factories and warehouses. The evening was miserable with drizzle. The man arrived at a building which seemed to have had all the life squeezed out of it by its bigger, taller neighbours on either side. At the bottom of a flight of steps was a basement door. Above the door there swung and flickered an oil lamp, hanging from a rusty bracket.

The man knocked twice on the wooden door, and, after a pause, once more. There was a shuffling from the other side, the sound of a bolt being withdrawn, and the door swung open. Whoever had unfastened it was no more than a shape in the dimness, a shape so slight that it might have been a child but one which appeared to acknowledge the man by the slightest of nods as he walked in. At the end of a short passage hung a tattered curtain. Beyond the curtain stretched a long, low-ceilinged room similar to the Tween Deck region of a ship. There were storage places here too, arranged in tiers with a narrow aisle between them. Instead of goods, people were stowed away on tiny bunks. Once the visitor was accustomed to the very subdued lighting, he would have seen slight signs of life. The shift of bodies sitting or squatting, the glow of red embers, now brightening, now fading. From all around he would have heard sounds of disturbed dreamers: garbled phrases, groans and sighs. Above all, there was a sweet and pungent odour smothering the smell of the damp fustian which clothed most of the dreaming bodies.

A dangling hand clutched at the man's face as he went down the aisle between the wooden tiers. He didn't flinch or jump but brushed the hand aside. He moved by instinct rather than by sight. At the far end of the room was a second tattered curtain, beyond which was a short flight of stairs illuminated by a single flaring gas lamp. At the bottom was a door. The man knocked again – the same pattern, two quick raps followed by a third – and was told to enter.

The interior was scarcely bigger than a boxroom. A cadaverous man was sitting on a low three-legged stool. He had a long pipe in his hand which he had evidently been about to lean forward and light from a candle on the floor when the knock came at the door. The sweet, pungent smell was even stronger in this little underground chamber where there was no apparent ventilation.

A woman lay on a mattress which was pushed against the wall and which took up half the floor space. One of her legs was cocked up and her skirts had fallen back to reveal pale thighs. Her white face was turned towards the door and her eyes were half-closed. She did not acknowledge the newcomer. Her white complexion by the light of the single candle, together with the gash of her red lips and the dark rings around her eyes, gave her a clownish look.

'Evenin', sir,' said the newcomer.

'Good evening to you, George,' said the man crouched on the stool. He spoke with an odd formality as he gestured with his unlit pipe in the direction of the woman. 'The lady is in the arms of Morpheus. She's two pipes down and I haven't even started. But I am glad of it, George. Why am I glad? Because I can listen to you with full attention before I take my pleasure. Sit yourself down on the mattress.'

The man called George – or in full George Forester – took off his cheap mackintosh and lowered himself on to the mattress. He sat cross-legged with the damp garment over his knees. He was small and lithe and did not find the position uncomfortable.

'How can you breathe in here?' said George. 'It's stiflin'. The air is wicked.'

Even as he spoke he felt the thick atmosphere in the room settle inside his throat like wet flannel. He would have preferred to be on the outside, drizzling and cold as it was.

'It's what you're used to,' said the other man. 'Me, I take to this like a fish to water – or is it a duck?'

'Anyone would think you own this place,' said George, meaning it as a compliment.

'Ssh, less of that now. I have my reputation to think of. The owner is a Malay whose name is so polysyllabic that no one can pronounce it apart from me. The fact that I *can* pronounce it and that I reminisce with him about Penang are reasons enough for him to respect me, and give me a private room when I require it.'

George did not know where or what Penang was. And, although he got the general drift of the other man's words, the meaning of 'polysyllabic' was unfamiliar to him. The individual who'd been about to light an opium-pipe was someone of education and breeding, no doubt about it. You only had to listen to his talk for a few moments to realize he was a cultured gentleman. He might have come down in the world and grown thin and pinched in the face. He might have lost most of what he once had but he still possessed a certain authority. Perhaps it was on account of his old profession, George thought. That was how they had met, through his old profession. George had good reason to be grateful, eternally grateful, to the man he always referred to as 'sir'.

'Well, what have you learned?'

'It's quite simple, sir. I hung around their drum and asked around their neighbourhood today and yesterday and I visited the shops and picked up a few titbits.'

'Such as?'

George raised his left hand and enumerated the points, one finger at a time. 'They are newly married. They recently moved into Abercrombie Road. They've got a maid called Hetty who's got a sister livin' a few streets away.'

'I'm not interested in the maid or her sister,' said the cadaverous man, gazing up at the low ceiling where the shadows jumped.

'What I'm gettin' at, sir, is there's just the three of 'em in the house.'

'No little ones?'

'Not yet.'

'That's good,' said the gentleman.

'Why's that, sir?'

'Never mind. Give me more details.'

'His name is Ansell, which you already know. First name Thomas. Hers is Helen. He works at a lawyers' in Furnival Street, he does. She's the daughter of a lawyer, deceased, of the same firm, so it's all very cosy.'

'What time does he get back in the evening?'

"Bout six or so.'

'And go to bed?'

'I saw no lights after ten,' said George.

'Hmm,' said the other. 'Well, they're newly married, I suppose. Street lights?'

'Nearest one's many yards away. You want any more help, sir? Any more kit? Just ask. I got one or two pieces left over. An' I got the know-how.'

'No, I don't want any more help, George. I am not yet decided what to do.'

'What about the other two, the ones I've already reported on?'

'I am still thinking about them as well. You may leave now, George.'

And the cadaverous individual leaned forward and started his pipe going at the candle. It was a sign of dismissal. George sprang up from the mattress where the white-faced woman slumbered oblivious, her eyelids completely closed by now. He put on his mackintosh, almost knocking over the candle as he did so. The shadows swirled across the tight walls and low ceiling.

'Careful,' said the other. 'We don't want to be left darkling, do we? Shut the door behind you.'

George did as he was told. He climbed the stairs, pushed aside the tattered curtain and paced through the long low room full of men and a few women banked in tiers and sprawled in various attitudes in their roosts. The red embers pulsed in the furthest shadows like the eyes of nocturnal beasts. The individual who attended on the outer door was revealed, now that George's eyes were more used to the gloom, to be an oriental woman, very diminutive and antique.

Once he had been let out and climbed the worn steps to street level, George paused and took in great lungfuls of the drizzly air as if he were striding along the North Downs rather than standing heel-deep in the filth of Penharbour Lane. He disliked his occasional visits to the smoking den – he had never been tempted by the habit himself – and he went only because it was the spot where he could almost definitely count on finding the gentleman he sought.

As he returned to Lower Thames Street, he wondered what use the gentleman was going to make of the information he'd given him. He wondered too why his offer of help had been turned down. For it would have been a simple matter for George to worm his way inside the house in Abercrombie Road. In his younger days he had been apprenticed to a sweep and the training was an excellent introduction for burglary, since climbing boys had to be fit, nimble and small. George dabbled in crime, acting as lookout for burglars, going to the scene of the crime beforehand to check that the coast was clear, then keeping watch while his two mates were at it. He had slithered through the odd window space himself. But he was not really cut out for a criminal life, never felt truly comfortable, and he did his best to turn away from it. Why, he even settled down and married. Now he and Annie had kids, a few of them, which was how he encountered 'sir' in the first place.

It was when one of their children had fallen ill of a fever. Someone said there was a doctor down on his luck who lodged round the corner in Rosemary Lane. He'd occasionally attend on a sick child if you caught him at the right time, if you found him in a kindly mood. His name? No one knew his surname. He answered to Tony. So George had hared round to Rosemary Lane and knocked on doors and toiled up rickety staircases and several times risked a punch in the phizog to track down this geezer. He'd inquired with increasing desperation of dozens of loungers and passers-by whether they knew a Tony, a medical gentleman. And, lo and behold, after half a day and when he was about to give up, he asked the man himself without realizing it. Doctor Tony was a tall, thin, long-haired gent with skin that, even by the vaporous daylight of Rosemary Lane, was decidedly sallow. George Forester did not discover his surname then or ask for it later.

The medical man accompanied George back to the two rooms in the Old Mint where he lived with Annie and the kids. He examined the child, a boy called Mike who was three years old and very hot to the touch. He prodded and poked with his long yellow hands as Mike lay on the ticking of the cheap mattress.

The other children looked on curious and silent. After a while Doctor Tony nodded to himself. He reached inside the pocket of the greatcoat which he still wore indoors – it was midwinter and freezing in the room – and withdrew a queer kind of wallet from which he took out a phial of amber liquid. He asked Annie if there was any water and she brought him some in a chipped, dirty cup. Doctor Tony poured a little of the amber liquid into the water and swirled it round. He squatted on his haunches, propped up Mike's head with his left hand and eased some of the preparation into the child's mouth. Mike spluttered but he swallowed a few sips and then more, until the cup was almost empty. The tall man stood up. He said, 'The crisis should soon be past.' And he left.

George and Annie could only pray that he was right. They despaired when the boy seemed to sink further into his fever and grow yet hotter in the chill of the room. But by the next morning Mike's temperature had fallen and his eyes were open and he was uttering a few feeble words. 'That man's a saint,' said Annie, referring to Doctor Tony. 'I don't mind telling him so.'

But it was George who next encountered the good doctor a few days later in Rosemary Lane, by which time Mike was back to his normal mischievous self. George Forester was so grateful that he not only passed on his wife's comment about saintliness but offered to do anything for the man he could only call 'sir'.

So it was that he found himself running odd errands for Doctor Tony, who seemed to know without asking that George had a dubious past and that, however respectable his current employment, he retained a few of his old skills. For his part, George came to know Tony a little better but remained in awe of the gentleman who had, surely, preserved his son's life.

As he sheltered inside his thin mackintosh and made his way along Lower Thames Street and towards the east, he pondered again on why Doctor Tony had instructed him to observe the habits of the newly married couple living in Abercrombie Road.

Back inside the opium den in Penharbour Lane, Doctor Tony drew for the last time on his pipe. He placed it carefully in the brass bowl by the candle and lay back on the mattress beside the sleeping woman. He left the candle to burn itself out, watching the rising spiral of smoke. He observed the smoke-thread joining the other shadows overhead, all of them swelling and shrinking as if they had life. He turned his head sideways and watched the woman. Poor as the light was, everything his eyes lingered on seemed to stand out with an unnatural clarity. He admired the white curve of her cheek and the generous red of her lips. A delicate handkerchief, lilac coloured, had fallen from her sleeve. He picked it up and held to his nose. He inhaled her scent.

He was conscious of the mattress against the back of his head, against his stockinged calves. He knew that the mattress was a rough, thin, cheap thing but just now it felt as soft as down. Doctor Tony was engulfed in a wave, a gradual wave, of warmth and safety. He sighed and gave himself up to his imaginings . . .

But it was no piece of imagination when, at about one o'clock of that same night, he found himself standing on a street of solid respectable houses; found himself there as if transported through the air. He was clear-headed but still under the influence of the three pipes he had smoked in Penharbour Lane. The sensation was not unpleasant, not at all. Rather, it made him feel secure to the point of invincibility.

So here he was, far from the riverside wharfs. Gaslights bloomed along the street and glistened off mud and stone that were still wet from the evening rain. Between the lights there were larger areas of darkness. The house he was interested in lay within one of these patches of dark.

The Doctor was calm, convinced that what he was about to do was not merely a fitting act but also in accord with the laws of justice, the higher laws. He pulled his greatcoat tighter about him and, despite the weight which caused the coat to pull unevenly to one side, he moved smoothly along the street until he reached the house which he was looking for. He slowed for a moment to make sure there was no stray gleam of light anywhere from within. There was no light. The occupants were tucked up asleep like the other occupants of the other houses in this solid, respectable thoroughfare.

Doctor Tony glided further along the street, counting as he did so, until he came to a narrow passage between two houses. He turned right, entered the alley and then turned right again when he reached the area behind the houses. There was a ragged stretch of ground here, neither cultivated nor wilderness. No doubt it would soon be parcelled into building plots and covered over with brick. Tony paused to let his eyes become accustomed to the greater dark on this side. Then he moved parallel to the direction in which he'd already come along the road, counting off the houses in the row one by one according to their chimney stacks. It would not do to enter the wrong dwelling.

It was awkward walking back here and more than once he almost stumbled over a tussock of grass or kicked a lump of stone. When he arrived at the eleventh house, he scrambled across the wooden palings which separated the garden from the land beyond. By now he could see quite well. There were tent-like supports for runner beans and a faint sheen of light reflecting off what was probably a cucumber frame.

Doctor Tony crept up to the rear of the house. He ignored the back door which led to the kitchen and pantry area and concentrated instead on an extension containing the water-closet. A small barred window was positioned at about head height. Tony drew from his greatcoat a length of thick rope and a steel rod. Working by touch rather than sight he passed the rope twice around two of the bars and inserted the rod between the strands. Holding the rope ends with his left hand, he turned the rod end over end with his right. After a few moments the traction on the ropes began to loosen the bars from their sockets. The row of houses might have been fairly new but the building work was not of high quality. George Forester had done a good job casing the back of the property.

In a few more seconds, one of the bars popped right out with a shower of dust and plaster. Tony placed it on the ground and eased the other bar free with his hands alone. He put the ropes and the steel rod and the bars in a pile at the foot of the wall. Beyond the bars was a pane of opaque glass. The wood of the frame was half-rotten with damp. He worked at the area round the catch with the point of a knife and it did not take long for him to insert the blade and force the catch up. Then he pushed the window open.

Tony was tall enough that he had to stoop slightly to operate on the window. But he was also thin as one of the beanpoles in the garden. Now there was a space of perhaps two-feet square through which he was able to scramble. He took off his coat, shoved it through the space and began to worm his way in. Someone as slight as George Forester would probably have accomplished the task even more quickly and easily but although Doctor Tony was prepared to borrow the little man's kit and also to listen intently to his burgling tips, he was reluctant to involve the other man in the business itself. He knew that George was trying his best to keep on the right side of the law. More to the point, he knew that George would be horrified if he was aware of what the good Doctor was about to do. In fact, he'd probably attempt to stop him.

Once through the window, Doctor Tony wriggled awkwardly to the floor of the closet. Then he was on his feet, brushing himself down, and so out of the closet and into the main part of the house. He was standing in the kitchen, his senses heightened to the degree that it was almost painful for him to hear and smell. He picked up the just audible ticks and creaks made by an occupied property at night. He thought of the married couple asleep upstairs. Innocent, oblivious. No, they were not innocent. The man and wife deserved what was about to happen to them. The Doctor dismissed them, the man and his wife, dismissed them with a metaphorical snap of the fingers.

Now he could smell the smells of this dwelling-place, so distinct yet so like the smells of tens of thousands of other households. Lingering scents of cooking, of furniture polish, of flowers that should have been thrown out a day or two before. And the faintest odour of gas.

Tony felt his way around the kitchen before going into the dining room, which was adjacent to it. The door was slightly ajar. With eyes well used to the dark, he moved towards the fireplace and examined the wallpaper and fittings on either side. Whatever he found evidently pleased him because he gave a small grunt of satisfaction. He repeated the process at various places in the parlour at the front of the house and then out in the hallway. After that he crept upstairs, keeping close to the wall where the treads were less likely to creak. Once on the landing he waited for several minutes, accustoming himself to the slightly different atmosphere of the first floor of the house. Different because there were human beings up here. He could hear a soft snoring from behind one of the three doors which opened off the landing. The door wasn't quite closed. There was the creak of a bed as one of the sleepers shifted. It crossed Tony's mind that he might actually enter the bedroom, but no, it would be enough if he just pushed the door a little wider . . . like so . . . and after he'd done that and one further thing he crept back downstairs.

Now he was standing near the front door. There was a gleam of light coming through the stained glass of the fanlight. It was enough for him to see the shape of what he was looking for, near the fanlight and just above head-height, out of a child's grasp. He reached out, then stopped, his hand poised in the darkness. From outside there was the sound of feet going by, a steady, heavy plod. A constable on patrol? What George Forester would have termed a 'peeler' or 'crusher'? Doctor Tony waited while the foot-steps passed the house. He heard a humming sound, a few slurred words. The man was singing under his breath. No, it was not a police constable but a drunk stomping home to bed. The noises faded.

Tony realized he'd been holding his own breath all this while. His hand was where he'd left it, suspended near the fixture on the wall by the fanlight. He let out his breath in a long sigh. He lowered his arm and savoured the tension in his muscles. Then he reached up and pulled down the lever on the gas main until it was fully in the 'open' position.

He waited a few seconds. Already he thought he could smell and taste it, the acrid smell of household gas as it poured out of the unlit jets in every room of the house. Some Tony had found carelessly unclosed, others he had opened. Like so many people, the couple who were sleeping soundly upstairs did not turn off the gas lights one by one as they went to bed every night. Perhaps they were fearful of leaks and tried to guard against them by shutting off the supply at the main. Perhaps the husband could not be bothered to turn off the gas lights one by one. Doctor Tony did not know whether the gas jets in the sleepers' bedroom had been left open but, in any case, the poisonous fumes from downstairs would soon rise to the first floor, seeping through floorboards and creeping around doors.

Clasping a handkerchief – lilac-coloured, with a woman's scent – to his face, Doctor Tony swiftly paced to the back of the house.

He did not make his exit via the water-closet but through the kitchen door which, he had already ascertained, was not locked but bolted. In fact he might have got into the house through the back door, he realized, although he had enjoyed the surreptitiousness of wriggling through a window, making use of George Forester's simple equipment.

The odour of gas penetrated the handkerchief which he still held to his nostrils. He shut the door behind him, and gathered up the rope and rod together with the bars from the closet window. Then he was striding past the beanpoles and the cucumber-frame and almost vaulting over the palings at the bottom of the garden. He paused to fling the objects out into the dark where they landed with a distant clatter.

By the time he reached the street he was breathing hard. He went back up the street, past the house where he had been prowling only moments before. All was quiet, no light showed, no sound came from the occupants. No sound would ever come from those particular occupants again, thought the Doctor. There would be something appropriate about the way they died, deprived of breath, choking for good honest air. He might have gone about the business in a more straightforward way. He could have shot the sleeping couple, for instance. He carried a gun, which he had possessed for many years. But there was a crude aspect to a shooting. And, besides, the noise of gunshots might have alerted neighbours and made it harder for him to get away. Here he was, striding along the street, free as a bird flying by night.

It was only after he had walked several hundred yards that he realized that he had left his greatcoat behind. He had taken it off before he wriggled through the window and then left it on the floor of the privy. He stopped in the middle of the street. Should he go back to get the coat? He did not want to break into the house all over again, especially a house that was filling up with choking gas. Doctor Tony did not think he could be traced or identified by the coat. It was as old and shabby as the rest of his garments, and any tailor's or manufacturer's mark had long disappeared.

Tony decided to leave it. If it was discovered, let the police make of it what they would. Of course, they might never find the coat. The house, and the overcoat with it, might be blown to blazes if someone was careless enough to cause a spark in the vicinity.

Tony was almost indifferent to his fate. He had a mission to accomplish, and once that was finished then he too was finished. There were more individuals to dispose of. But, that done, his work was over.

Act Two

The Major comes forward to the footlights. He says to the audience, 'In my time I have brought to many audiences a veritable extravaganza of extraordinary feats deriving from the lands of the east, lands whose denizens have access to secrets of life which we in the west have long forgotten or never knew. But none, in my humble opinion, is so truly remarkable as what I am about to show you.'

He claps his hands and the curtains behind him are parted to reveal a wide plank of wood resting on the backs of two chairs. The backdrop is as highly patterned as suburban wallpaper. Dull but not restful. An Indian gentleman comes on, dressed in a dark suit, western style. He is elderly and stooped, with flowing white hair. He acknowledges the audience with a slight inclination of the head. He does not smile.

'Ladies and gentlemen,' says the Major, 'allow me to present to you the mystical Mahatma of Agra. He has made a lifelong study of the methods by which a privileged few may escape our earthly bounds, our mortal bonds. Even I do not know how the mystical Mahatma accomplishes the feat he is about to demonstrate. It quite contradicts all that we know of the laws of nature. Sit back, ladies and gentlemen – no, do not sit back but lean forward – perch with eagerness on the edge of your seats – and marvel!'

With the Major's help, the Mahatma clambers awkwardly on to the plank supported by the chair backs. He lies on his back, steepling his hands on his chest like an effigy on a tomb.

Once more Major Marmont turns to confide in the audience.

'The incantation I am about to utter was taught to me by the Mahatma himself. We were standing on the shores of the Ganges River as the sun was setting. I can remember the scene as if it was yesterday. You will not understand the words I say for I can scarcely understand them myself. But see their result!'

Major Marmont swivels towards the figure on the plank, who is so still he might be in a trance. He mutters several sentences in a foreign language, very fast, at the same time raising his hands in the gesture of a blessing. Slowly, very slowly, the plank bearing the aged Mahatma of

Agra lifts itself clear of the chairs. When the Mahatma is about three feet above these makeshift supports, the Major whisks away the chairs with the dexterity of a waiter. The plank and the man continue their steady ascent. The audience is split between wonder (this is indeed a denial of the laws of nature) and a futile attempt to discover how the trick is worked. They strain their eyes searching for cords and levers; they listen for the whirring of cogs and pulleys. They see nothing except the levitating Mahatma; they hear nothing apart from their own gasps of amazement.

Once the Mahatma of Agra has reached a height of about fifteen feet above the stage there is a queer kind of shimmering in the air. He begins to come down again. The Major watches his descent. When the Mahatma – unmoving, hands still steepled – is at shoulder height, Marmont runs his own hands over and round the head and feet of the body. He is showing that there are no hidden supports here. The chairs are replaced in their original positions. The plank bearing the Mahatma settles itself on the chair backs once again. The Major utters a few more incomprehensible words and raises his arms.

The Mahatma climbs quite nimbly off the plank, without Marmont's aid, and stands on the stage. But what has happened? The man who floated up through the air was old and stooped. The one who now appears before them is upright and handsome. The hair that was white and flowing is now a gleaming black. Major Marmont seems almost as surprised as the audience. He bows at the applause but the Mahatma only inclines his head.

Afterwards the audience conclude that the Mahatma has not merely travelled magically through space but also through time. He has shed his years.

It is all a trick of course, somehow emphasized by the simplicity of the props and the wallpaper backdrop. It must be a trick. But who is to say that the sages of the East do not have access to secrets of life which we in the west have either long forgotten or never knew?

On the Train to Durham

It was only when they were travelling north by train that Tom Ansell thought to ask Helen why her aunt Julia Howlett had chosen to live in Durham. They had a compartment to themselves once they'd changed lines from the Midland to the North Eastern at Doncaster. Their thoughts were turning to the different missions with which they'd been entrusted.

They were going to stay at Miss Howlett's house for a few days. Helen had written asking whether they might visit. It had been many years since she'd seen her aunt and, besides, she wanted to show off her new husband. She said nothing about the main reason for her trip. Meanwhile Tom arranged through Scott, Lye & Mackenzie for a meeting with Major Marmont, who happened to be performing in Durham for a week.

So, why had Helen's aunt gone to Durham when the rest of the family lived in the south?

'It's rather a sad story as I understand it from the hints my mother has given,' she said. 'Many years ago Aunt Julia moved to Durham in pursuit of a man. She was engaged to be married to a curate but something went wrong. He was working in a parish somewhere in the city. I do not know whether things went wrong before or after she visited him but anyway the engagement was broken off and then the curate was moved to a different parish. Aunt Julia was reluctant to come back empty-handed, so to speak, and decided to prolong her stay in Durham. She must have fallen for the place because a few weeks turned into months and then became a year or two. At some point she acquired a fine house in the old part of the city on the bailey, where she has been living, a prosperous and respected spinster, these many years. I don't suppose she'll ever return to the south now.'

'She must have an independent streak,' said Tom.

'Mother says I take after her but I am not certain whether it is altogether a compliment. It's only recently that Aunt Julia and she have started corresponding again.'

'I had the feeling that your mother was not so concerned about your aunt but more about – I don't know – about family honour, the memory of her father.'

'It is this business of the medium using grandfather Howlett to get what he wants from Julia that is so distasteful. I agree with mother there. But, Tom, I am not looking forward to this one bit.'

'After the trouble in Tullis Street?'

'It does not give me much of an appetite for confronting mediums.'

Neither Tom nor Helen had talked a great deal about the apparent suicide of Ernest Smight. When they did discuss it, they tried to persuade themselves they had no share in the man's death, that it was a result of his despair at the police action and imminent prosecution. But even so they felt twinges of guilt. They had been present at the séance; they were witnesses. Like the authorities, they too regarded Smight as a trickster who deserved exposure, for Helen had by now begun to revert to her old suspicion of mediums and Tom had almost forgotten the encounter with his father.

'Never mind,' said Tom. 'You will not have to confront this Flask fellow by yourself, if it comes to that. I'll be there. And maybe you will be able to convince your aunt without any confrontation, maybe she'll have had a change of heart by the time we arrive and be all for leaving her money to a local orphanage.'

'I hope so,' said Helen. She gave up any pretence of reading her book and gazed out of the window at the countryside rolling by. They had stopped at several great manufacturing conurbations, each announced by a pall of smoke not merely overhanging but spreading out into the surrounding countryside. In between the towns the landscape was largely low and level, stretching away in the summer's afternoon.

'I feel life must be more serious up here,' said Helen after a time. 'More earnest.'

'Is that because the Brontë sisters and Mrs Gaskell tell you so?'

'Why, Tom, I did not know that you read female authors.'

'I may have glanced at them from time to time.'

Tom had taken an interest in female authors ever since he had met Helen and she revealed to him her ambition to write a novel. He had even read a few of their books to get a sense of the competition. But he did not have much to say about his experience of women authors, except that there seemed to be an awful lot of them. This would not have been a tactful remark to make to Helen under any circumstances. He went back to reading the Cornhill Magazine and Helen returned to her book.

They were joined by a tall, well-dressed gentleman who got on at York. After putting a small valise in the rack, he settled himself in the opposite corner of the compartment. He stretched out his legs in front of him and flexed his gloved fingers. His glance flicked from Tom to Helen and back again.

'Newly weds?' he said.

Helen looked up, a very slight blush on her cheeks. Tom was about to tell the man to mind his own business but his wife said, 'Not *that* new. But how do you know? Is it so obvious?'

'When I was putting my bag up there I noticed that the initial, the last initial, on your case had recently been painted over and a different one substituted. You started out as an S but now you are transformed to an A.'

The man addressed Helen. The familiarity in his words might have been offensive in someone else but he had a curiously insinuating manner of speaking. His voice was warm and low.

'Very observant of you,' said Tom.

'It is not only a question of letters and paint and luggage. Do not take what I say amiss but there is a kind of bloom on the both of you,' the man persisted. 'The bloom of the freshly married when the voyage of life lies all before you.'

'Yes, we have lately cast off into the sea of marital life,' said Helen, 'marital life with its many shoals and shallows, its storms and its sunny days.'

'My dear lady,' said the man, his voice taking on a quality that was positively flowing and syrupy. 'My dear *young* lady, you can certainly take a metaphor and stretch it. But to move from metaphor to actuality, are you travelling far today?'

'To Durham,' said Helen.

'What about you?' cut in Tom. 'You cannot be going any distance since you're travelling light.'

'Durham is also my destination. A city on a hill.'

'Going there on business?' said Tom, giving the stranger a taste of his own inquisitiveness.

'I reside there for the moment,' said the man. 'But I am always about my business. It never ceases.'

By now they were approaching the outskirts of the city. The green of the countryside was blotched with heaps of slag and skeletal pitheads and pinched lines of housing. Even the sheep in the fields seemed to have been dipped in a sooty dye. Helen looked as eagerly out of the window as she would have at an attractive prospect. Then the train ran across a gently curving viaduct and they had their first sight of the castle and the cathedral. The afternoon sun gave the stone a warm glow but the buildings were still massive and imposing.

'Here we are!' said the man, waving his hand as if he'd conjured up the scene himself. 'The city on a hill.'

The train had scarcely begun to draw up alongside the platform when the tall gentleman leaped from his seat and took his valise from the rack in a single movement. He had the door unfastened before the train was fully stopped. He paused for an instant and made a kind of mock-bow towards Tom and Helen.

'*Au revoir*, Mr and Mrs A.'

And with that he stepped out on to the platform. By the time Helen and Tom had gathered their own luggage and got down, there was no sign of him. A few other people got off the train at the station, which was so new that the stonework had only just started to take on a darker, grimy colour. Among the alighting passengers was a tall, shabbily dressed man who stared at the retreating backs of Tom and Helen.

The Ansells took a battered old hansom from the railway station. Helen gave the driver an address in the old part of town called the South Bailey. As they were being driven downhill past terraces of new housing, Helen said, 'I wonder if the man on the train is typical of the inhabitants of the city? I thought it would be full of miners.'

They drove across a bridge that straddled a river so dark in patches that it might have been running with liquid coal. Tom thought it was the River Wear. He had studied a town map before leaving London and recalled how the river looped round and back on itself so that the older part of Durham was isolated like a peninsula. Some loungers in artisan clothes turned from gazing into the black waters to look at the cab go by. To the right, high up on the bluff overlooking the river, were the castle remains and the twin towers at the western end of the cathedral. The carriage ascended slowly into this fortress-like area by a round-about route, passing through a wide marketplace and then up cobbled streets that were lined with tearooms and confectioners and dress shops.

The road began to level out and they passed beneath the cathedral on its eastern side. Helen had never seen her aunt's house before and had only the name to go by: Colt House, named for the mine-owner who had once lived there. Tom stuck his head through the trapdoor in the hansom roof and repeated the name to the driver who shook his head. Tom added that it was the residence of Miss Julia Howlett. The driver's seamed face registered some kind of recognition at the name. Within a few moments they had drawn up before a broad-fronted house with a handsome pillared portico.

The Ansells got down. The driver produced their cases. Before Tom had finished paying him and while Helen was still studying the facade of Colt House, the front door flew open. A small woman came out at a run and nearly collided with Helen.

'Helen, is it really you?'

She held Helen by the elbows and looked up at her face. She was tiny, bird-like.

'Aunt Julia!' said Helen. 'You have not changed.'

'But you have, my dear. Last time I saw you, you were so high – or so low, I should say. And this must be your husband Thomas.'

Tom shook hands with Miss Howlett. She had a darting eye, and he felt assessed within seconds. He wondered whether Helen felt the same twinge of discomfort. They weren't exactly innocent visitors. They had come to persuade this woman to do what she probably had no wish to do.

Colt House

As they were talking in the hall, a stout and quite elderly man entered. He was carrying a bundle of papers under his right arm. White hair straggled from beneath his hat. He looked at Tom and Helen with curiosity.

'Septimus!' cried Aunt Julia. 'You must meet my niece and her husband.'

The gentleman came forward. He awkwardly shifted the papers to his other arm and shook hands with the Ansells.

'I have heard a deal about you,' he said. 'Miss Howlett has been greatly looking forward to your visit.'

'Mr Sheridan – Septimus – is a lodger in Colt House,' said Julia. 'He has been here for so long that I may say he is almost part of the furniture!'

Far from being insulted, Septimus Sheridan smiled gently and bowed his head. He said to Helen, 'You aunt is very good to me, Mrs Ansell.'

'Now then, you two must be tired after your long journey. You will need to wash and change before dinner. We will be dining early because I have invited a few friends and neighbours for this evening.'

'Not on our account, I hope,' said Helen.

'My dear, do not be so modest. But no, I had arranged this, ah, event before I knew you were coming. Even so your arrival is very timely. You see, I have asked a good friend of mine to provide us with a manifestation tonight.'

'A manifestation, Miss Howlett?' said Tom. He had an uneasy feeling he knew what was coming.

'Oh do not call me Miss Howlett, Tom. If I am an aunt to Helen, I shall be one to you also. But, yes, we are having a *manifestation*. A gentleman by the name of Eustace Flask is to show us his powers. He will communicate with the other side, he will bring us messages from beyond the grave. I am sure your mother has mentioned Mr Flask, Helen? I have been filling my letters with him. He is a remarkable individual.'

'She did mention someone of that name,' said Helen, glancing at Tom. Her look gave nothing away. Well, thought Tom, this has come sooner than expected. But it was good to have an early opportunity to get the measure of their opponent.

Aunt Julia talked with enthusiasm on the subject of spiritualism while they ate their early dinner. But her enthusiasm was oddly impersonal. She wasn't attempting to make contact with the 'other side' for herself or to soothe some recent grief. Rather, she was genuinely eager to further the work of those 'brave and pioneering' individuals who, in the face of misunderstanding and even persecution, were attempting to 'pierce the veil between the mortal and the eternal.'

Tom caught Helen's eye while she was coming out with all this. Yes, their task was going to be a difficult one. It did not seem to him, either, that Aunt Julia was physically weak or mentally failing and about to give away her worldly wealth, as Helen's mother had implied. Perhaps that had just been Mrs Scott's way of getting them to go on their mission to Durham.

It was difficult to work out Septimus Sheridan's exact position in the household. From some comments he let slip during the meal, Tom understood that he spent most of his time in the cathedral library engaged on some scholarly work or other, which explained the bundle of papers he brought to the house. Certainly, he had the dry and dusty look of one who most enjoys old libraries. Even his hair was the whitish-yellow tint of old parchment. But every so often he'd glance at Julia Howlett in a way that was half admiring, half timorous. Whenever she was speaking he listened with particular attention and he was quick to agree with her, whatever the subject. She, for her part, treated Septimus with a weary familiarity. He called her 'Miss Howlett' while she called him by his first name.

He'd been introduced as a lodger. A lodger! It was just the kind of description which might have provoked a bit of scandalized gossip, a situation where a single man, however old, was living in the house of a spinster lady, however ancient. If so, Aunt Julia didn't seem to care. In the brief time since they'd been introduced, Tom had realized that here was a woman who went her own way – something which would make Helen's task even harder.

Julia Howlett referred to Eustace Flask several times more. His visit this evening to Colt House was a privilege. Helen and Thomas were truly fortunate that their own visit should coincide with one of Flask's appearances. Aunt Julia's face grew even more animated while she was saying all this. Her eyes sparkled.

'What does this Mr Flask actually do during his evening sessions?' said Helen.

'I think you'll find he puts on a good show for the audience,' said Septimus Sheridan.

'A show, Septimus! How can you describe it as a show! He is not some vulgar magician or entertainer. What Mr Flask provides is a *manifestation*. He is not unlike you.'

'Me?'

'Both of you toil to uncover the truth. You do it among piles of manuscripts, Septimus, while dear Eustace ventures into the trackless world of the spirits.'

'Of course, Miss Howlett, you are quite right. He is no showman but a serious seeker of truth.'

Tom strained for any touch of irony in Sheridan's words but could not detect it. Further discussion of the medium wasn't possible because the advance guard of his party arrived at the house. They were called Ambrose and Kitty. Ambrose was a squat young man who at once started lugging planks and panels of wood out of a handcart which had been wheeled not to the tradesmen's entrance but to the front door of the house. He carried the wooden sections into the morning room. Since the room was on the ground floor it was the most convenient place for the session. Kitty was introduced as the niece to Eustace Flask. She busied herself with bits of material, little muslin curtains, and an assortment of musical instruments which were also required for the evening.

The bits of wood were rapidly assembled by Ambrose into the framework for a large cupboard-like structure with double doors, each of which had an oval hole cut into it. The cupboard was on a stand so that the base was about a foot above the floor. Meanwhile, the household maids were bringing extra chairs into the room and being instructed on how to arrange them. Julia Howlett was obviously expecting a good turnout.

There was a bustle in the hall and a figure suddenly material-ized at the door of the morning room. Tom and Helen had been watching the preparations with mild interest but they became very alert when they saw the newcomer. There could be no doubt over his identity. Afterwards Tom wondered why they hadn't recognized him in the first place, not now but earlier. After all, they had seen his photograph. But the quality of the overexposed picture was poor and his heavily ringed fingers had been hidden by gloves. The new arrival in Colt House was the well-dressed gentleman from the train. It was Eustace Flask.

He noticed Tom and Helen on the far side of the room. Aunt Julia, however, had not seen the medium arrive since she was examining a tear in the fabric of the cover of a chair just put in place by a maid. She was tutting and shaking her head, as if debating whether to have the chair taken out again.

Meantime Flask walked briskly towards the Ansells. He came close to them. He said, 'What did I say, Mr and Mrs A? I knew that we should meet again – and meet shortly.'

Tom and Helen did not have long to get over their surprise at the fact that Eustace Flask was none other than the insinuating individual who'd boarded the train at York. Now, with rings twinkling on his naked fingers, the dapper spiritualist was directing his two assistants to put the finishing touches to the cabinet or wardrobe which sat at one end of the morning room. Flask would have stood out in a crowd. He favoured colourful clothes, if his bright green frock-coat was anything to go by, and was of more than average height and very pale in the face. His hair was a light red and seemed to spring away from his head as if eager to escape. Helen whispered to Tom that he made her think of a walking candle, his flame-like hair wavering as he directed his helpers.

Ambrose was doing the finishing work of fitting panels into place and tightening screws while Kitty was fussing over the decorative curtains which hung over the oval windows in the upper part of the cabinet, a bit like a Punch & Judy booth. Tom took a more careful look at the assistants. Ambrose was a short fellow with a squashed nose who looked as though he'd be happier sparring in the ring than sitting around a table at a séance. Flask's niece, Kitty, had an elfin sort of face on a well-padded body. Tom noticed that her uncle frequently touched her arm or shoulder as he was giving instructions. Meantime Aunt Julia was bustling about, welcoming the twenty or so visitors who had come for the show.

No, it was not a show, Tom reminded himself, but a 'manifestation'. The visitors, men and women, were a mixture of ages but all of them had the look of solid citizens, not easily taken in. It was much more elaborate and professional than the session in Tullis Street.

Eventually everything appeared to be ready. The curtains had been drawn on the remains of the summer evening outside and the indoor lights – a mixture of gas and candles – turned down or extinguished. Nevertheless, the illumination was stronger than it had been at the Smights' house. Eustace Flask stood before his audience, with Ambrose just behind him and Kitty to one side. In a well-practised move Flask slipped off his green frock-coat and handed it to Ambrose.

'Ladies and gentlemen,' he began in a style that was smooth as oil, 'I customarily ask for a volunteer at this point to search my person and ascertain that I am not wearing any concealed devices. We live in such a suspicious age that all of us are forced to show ourselves beyond reproach, even Eustace Flask. I look around and I am delighted to see some familiar faces but it would be best if someone who was not known to me came forward for this *personal* examination. I might of course ask a lady here who is not known to me . . .'

His eyes lingered on Helen. Tom felt her shift on the chair next to him. But Flask was saying this only to tease for his glance then moved to Tom.

'. . . but perhaps it would be more appropriate if an unknown *gentleman* volunteered. After all, we shall have no imputations of indelicacy here!'

Tom got up and walked the few paces to where Flask was standing in his waistcoat, shirt and trousers. Close to, Tom noticed a sheen of sweat on Flask's pale face. He spoke quietly, hardly above a whisper.

'Place your hands where you like, Mr . . ?'

'Ansell.'

'We have not been introduced before?' said Eustace Flask speaking loudly enough for the whole room to hear.

'No, we have not been introduced,' said Tom. The man was

quick, no doubt about it. They had met on the train but they hadn't been *introduced*.

'Place your hands where you like, sir, within the bounds of propriety.'

Flask looked out at the audience over Tom's shoulder with a roguish twinkle in his eye. The voice was more brown and syrupy than ever. Tom put out his hands as if he were being invited to catch a ball. He felt uncomfortable and self-conscious, which was probably Flask's intention. No doubt the medium counted on not being examined or searched thoroughly. God knows what he had concealed behind his waistcoat or inside his trousers.

Tom, suddenly provoked, decided that he would not be embarrassed. He would give this man as thorough a going-over as a criminal would receive in the police-house. So he ran his hands along the other's extended shirtsleeves and over his sleek chest, he felt about his waist and up and down the trouser legs. To his slight disappointment, he felt nothing, not even a purse or a pocket-watch. Flask's clothes were snug and well-fitting. They were also expensive. A fine stickpin topped by a pearl fastened his burgundy cravat. The thought crossed Tom's mind that one of Aunt Julia's cheques might have paid for the brocade waistcoat and, although it was really nothing to do with him, the idea irritated him.

He turned to face the people in the room. He shook his head and said,

'As far as I can tell, Mr Flask is . . . clean.'

There were one or two titters from the audience, whether out of genuine amusement or from nervousness because Tom had shown a touch of disrespect towards Eustace Flask.

'Thank you, Mr Ansell,' said Flask from behind and then more quietly he spoke directly into Tom's ear, 'Your hands have such an expert touch that I thought you might be a tailor.'

Tom could have jabbed his elbow into the other's gut at the little insult but he restrained himself and went back to sit beside Helen. Aunt Julia was beaming, gratified that Flask was acquitting himself so well. She was sitting beside Septimus Sheridan, who looked generally uncomfortable at the course of events.

Now Flask turned his back on the audience, his open hands stretched behind him. Ambrose produced a little bag from which he poured what appeared to be flour into Flask's hands. The medium grasped the flour. Then Ambrose wound a coil of thin rope several times around Flask's wrists. He made a show of knotting the cord tight and beckoned to a gentleman in the front of the audience to test the knots. This was quickly done and then Flask moved towards the wardrobe, where Kitty was standing by the open doors.

The interior was empty apart from a ledge or bench which ran along the back. Flask sat on this, rather awkwardly because of the position of his hands behind him. There were holes in the bench through which the ends of the rope were passed before being secured round Flask's ankles by Ambrose. The same man from the front row was asked to test the new knots, which he did willingly. Now Flask was trussed up inside the wardrobe.

With a flourish, Kitty closed the double doors. She made sure that the windows were covered by the muslin curtains which hung on the inside. Within a few moments there was a stir from inside and an arm was thrust through the material. There was a collective noise from the people in the room, somewhere between a gasp and a sigh. The arm was bare and, for sure, it did not belong to any grown man. Judging by the thinness and pallor of it, the arm was a girl's, even a child's. Tom's eyes automatically flicked sideways to see where Kitty had been standing but he could not immediately spot her. Now a second arm was thrust through the curtain covering the other hole in the other door. The two limbs were the same size but seemed to belong to two different bodies. In fact, they must do because the gap between the two holes was too wide even for a grown man to extend his arms any distance beyond the openings. The arms waggled their hands and the hands flexed their fingers, and the whole effect was unnerving.

All at once Kitty was in front of the cabinet again and the arms had scarcely time to disappear before she was unlatching the double doors and flinging them open to reveal – ah ha! – Eustace Flask sitting on his bench, the rope apparently securing his hands and feet, and with no sign of any bare arms floating about. But this was not the most extraordinary part of the manifestation. It was rather that Flask sat there quite still and calm, a seraphic smile on his face. There were noises of muted approval from the audience.

Helen whispered to Tom, 'I'm impressed but I don't see the point of it. What's he trying to prove?'

'That he is in touch with the spirit world, I expect,' said Tom, wishing that he felt as calm as Flask looked.

The next part of the evening session followed when the various musical instruments – guitar, tambourine, violin and trumpet – were hung by Kitty upon hooks on the inner walls of the cabinet. All this while Flask had remained tied up, smiling benignly out at the room. The same man from the front row of chairs once more checked the knots and this time it was Ambrose who closed the doors to the cabinet. A few seconds passed before a terrible din emerged from within, the sounds of thumping and rattling, tooting and screeching. It was as if a pack of monkeys had got hold of the instruments and were doing their best to play them, or to destroy them. At one point the tambourine was thrown through one of the holes and almost struck a member of the audience in the face.

Ambrose now did duty by unfastening the doors as the cacophony faded away. Again Eustace Flask was revealed on the inside, securely trussed up on his bench, with the instruments hanging limply on their hooks. Ambrose untied him and the medium stood up, flexing his arms in front of him. He opened his hands so that a little shower of flour tumbled down from each of them. That proved – beyond a doubt, surely? – that his hands had been fully occupied grasping the flour all the time. Then he rubbed his chafed wrists and acknowledged the crowd in the room with little bows to left and right. He stood while Ambrose helped him back into his green frock-coat.

This concluded the second part of the evening. The trio of Flask, Kitty and Ambrose left the room whilst the medium paused to exchange a few words with Julia Howlett who was still beaming with pleasure at the success of it all. Tom observed that Septimus Sheridan, standing near her, looked less enthusiastic.

There was a gap like the interval in a play. Candles were relit and the gaslights turned up higher. Tea was brought in by a couple of housemaids and the visitors stood around chatting in small groups. Mr Sheridan came towards them. He said to Helen, 'I understand, Mrs Ansell, that it is many years since you last saw your aunt.'

'Yes. It was when I was a child, quite a small child.'

'Whatever you may think of events this evening, she is a good woman, you know, a very good woman.'

'I was too young to know it then but I see it now.'

'We are of one mind then,' said Septimus Sheridan with satisfaction.

Tom had half his attention on this exchange but he was also looking at the behaviour of the gentleman in the front row, the one who'd been asked to test the knots in the ropes securing Eustace Flask. He was a short, spruce-looking figure with a fine moustache. He was peering into the interior of the cabinet to scrutinize the musical instruments on the hooks as well as the ropes which had been left coiled on the shelf and the flour smeared on the floor. He was squatting and looking at the raised underside of the cabinet before walking round it to examine the back. Tom, his curiosity stirred, joined him.

'Everything is in order?' he said.

The man tugged at his moustaches and gave Tom the same careful study he had given Flask's cabinet. 'Oh yes, it is in good order. I wouldn't expect anything else. This cabinet would not have been left so carelessly open for inspection had it been otherwise.'

'You're not a . . . believer in all this?' said Tom, indicating the cabinet.

'I am no believer.'

'But you were the one who checked the ropes and knots securing Mr Flask and you seemed to be satisfied.'

'Just as you were satisfied when you searched him, sir. He wouldn't offer himself for inspection if he wasn't confident of getting away with it. You are not from this city or this county?'

'From London. My wife and I are visitors here. From your voice, you are not local either.'

It was easy to detect those who hadn't been born or brought up in Durham. Although neither Julia Howlett nor Septimus Sheridan had acquired the local accent, Tom had been hearing the distinctive flattened vowels in undercurrents of conversation about the room. But Tom and the inquisitive gentleman could talk no further for Eustace Flask and his little entourage now returned to the morning room for the other half of the evening's manifestation. The lights were lowered once more. Tom thought it was dimmer than it had been for the cabinet show. This time the medium sat at a small table. Aunt Julia was invited to sit on one side of him and Helen on the other. Four more of the guests joined them, but not the individual who'd been examining the cabinet even though he was hovering about as if he wanted an invitation to sit down. The other dozen or more guests stood around the group at the table.

The elfin-faced Kitty brought a hinged slate and a stick of white chalk to the table. Flask lodged the slate on his lap so that the edge of it was resting against the table. He propped both his hands on the table and invited Helen and Julia to rest one of their own hands on the tops of his. After a few moments Flask jerked violently and Tom heard a whisper from one of the group, 'That is his control.' Questions were asked for by Kitty. Almost everyone in the room seemed familiar with the form. Someone said, 'What is twenty times thirty?' and someone else said, 'Who is your control?'

Each time there was a pause then a scraping sound like chalk being dragged across slate. Tom, straining to see through the gloom, thought that Flask's hands stayed without movement on the rim of the table with the slate between them. Oddly, the whole thing was more unnerving than the cabinet display, perhaps because he was only a couple of yards away from Flask or perhaps because the scraping noises set his teeth on edge. More questions were invited by the medium, who spoke now with a queer trembling unlike his usual oily tone.

'Have you a message for me?'

This was Helen. Tom was amazed that she should have asked something and faintly alarmed when her question was followed by more scratching. Then Aunt Julia asked, 'Whom should I trust?' Further scraping sounds.

Flask began to wobble his head violently as if an invisible person had seized him by the back of the neck. The slate clattered to the floor. Someone – Ambrose or Kitty? – turned up the gas, signalling the end of the session. By the better light, Flask looked paler than ever, as if he had just woken from a deep and unpleasant sleep. He seemed to come to himself. He picked the slate up from the floor. He displayed both sides of it to the room. They were blank.

Tom was relieved – and a fraction disappointed. The man was a charlatan after all and an incompetent one at that.

But then Eustace Flask unhinged the slate to reveal some writing on the inside. He nodded as he scanned the words before handing the slate round the people in the room who were pressing closer. They treated it reverently, passing it from group to group. When the slate got close to Tom he saw the following answers, written in capital letters and on separate lines.

The number: '600'

A scrawl that looked like: 'RUNNING BOOK' or possibly 'BROOK'.

The sentence: 'BELIEVE HELEN.'

The words: 'LIKE A SON'.

Apart from the first answer to the arithmetic question, none of these made much sense but it gave Tom a jolt to see Helen's name scrawled on the tablet for everyone to read. Now Kitty took the slate and, for the benefit of those who hadn't yet seen it or did not understand the responses, explained that 'Running Brook' was the name of an Indian maid who was Flask's 'control'. Indeed, the maid had already manifested herself that evening. Yes, it was Running Brook's white limbs that had appeared through the cabinet doors. Kitty, with a voice straining to be genteel, said she believed that Helen was the lady sitting next to her uncle and that the message to her was plain. She must place her trust in the reality of the spirit world. She should 'BELIEVE'. As for the final answer – the cryptic 'LIKE A SON' – Kitty was not sure of the application of these words but no doubt all would become clear in the fullness of time.

'I know what it means,' said Julia Howlett. 'It was I who asked the question 'Whom should I trust?' and the answer has come from Running Brook. I should trust my dear Mr Flask here. I should treat him *like a son.*'

Flask put his hand on his shirt-front as if to say, 'Who? Me?' But his surprise, and everyone else's, was greater when the spruce, moustached gentleman stepped forward and snatched the slate from Kitty.

'Wait a moment, Mr Flask. I think you should explain first of all how the writing on the slate is in blue chalk when there is plainly a white piece on the table.'

All eyes swivelled from the blue lettering on the tablet to the stick of white chalk on the table top. It was strange, thought Tom, that he hadn't noticed the inconsistency in colour.

'The spirit moves in mysterious ways, sir,' said the medium, perfectly self-possessed. 'What matters is the message not the colour of it.'

'You might also explain, Mr Flask, how you have left blue marks on your shirt . . .'

Flask gazed down at where he'd just patted his chest in his 'Who? Me?' gesture. There were smears of blue on his starched front. Automatically he glanced at his fingertips and there too were traces of blue chalk. For a moment he looked baffled. Then he looked angry as he saw the other man holding up a stick of blue chalk.

'I was standing near the table just before you started your folderol and your fiddle-faddle, Mr Flask, and I switched the white chalk for the blue. Then at the end of your performance, I switched them back again.'

'And what follows from that, *sir*?' said Eustace Flask.

It was fairly obvious what followed. Flask had written the words himself. By now Helen had come back from the table to stand next to Tom and they turned to look at each other. The same thought was in both their minds: was this another police exposure as in Tullis Street? Yet although the moustached man had an odd air of authority he did not seem to be a policeman. What he did next made it even less likely that he was one. He dived for Flask's ankles – the medium had not risen from his chair – and tugged at the bottom of the man's trousers like an angry dog. A shower of flour rained on to Julia Howlett's carpet.

'There we are,' said the man, standing up and gazing round the room, his own hands now white and floury. The guests looked bemused and shocked. 'I ask you why a man should need to keep flour in little secret bags at the bottom of his trousers. There is no sane explanation unless it is to replace the flour that the same man has let drop while he is fiddling with his knots and jangling his instruments.'

When they discussed it afterwards, Tom and Helen both confessed to a touch of admiration at the way Flask responded, even if it was only admiration at his impudence. In their eyes, he'd been caught red-handed, or rather caught with a piece of blue chalk and with piles of concealed flour.

Instead of shrivelling up or admitting defeat, as Ernest Smight had done, Flask rose from the table. Ambrose shouldered his way towards him but the medium lifted a ringed hand, the tips of his fingers still tinged with blue chalk. It was like the benediction of a bishop. The gesture said, 'Blessed are the peacemakers.' Flask paced slowly towards the gentleman with the fine moustaches, who did not shift one inch. He halted when he was within striking distance. When he spoke next it was not to his opponent but to the rest of the company.

'Our Lord tells us that when our enemies assail us, we should turn the other cheek. I do not know what your reasons are for coming here tonight, sir, but you have fallen among people who seek no quarrel with you and rather wish the scales to fall from your eyes.'

There were nodded heads at this and whispers of agreement. Tom realized that, whatever the exposer's motives, he had badly misjudged the occasion. Apart from the Ansells and possibly Mr Sheridan, Julia Howlett's guests were true believers. It would take more to convince them than the uncovering of a trick or two. They blamed the accuser and not the accused, who was adopting the role of injured innocent. The man with the moustache understood this. He smiled. He bowed in a way that was slightly stagey. His departing remark too had a melodramatic ring. 'Next time, Mr Flask, we shall do battle on a ground of my choosing.'

He turned smartly on his heel and strode from the morning room. There was a pause and then a woman began to clap and soon Eustace Flask had earned a round of applause for the way he stood up to the outsider. Aunt Julia clasped him by the arm and other women gathered round him with praise and reassurance. Everyone seemed to have forgotten the business of the blue chalk and the surplus flour, even though there were little mounds of the stuff on the floor by Flask's seat. There was some talk about the identity of the impertinent fellow who'd tried to ruin their evening but no one seemed to have an idea of who he was. Yet, equally, Tom and Helen had the impression that, in the spiritualist community, such hostility and persecution were routine matters.

These things were to be expected and, in a perverse way, they fortified the true believer.

Ambrose started to dismantle the cabinet and Kitty to pack away the curtains and muslin. Aunt Julia was sitting and writing at a roll-top desk in the corner of the room and Flask was standing over her like a shield. She handed a slip of paper to the medium who promptly tucked it away. Tom would have bet a month of his own salary that the medium was receiving his reward for the evening. The task which Helen's mother had entrusted to her, that of weaning the aunt away from her devotion to the medium, seemed more impossible than ever.

Flask's Family

Eustace Flask and Ambrose Barker and Kitty were renting a tiny end-of-terrace house outside the city walls in the old borough of Elvet. The medium and his companions were better dressed and kept odder hours than most other inhabitants of the borough, which lay to the north-east across the River Wear. If anyone asked, the trio was a family of sorts, with Flask as the uncle, Kitty his niece and Ambrose some kind of cousin. But no one did ask because in this area of back-to-back terraces, boarding houses, small shops and drinking places on the fringe of a colliery, there was little neighbourly curiosity. Besides, Ambrose had a faintly threatening air to him that discouraged questions.

If the old part of the city was dominated by the cathedral and castle, this more recently built quarter was the location for the new court and police-house and an imposing prison. Ambrose might have seen more than one prison from the inside – he looked the type – but if it disturbed him to glimpse the high walls of Durham Gaol first thing in the morning and last thing at night he did not show it.

Now he finished stowing away the handcart containing the dismantled cabinet which he had wheeled down from the old maid's place in the South Bailey. The terrace house was backed by a tiny yard, convenient for storing the equipment required by the guv'nor. The guv'nor! Ambrose was able to maintain a sober face while Flask was pulling his tricks but the moment the show was done with and they were away from the spiritualist mob and their trusting sheep's eyes he could hardly keep himself from sneering and cackling at the stupidity of humankind.

This attitude did not extend to Eustace Flask himself for, although Ambrose was often nettled by the airs and graces of the medium, he recognized that the man had a real talent for deception and moneymaking. He called him Eustace but also the guv'nor sometimes and it was not altogether ironic. It was his appreciation of Flask's skills that made him bite his tongue as he watched the medium and his 'niece' Kitty walking ahead while he trundled the cart behind them over the cobbles, feeling a bit like some beast of burden. He knew that if they were to be stopped by one of the town police – which had happened more than once – Mr Flask would soon knock any suspicions on the head. He'd talk in that superior way of his and refer in a familiar style to the Chief Constable and his superintendents and other town worthies as if he dined with them every day. Nevertheless, it hurt Ambrose in the heart to see Kitty next to Flask and touching his arm so constantly with her little paws as they walked so close, to see her whispering and giggling all confidential in his ear, and altogether behaving like a silly chit.

Ambrose had always taken Flask for a molly, a Mary Anne. The guv'nor slipped into the manner easy enough and he was relaxed in the company of women, especially older ones, which could be a sign of molly-hood. But perhaps the truth was that he was something in between, or a nothing in between, neither fish nor fowl. Yet it disturbed Ambrose to see Eustace and Kitty so cosy. He'd have words with Miss Kitty Partout later on, he would.

He pronounced her name Par-tout, putting the stress on the second part and rhyming it with 'out', which she said was wrong because it was French and she should be pronounced Par-too. Kitty claimed to be French originally, a generation or two back. In that case, said Ambrose, what's *Par-too* mean? Does it have a meaning? Dunno, said Kitty. My mum never said and my dad wasn't around to ask. But Ambrose did believe that Kitty might have Frog blood in her. She had a saucy air sometimes and a way of looking up from under her lowered lashes that was, well, *foreign* as far as he was concerned.

Ambrose made certain that the gate to the yard was locked before he entered the house by the back passage. He heard rustlings from the parlour and walked into the room just as Mr Flask and Kitty sprang apart from each other. Ambrose thought that his guv'nor's hand might have been on her tit. Trying the goods, eh? He almost laughed to imagine what that old maid and the other worthies up in the high town would say if they could see their precious medium fondling the boobies of his 'niece'. He almost laughed. Instead, he promised himself he'd definitely be having words later on with Miss Kitty.

'Ah, Ambrose,' said Flask. 'Everything tucked up for the night? Join us for a libation?'

There were glasses of some sticky pale brown stuff on a table. Sherry or something.

'There's a jug of porter in the kitchen. I'll have some o' that. Run and fetch it, Kitty Par-tout, there's a good girl.'

Kitty hesitated for a second and Ambrose saw Flask nod almost imperceptibly before she scampered off to the kitchen. But he put his best face on it and said, 'Find anything in York, Eustace? That's where you was this afternoon, wasn't it?'

'A couple of likely prospects,' said the medium. 'One of them a widower.'

'Thought you found women easier to work with than men, guv'nor. More – what's the word? – pliant.'

'It depends,' said Flask.

Kitty returned carrying the jug of porter and a tankard. She made a show of pouring it out for Ambrose and not spilling more than a drop or two, as if she wanted to demonstrate what a careful girl she was. Then, picking up her own sticky brown libation, she flung herself into a battered armchair, one of a pair. Eustace Flask settled in the other while Ambrose had to content himself with an even more dilapidated rocking chair which was hard on the bum and pinched the hips.

'We did well tonight. Here is a contribution for the cause,' said Flask, producing the cheque which Julia Howlett had presented to him. Ambrose noticed that he didn't let it out of his hands or even say how much the cheque was for.

'Who was that terrible man with the moustache?' asked Kitty.

'I think I know who he is,' said Flask, without enlarging on it.

'He nearly spoiled everything.'

'That's where you are wrong, my dear Kit. He made an exhibition of himself and, far from convincing the congregation he was right, he made them feel I had been hard done by. I am sure that Miss Howlett gave us more than she would have done without his intervention.'

Eustace Flask sometimes referred to his audience as a

'congregation'. He did it with a straight face, which you had to admire him for.

'What about that other couple, Eustace?' said Ambrose. 'The tall, dark-haired geezer and the pretty piece with fair curled hair. What were they up to?'

'I understand from Miss Howlett that the woman is her niece and the man is her husband. They are newly married and visiting Durham for the first time. As a matter of fact, I met them on the train from York. I don't think there is any harm in them.'

'Oh, we know all about nieces, don't we Eustace?' said Ambrose.

Eustace ignored the remark. He said, 'We must tread very carefully over the next few days. That is why I responded with calm and dignity to the attack on me this evening. We have reached a critical moment. Miss Howlett is primed to provide me with an allowance so that I can continue with my good work for the *cause*. And I have high hopes of something more . . .'

Ambrose was wondering what the 'something more' could be when Kitty broke in. 'Does that mean we'll have to stay in Durham, Eustace? I am getting tired of the city.'

'We shall not be staying here for much longer. I shall make it a condition of any allowance that I – or we, rather – would have to continue with our journeying, to spread the word. Now, Kit, we are ready for a little supper after our exertions. You purchased some pork chops earlier today, did you not? It must be time for you to go and cook them up.'

Kitty refilled her glass and then busied herself in the kitchen frying the chops. Eustace and Ambrose sat in silence in the parlour, drinking. By the time the food reached the table, all three of them were sozzled.

When he got Kitty to bed that night, Ambrose had more or less forgotten his earlier irritation at seeing Eustace and her so comfortable and familiar together in the street and the parlour. He did give her nipples a few extra twists but it was half-hearted, like her little shrieks in response. The two shared a room at the back of the house, with a view of the stern prison walls, while Mr Flask had the bigger room at the front.

The nipple-twisting had turned to stroking and fondling, and Kitty's little shrieks to sighs. But before they got on to the main matter, Ambrose had something he wanted to ask her. 'What's the guv'nor hoping to squeeze out of the old maid? She's going to give him an allowance – more fool her, if she does – but he was talking about something more. What's he mean?'

'I don't know, Ambrose. Ah . . . yes that's it. And I'll just put my hand here . . .'

There was an extended pause but suddenly Kitty said, 'Maybe he's trying to get her to put him in her will.'

'Who? What you talking about?' said Ambrose, who was rather distracted at this point.

'Eustace and Miss Howlett. He thinks she might leave him something in her will.'

'She's not dead yet.'

'She's old.'

'Looks in good health to me.'

'You never know with old maids though. They can go sudden.'

'Or be pushed sudden.'

And the two, in the middle of their pleasure, giggled at the thought.

Ambrose Barker was familiar with the use of force. It was one of his attractions for Kitty Partout. She had first admired him while he was wearing no more than knee breeches and practising his trade at the Black Lion near Drury Lane. Miss Partout was keeping company with a young Corinthian or swell who enjoyed seeing men of a lower class beat each other to pulp. Usually Kitty enjoyed it too. Most of the fighters showed the marks of their trade in broken noses and ripped ears and swollen hands. Although Ambrose possessed a dented nose he still had a touch of youth about him. But that evening he came off badly at the hands of a negro called Turner. As he was being dragged from the ring – which was nothing more than a chalked-off square on the bare pine boards of a back room – he managed to exchange glances with Kitty. She felt a thrill go through her.

About an hour later, when 'Ebony' Turner had disposed of several more contenders and Kitty's swell had drunk so much that he was staggering worse than the fighters, they left the Lion. Ambrose was waiting outside, lounging against a wall, holding a flannel to the side of his face where Turner had torn a great rent in it. Apart from that wound he had quite recovered as he demonstrated by what he did next. With his free hand he seized Kitty's arm and said, 'You're coming with me.'

'Where we going then?' she said, as her Corinthian swell fell into the gutter without needing so much as a shove. 'Where are we going? Gretna Green?'

It was such a good joke that she was still laughing as they stumbled, hand in hand, towards Covent Garden. They didn't end up in Gretna Green but in a nethersken in Hackney – two pennies for a room to yourself – where they stayed for that first night and plenty more of the nights to come. When they eventually found time to talk, Ambrose explained that he'd had enough of the fancy or P.R. as he called it, meaning Prize Ring. The ring was on its last legs in these new respectable days; he'd come at it too late and maybe – he didn't say this but Kitty guessed it – he was not quite ruthless enough or sufficiently indifferent to his own injuries. There must be safer means of getting by.

Ambrose and Kitty tried a couple of the safer means. He worked on the docks and in a carpenter's while she tried her hand as a milliner's assistant. But there was always the pull of something darker and more lucrative – and more dangerous. Ambrose had links with the fancymen who hung about the prize ring, and obligations to one in particular. It was suggested that, to fulfil one such obligation, that he work as a bearer-up – a robber – while Kitty would be the decoy. He might have done it; he wasn't averse to a spot of outright robbery. But Kitty balked at being his accomplice. She had never, yet, broken the law, at least not so nakedly or violently.

But they had to leave Hackney in a hurry and somehow they decided to quit London altogether. They made a slow zigzag progress north, going via Newport Pagnell and Birmingham and then across to Derby and Nottingham. It was as if they were giving substance to her original jest about Gretna Green. Eventually they arrived in Durham, a city that neither of them knew. They were on their uppers.

It was then that, in desperation, they tried a form of mild extortion. Kitty was to accost a man in one of the city vennels or alleys and after a brief time Ambrose would appear on the scene as her outraged mate demanding payment by bluff and bluster. They were depending on Kitty's good looks and Ambrose's pugnacious ones. They selected a fine-looking gent on account of his clothes and swagger. They watched as he turned off Saddler Street down one of the alleys, and Kitty cooeed softly after him. The pair got to talking in the covered passage. Kitty started to fondle him, even though he was not very receptive, and she wondered whether she'd laid her hands on a molly. Then, too soon, Ambrose clumped down the alley, full of useless outrage.

The gent was Eustace Flask. Unfortunately for Kitty and Ambrose, Flask was better at the bluff and bluster business than they were. He saw through them, saw that they were not as ferocious or threatening as they seemed. Rather than taking his money, the couple found themselves listening to a proposition. He, Flask, was in need of a couple of assistants for his work. What work? It's legal, he said, it's legitimate. It will take you into the better houses in the city. It will make us some lucre. They were impressed by his smoothness, by his way with words. He explained that they would have to smarten themselves up, be on their best behaviour. They agreed.

The threesome established themselves in the rented house in Old Elvet. Kitty was Eustace's niece, if anyone asked questions, while Ambrose was a cousin. Flask was ready to develop his spiritualist show. No longer content with table-rapping and such minor manifestations, he realized that more elaborate and impressive effects were required. He was cultivating a wealthy spinster who lived in the old part of town. Ambrose constructed the spirit cabinet and Kitty purchased the material for the curtains and painted the cabinet.

This was a new world for them. Flask instructed them in some of his methods. He demonstrated how one could write on a slate even while one's hands were seemingly at rest on top of a table. He showed them how to tie knots which could easily be slipped. He taught them how to use two of the key techniques of the performer, which are expectation and distraction.

Kitty in particular took to her role as Running Brook, the Indian maid who was Flask's 'control'. She was an adept performer. Ambrose wasn't so willing or useful but he acted as a combination of handyman and valet. He still believed that Flask was a molly but Kitty wasn't so sure. Some day she would have to put it to the test, to put him to the test. But not yet. She was happy to be in bed with Ambrose, even if he was somewhat coarse and brutish compared to Eustace. She was happy that they were all together, that they had a roof over their heads and a bit of cash in their pockets. They were almost like a family.

By the River Wear

'It felt like a real hand,' said Helen, 'though now I think about it I was only touching one of his fingers with one of mine, which is what the medium told me to do. And the lights were low.'

'Well, we know that Flask somehow managed to write those words on the slate and at the same time make you and your aunt believe both his hands were resting on the table.'

'Unless he's got three hands,' said Helen. 'Or unless he was using his feet to write. Or unless there was a dwarf concealed beneath the table and busy scribbling away.'

'That wouldn't explain the blue chalk on his fingers,' Tom couldn't help pointing out, though he admired his wife's skill and imagination in coming up with all these possibilities.

'Whatever the explanation, whether it's three hands or feet capable of writing or whether it's dwarves, it is all rather horrid. I did not like the way he employed my name. Writing 'BELIEVE HELEN' on the slate.'

'But you asked him a question,' said Tom.

'I felt that he wanted me to. It gave me goose-bumps.'

'And he was using your name to show how familiar he is with the household,' said Tom. 'He's clever all right.'

'Clever and sinister. I'm glad we've got this romantic view all around to distract us from Mr Eustace Flask.'

It was the morning after their arrival in Durham. Helen and Tom Ansell were strolling beside the river and below the rise dominated by the castle and cathedral. They could feel the presence of those great edifices although the buildings themselves were hidden by the rise of the bank and thick tiers of summer foliage. A walk had been created under the overhanging oaks and chestnuts, and there were other people ambling along in the morning sun. Among the casual walkers was the individual who had alighted at Durham Station from the same train as Tom and Helen. Once again, his attention seemed to be fixed on the backs of the young couple who were perhaps fifty yards ahead of him.

It was warm and Helen had brought a parasol although it was still furled. In front of them was a fulling mill and a line of dirty foam where the river level dropped and the water tumbled across rocks. For all the coal-black streaks which ran through it like threads, the water sparkled in the light.

They'd spent most of the walk discussing the session of the previous evening. They thought they'd worked out how the thin white arms might have been done: Tom said it was significant he hadn't been able to spot Kitty during the time when the limbs were being waggled through the muslin curtains. Although she'd appeared in *front* of the cabinet just as the arms were being with-drawn inside, perhaps some trickery had occurred. Make-believe limbs of wax or plaster which might be substituted for real ones at the last moment? The light was low and everyone was in a state of heightened expectation in which they might see what they wanted to see.

But it was one thing to use common sense and discuss how it might have been done while walking along the riverbank on a bright summer's morning, and another for Helen to per-suade her aunt to see Eustace Flask for the fraud he really was. Indeed, she was wondering whether it was even right for her to try.

'After all, Tom, we've already had an unhappy experience with the spiritualists. That man in London who drowned himself. Suppose Mr Flask did something so desperate.'

'Flask isn't like Smight. He is a – I don't know – he's a profes-sional. If he fails here then he'll go and try somewhere else. Besides, he is not failing, unfortunately, but doing rather well. Making money.'

'I know it is my aunt's money. But it is also her life. I do not think I can dictate to her how she should use them.'

'Even though Flask is no better than a confidence trickster. It was very clever how he nudged your aunt into believing that he should be treated "like a son".'

'*We* can see that he is a trickster but no one else there last night was willing to accept it.'

'Apart from the gentleman who exposed him,' said Tom.

'Who was he, do you think?'

'I've no idea except that he is an outsider here, like us. But

he was very accomplished with his own sleight of hand.
Substituting the sticks of chalk and then knowing that Flask had
flour hidden away at the bottom of his trousers.'

There was something so absurd about the flour and the trousers
that Tom and Helen laughed out loud. Then a thought occurred
to Tom. It was to do with an outsider who was skilled with his
hands . . . the techniques required by a fraudulent medium . . . or
by a magician. Now Helen was saying something else and he
wasn't listening.

'I said that the unknown man wasn't the only person to be
sceptical about Flask. There's also my aunt's lodger, Septimus
Sheridan.'

'It's true he expressed just the tiniest doubt about Flask and
he was looking a bit unhappy during the evening. But I noticed
he was very quick to agree with Aunt Julia about everything.'

'Here is a strange business, Tom. I was talking to Septimus and
he let slip two or three things. In fact, he didn't reveal them acci-
dentally. I think that he wanted me to know them. He used to
live in the city of Durham. He has been friends with my Aunt
Julia for many years although there was a long period when they
did not see anything of each other. While he was saying this, he
let out a deep sigh as though he regretted that long absence. And
from something else he said I understood that he had once been
in the church . . .'

'Had been in the church? I don't understand. Doesn't Mr
Sheridan spend his time researching in the cathedral library?'

'Yes, he does. But I mean that he was once a minister, that he
was ordained.'

'He's been defrocked!' said Tom.

'No, no. Does he have the look of a man who's done something scandalous? Septimus mentioned a 'crisis of faith'. I believe
that he quit the church but that he continues to do his work or
research in its shadow. And I think too that *he* was the man that
my aunt was engaged to, the man on whose account she first
came to Durham.'

'Aren't you letting your imagination wander, Helen?'

'Do not say so, Thomas, otherwise I shall push you into the
river with the tip of my parasol, like this.'

They were passing a section of the bank which dropped sheer

to the river. Helen jabbed at Tom in a way that was almost entirely playful. Tom looked round. He noticed a tall man behind them who quickly averted his gaze.

'Supposing you're right,' said Tom after a moment. 'Does that mean that Septimus Sheridan has come back in the hope of marrying your aunt after all these years?'

'He has no ambition that way as far as I can tell. Nor has she. Haven't you noticed the weary manner in which she talks to him? On her side, it's as if they've been married years already while he defers to her and then talks about her in a way that's almost reverential.'

'Oh dear,' said Tom gloomily. 'I didn't know you were such a dissector of the right conditions for marriage. Weariness from the woman and deference from the man.'

'Whatever is between my aunt and Septimus is not a marriage,' said Helen. 'Septimus is – I don't now – he's a mixture of a hermit and a lodger.'

'It's all very odd,' said Tom.

'That's what you said about our journey before we started. The coincidence of Aunt Julia and the medium together with your Major Whatnot and his dagger. You must tell me what he says. Unless it's confidential and legal and all those things.'

'I think Major Marmont wants the world to know how he came by the dagger. Anyway I shall tell you everything after I've met him.'

'Pardon me,' said someone loudly.

Helen and Tom stopped and looked back. A man was standing there, the same individual whom Tom had observed earlier.

'Pardon me,' he repeated. 'I believe you may have dropped this, madam.'

He was holding out a lilac-coloured handkerchief. Helen stepped closer to examine it. 'No. I don't think so,' she said. 'Thank you but it doesn't belong to me.'

'I could have sworn you let it fall as you were walking. I saw it fluttering to the ground.'

The man was tall and dressed in clothes that had been of good quality but now showed signs of wear. He was well-spoken. Since he was so insistent, Helen made a show of looking at the lilac handkerchief more carefully. She shook her head.

'Ah well,' he said, 'I must be mistaken. Good day to you, madam, and to you, sir.'

He touched his hat in salute and walked off in the opposite direction.

'It might have been your handkerchief,' said Tom. 'He seemed very convinced.'

'I recognize that man,' said Helen. 'Or not recognize exactly, but there was something familiar about him.'

They both turned round again to watch the man striding along the riverside path. He had a rangy, loping walk.

'No,' said Tom. 'Doesn't look like anyone I know.'

The Cathedral Precincts

At about the same time as Helen and Tom were beginning their stroll along the riverside path below the cathedral, Eustace Flask was taking a walk on Palace Green, in the precincts of the cathedral itself. He reached the north porch where a man was waiting for him. They nodded to each other before entering the building. If they had been interested in such things they might have remarked on the great pillars in the nave which were incised with zigzags or lozenge patterns, or commented on the way the sun poured through the rose window in the east. But the two were not attracted by ecclesiastical architecture or the morning light. Instead, the cathedral served as a convenient meeting place where they might go unnoticed on account of the regular visitors and the coming and going of the masons and carpenters who were presently rebuilding the choir screen.

Flask's companion was a man of medium height with a florid complexion. His name was Frank Harcourt and he was a police superintendent, one of six holding that rank in the Durham City Constabulary. He was off-duty and so wearing civilian clothes, a three-piece suit which he would not normally have afforded but which his wife Rhoda had encouraged him to buy. Of the two men Harcourt might have been the more easily recognized, perhaps by one of the clerics who were walking purposefully about the building, but he avoided meeting anyone's eye. By instinct the two kept their perambulations to the secluded or shadowed corners of the cathedral.

They didn't speak a word until they were standing in the north transept where Eustace Flask said, 'How are you on this fine summer's morning, Frank?'

'I cannot hold them off for much longer,' said Frank Harcourt who evidently had no time for pleasantries. He was sweating, despite the coolness of the place, and his red face was a contrast to Flask's pallor. Nearby was the scuffling movement of workmen up and down ladders, the discreet tap of chisel on stone.

'Hold them off? Whom do you mean?' said Flask.

'*Whom* do you think I mean?' said Harcourt, imitating Flask's oily tone. 'I mean Alfred Huggins. I mean the Chief Constable.'

'But you said *them*, which I took to be more than one person.'

This time Harcourt answered with real irritation. 'You know the situation, Mr Flask. There are quite a few people who do not care for your activities in this town or even your presence here.'

'Which people?'

'Do I need to spell it out? Some of them are probably in these precincts at this very moment. Men of the cloth. Not all of them approve of this spiritualist lark. They call it an offence against religion. Not to put too fine a point on it, they think that you are a fraud.'

'Spiritualist lark? *Lark*?' said Flask, putting his hand on his fine brocade waistcoat in the gesture he'd previously employed in Julia Howlett's morning room. 'Well, I suppose that true prophets and seekers of truth have always been mocked and persecuted.'

'Spare me the indignation, Mr Flask. You do not have to pretend with me. These important people, men of the cloth and the rest of them, are putting pressure on the Chief Constable who in turn is putting pressure on me to do something about it.'

'Frank, Frank, I can't tell you how disappointed I am to hear you talk in this unfriendly fashion. For we are friends, you know. Besides I am not breaking any laws.'

'Maybe not, but if I was to investigate I'm sure I could turn up something. And it's not only you. There is that Ambrose Barker fellow and the woman, Kitty with the strange surname. I could certainly turn up something on *them*.'

'If you *were* to investigate, perhaps you could. But you are not going to, are you?'

'Like I said just now, I cannot hold the Chief Constable off forever.'

'Keep your voice down, we are attracting attention.'

And, indeed, a gaggle of visitors assembled in the crossing place who'd been staring upward at the soaring interior of the tower as well as admiring the new work on the choir screen were now turning to look at Flask and Harcourt. The two men moved away to the south end of the cathedral before walking out to the cloisters. When they were out of earshot of the few other people ambling round the area, Superintendent Harcourt went on the attack once more.

'I heard there was trouble last night at that old lady's house in South Bailey. Someone tried to expose you.'

'How did you know?'

'I am a policeman, Mr Flask. It is my duty to keep my ear to the ground.'

'We must not forget you are a policeman, Frank. A pillar of the community. Yes, some troublemaker did try to "expose" me, as you put it. He did not succeed.'

'It doesn't matter. Your presence in Durham cannot be tolerated for much longer.'

'How is your pretty new wife, Frank? How is Rhoda?'

'She is well,' said Harcourt, in a subdued voice.

'Did she like the cameo I sent her? It was a nice piece. I know that she has fine tastes or should I say expensive ones.'

'She appreciated the cameo, thank you.'

'I wonder what Mr Alfred Huggins would say if he knew your wife had accepted gifts from a spiritualist. I wonder what he would say about the other little contributions I have made to your household economy?'

This time Harcourt was silent.

'All I require is a few more days to complete my, ah, work here,' resumed Flask. 'Then I shall move to pastures new. Why, only yesterday I took the train down to York to see the lie of the land.'

'I'll do my best,' said Harcourt. 'You can go to York or go to the moon for all I care but you *must* leave Durham very soon. Otherwise I shall have to begin an investigation of your activities. Only a few days, mind.'

'Good, good,' said Flask, apparently satisfied. 'I think I shall have a look at the library here. They say it is one of the finest ecclesiastical libraries in the country. Do you know it? Are you familiar with the cathedral library?'

'Do as you please,' said Harcourt but he spoke the words under his breath to the retreating back of Eustace Flask, who, with a nonchalant farewell waggle of his hand, turned into a doorway leading off from the cloister.

The superintendent of police made his way out of the cloisters.

He was still sweating inside his new suit, sweating with heat and irritation at the conversation with Flask, and he went into the cool of the Galilee Chapel to recover. Idly, he gazed at the tomb of the Venerable Bede which stood isolated and flanked at each corner by ceremonial stone candleholders. There was an inscription in Latin on the black surface of the tomb. Frank Harcourt wondered at the meaning of the words. No doubt Eustace Flask could have told him. Flask was an educated man. A plausible educated fraud.

Harcourt had encountered Flask a few months ago when the medium had first arrived in Durham and before he had set up with his retinue of Kitty and Ambrose Barker. In a moment of weakness the policeman had asked him if he might make contact with his late wife. Harcourt's marriage to Rhoda was scarcely a year old but, for all her comparative youth and relative attractions, he found himself missing Florry who had passed away three summers before. Florence Harcourt was like one of the old, comfortable, familiar suits which Rhoda had forced him to discard. He missed the way that Florry had been satisfied with his rank and his pay, or at least the fact that she had never complained about it. It was no mean thing to be a police superintendent, one of only six in the city, and to be bringing home a weekly wage of forty-two shillings. No mean thing for him, who had worked his way up from the ranks, but yet not enough for Rhoda. She made not-so-casual remarks about promotion, she regularly inquired about the age and health of Alfred Huggins, the Chief Constable.

So, after meeting Flask, he attended a séance without telling Rhoda and there he heard from Florry. Yes, she was more than content on the other side – oh, it was a place of such light and ease and wonder. A place where one breakfasted with angels and dined with the spirits of the departed. His first wife was also content that he had found happiness in the arms of another although she – or rather Eustace Flask – didn't put it exactly in those terms. But Frank Harcourt was no fool. He had spent too much time questioning felons and listening to their denials and evasions to be incapable of smelling a rat. Once the initial delight at hearing from Florry had worn off, he quickly concluded that he had been taken in. He wondered why angels should need to eat breakfast, or why his late wife needed to eat at all for that matter.

But by then it was too late. Flask was no fool either and he speedily realized how useful it would be to have a member of the Durham constabulary looking out for him while he pursued bigger game in the city. From hints dropped carelessly by Frank Harcourt, the medium understood the policeman's resentment at his new wife's nagging ambition.

Under the guise of paying his respects to Rhoda, he called at their house in Hallgarth Street when he knew the superintendent was at work. When Harcourt got home that evening and heard that Flask had visited, he was first angry then fearful. He expected Rhoda to give him hell over his secret consultation with the medium, he thought she would as good as accuse him of infidelity by wanting to be put in touch with Florence. But Rhoda Harcourt had been charmed by Flask. 'A real gentleman, so educated and refined,' she said. He had even given her a brooch as a token of his regard. It was the first of several gifts. Harcourt wasn't sure that Rhoda was aware that Flask practised as a medium, since he had introduced himself as someone who had encountered her husband in the course of 'civic affairs'. Perhaps she assumed that he had no need to earn money for it was well known that gentlemen, especially such educated and refined ones, could be idle all their lives.

But the fatal error that Frank Harcourt committed was to take money for himself. Or for the 'household economy' as Flask expressed it. The medium, with his perception of others' weak points, had seen that the police superintendent was strapped. One glance around the house in Hallgarth Street, with its furniture and curtains which were new but not quite expensive enough, was sufficient to tell him that. He presented the white five-pound note to Harcourt as a favour, one friend to another. To tide him over. Pay it back when you can. Best not to say anything about it to anyone.

The superintendent reached out and felt the white paper. He closed his fingers on it. Even as he did so, he knew that he was lost. But the note amounted to more than two weeks' wages! And he'd been having a particularly difficult time with Rhoda recently, who was insisting on the need for another housemaid.

He tucked the note into his wallet and muttered something about repaying it as soon as possible. Once the money was secure, Flask produced a small black notebook and wrote down the amount and the date of the loan.

'Why are you doing that?' said Harcourt. 'I've got a poor memory', said Flask, 'I note down everything. Don't worry, we're friends, aren't we?' Harcourt should have handed the money back there and then, he should have seized the notebook and torn out the offending page, but he did neither of these things. Instead the fiver lodged in his wallet like a lead weight while his hands hung heavy at his sides.

Other smaller loans had followed, two pounds here, a pound there. Having accepted one, Frank Harcourt found himself almost helpless not to accept more. These loans were never called in. Frank decided that he would prefer to be in the hands of the most grasping usurer rather than in Eustace Flask's. For it was evident that the medium expected not cash but favours, he expected the superintendent to protect him from the law or, indeed, any unwelcome attention from the authorities. As Harcourt had described it, there were plenty of important people in Durham – several but not all of them in the church – who objected to the presence of Flask in the city. They were particularly concerned about the spinster Julia Howlett, a wealthy and respected member of the community.

The Chief Constable, old Huggins, had personally demanded to know what they were going to do about this 'fraud' Flask. Was it true that Harcourt knew him? said Huggins in that gruff no-nonsense manner of his. Some whispers had reached his ears. It didn't look good, you know, for one of the senior members of the Constabulary to go round consorting with such a dubious creature. Frank protested that he was merely trying to gather evidence so that he could bring charges against the medium. 'Well, be quick about it, Harcourt,' barked Huggins. 'I'd like nothing better than to see him behind bars.'

This conversation had occurred a couple of days before Harcourt's meeting with Flask in the cathedral. What Huggins would say when and if he heard that there had been a scene involving Eustace Flask at Miss Howlett's house, Harcourt dreaded to think. It might be enough for the Chief Constable to demand

Flask's immediate arrest even though, in this case, it seemed that the medium had been the victim and not the assailant.

The superintendent might have been relieved by Flask's saying that he was planning to leave Durham in a few days but he wasn't. He did not trust the medium, not an inch. And there was the threat that the man had made today, the first time he had uttered it, the threat to let slip the story of the gifts to Rhoda and the household loans. He could deny them, of course, but he wasn't certain that his wife would keep quiet and there was the evidence in Flask's little black book. Besides, it was already known to Alfred Huggins that he had dealings with Flask.

No, if this ever got out, Superintendent Frank Harcourt could see disgrace stretching in front of him. Stripped of his rank and discharged from the force without a penny. Worse, banged up in the gaol alongside some of the very felons he had had the pleasure of putting there.

No less hot and angry, he stalked out of the Galilee Chapel and emerged into the sunlight on the north side of the cathedral. He wiped his sweating brow. He walked over to the parapet-like wall which gave a view over the thickly wooded slope leading down to the river. He wasn't aware of it but Tom and Helen Ansell were strolling down below him at that very moment. In fact, Harcourt was aware of nothing except his anger at Eustace Flask. Far from growing calmer, he was growing more desperate. If that fraud did not quit Durham very soon, there was no telling what might happen.

Meanwhile, the object of his fear and hatred was sailing into the cathedral library, which lay off the south side of the cloisters close to the old monks' quarters. Eustace Flask had no strong desire to enter the library but neither did he wish to accompany Superintendent Harcourt back through the cathedral precincts. He preferred to make a slightly stagey exit and he also wanted to leave the man stewing in his own juices, so he strode off with that nonchalant wave and climbed the stairs to what had once been a refectory.

Altogether, he was satisfied at the way the encounter with Harcourt had gone. The man was literally in his debt – those little presents to his wife, those small contributions to the household economy – but it was extraordinary how ungrateful some people could be. So the occasional reminder was necessary. He wondered whether it had been wise to threaten to tell certain things to the Chief Constable because Harcourt grew even more red-faced and anxious. But it was better that the man was absolutely clear about how things stood.

Flask was convinced that he was only a couple of days away from persuading Miss Howlett to make him an allowance for his 'researches' and for 'spreading the word'. He had higher ambitions than an allowance of course. An allowance, even a regular one, would cease when the old maid got some fresh bee in her bonnet and it would stop absolutely with her death, whereas a legacy would be something really worth striving for. Perhaps he should chalk a spirit message to that effect.

Flask was particularly pleased that he had succeeded in slipping the communication LIKE A SON on to the slate yesterday evening. He congratulated himself on his subtlety. He had left it to the old maid to jump to the right conclusion, namely that he, Eustace Flask, was the one who should be treated LIKE A SON. People were much more ready to believe if they did their own work in convincing themselves rather than sitting there, waiting to be convinced.

As for the message BELIEVE HELEN, that had come to him in a moment of inspiration. It established a further link between himself (or more strictly his control, Running Brook) and Miss Howlett's family. He rather thought that the old maid's niece and her new husband would need quite a bit of convincing. Nice-looking woman, the niece, Helen, someone with a bit of class quite unlike Kitty Partout. *She* had been especially attentive to him recently, perhaps because she saw him as a challenge, perhaps because she regarded him as a more secure source of income than Ambrose Barker.

Anyway, once his allowance had been signed and sealed he would set off to York, or elsewhere, secure in the knowledge that he had a guaranteed income for a time. He'd have to pop back to Durham every now and then to reassure the spinster and spin her a story or two, but essentially he was quids in. His investment in Frank Harcourt was paying off, and a nice irony was that the sums of money he had given to the policeman came indirectly from Miss Howlett, just as the gifts he had presented to Rhoda Harcourt were also from her or other ladies. (Not all of them were *gifts* freely made to Flask for the medium was light-fingered. It was one of his several talents.)

He poked his head round the door of the cathedral library. An individual in clerical vestments looked up from a desk by the entrance. Flask nodded and smiled at him. He walked confidently into the great book-lined chamber, knowing that if one acted with enough assurance one was rarely challenged.

There were a handful of men, mostly elderly, in the library, scribbling away or slowly turning the pages of single volumes or doing God-knows-what behind great barricades of books. Motes of dust hovered in the sunlight slanting through the high windows. Once inside, Eustace Flask found a secluded alcove among the banks of shelves. He took a letter from his pocket. He had already read the letter more than once but its contents baffled him. Or, more precisely, they raised his suspicions.

The letter, strangely affable in tone, was from the person who had done his best to disrupt the séance at Miss Howlett's the previous evening. It made only a passing reference to their 'unfortunate encounter' and, by way of compensation, invited the medium to attend a forthcoming event at which he would be 'enlightened, entertained and edified'. The letter-writer had given a time and a venue. These details and the signature at the end confirmed Flask's intuition about the identity of the séance-spoiler. Well, that was no great surprise. There was a long-standing hostility between individuals like himself who sought to pierce the veil separating the mortal from the eternal and those who followed this particular gentleman's . . . profession? . . . no, he would not call it a profession, but a trade. Or an activity. A cheap, crowd-pleasing activity.

There were several puzzling or worrying aspects to the letter. It had been delivered that morning to the dwelling in Old Elvet, and Flask wondered how the writer had found out the address of the house which he was renting. But that was a minor matter compared to this man's motives. *Why* did he wish the medium to be 'enlightened' and all the rest of it? Was he holding out an olive branch with one hand and hiding a knife behind his back with the other? Or if not a knife then a piece of blue chalk.

Flask's instinct was to keep his distance, to have nothing to do with this individual. Yet at the same time his curiosity was piqued. There could be no harm, surely, in his taking up the other's invitation? The old saying about 'knowing your enemy' crossed his mind.

He moved out from the shelter of the alcove and started to walk back towards the entrance to the library. On the way he was conscious of someone staring at him from behind a mound of books. There was a peculiar intensity to the stare. All he was able to see was a pair of dark eyes surmounted by wild white hair. It was not a friendly gaze. Flask did what he usually did when faced by hostility. He turned the other cheek. He dipped his head in slight acknowledgement and gave a half-smile. But the man kept on staring, if anything with greater intensity and dislike. As he passed, Flask recognized him. The straggling hair and dark eyes belonged to Septimus Sheridan, the permanent guest at Miss Howlett's house in the South Bailey.

Eustace Flask was already aware that Sheridan was no friend to him. Stray comments and quizzical glances during his visits to Colt House suggested that Sheridan was a sceptic about spiritualism. Fortunately, Sheridan was so indebted to Miss Howlett, so ready to follow her lead, that he would never dare to contradict her openly. If he was yet another enemy, he was an enemy too feeble to influence the old maid. Flask walked on, pale head held aloft like a high candle, deigning to give Septimus Sheridan one more tiny nod.

Flask would have been surprised, even shocked, had he been able to read the other man's thoughts. Septimus hadn't noticed the medium's arrival in the cathedral library. He was too wrapped up in his work (a study of the patristic fathers). It was only as Flask was leaving that he happened to glance up and see the familiar figure swaying towards him. All at once, and from nowhere it seemed, a great contempt and loathing for Eustace Flask welled up. What was that man doing here in a place devoted to study, to contemplation and religious history?

Although Septimus Sheridan had largely lost his faith, he had never lost his respect, even love, for the institutions which enshrined that faith. Hence his return to Durham and a life of undisturbed scholarship. He was glad to be allowed to live in Julia

Howlett's house under almost any terms, and he understood how much he owed to her. Understood how foolish he had been to reject her as a wife when they were both comparatively young and she had come up to the north searching for him – a typically independent action on her part.

He could hardly recall the reasons for his rejection of her now. He was sorry for it almost at once. He had moved away from the city and spent years in obscure parishes in grimy suburbs or even bleaker countryside until that terrible day, the worst day of his life, when he had written to his bishop explaining that he could no longer remain in the church with a clear conscience.

Ever since going to live at Colt House he had grown fonder than ever of Miss Howlett. Sometimes he imagined what it would be like if they were sitting round the breakfast table not as house-holder and lodger but as man and wife. If he were able to call her not 'Miss Howlett' but 'Julia'. How would the intervening years have been different if they had married? Septimus Sheridan could not know, but different – and better – they would have been.

He was fiercely protective of Miss Howlett while realizing that she was well able to protect herself. She had resources and good sense. Except when it came to spiritualism and to Eustace Flask in particular. Septimus had not trusted Flask from the start, and the distrust had deepened to an instinctive rejection of everything that Flask said or did.

Septimus would have done almost anything to wrest Miss Howlett away from the medium. But what could he do? Perhaps it was because he was so helpless that these feelings of contempt and loathing surfaced so abruptly in the hushed surroundings of the cathedral library.

The Military Magician

A meeting had been arranged between Major Sebastian Marmont and Tom by letter for noon of that day. The Major was staying at the County Hotel just the other side of the river. Tom was told that the Major had a suite of rooms on the first floor of the hotel, reputedly the best in the city. As he climbed the stairs he reflected that there must be money to be made through magic. But then the Major and his Hindoos were a big attraction. Tom and Helen had already glimpsed several posters advertising the 'Wonders of the Orient' show at the Assembly Rooms. *See the Miraculous Talking Head. Marvel at the Fabulous Perseus Cabinet.* All of this illustrated with a picture of a wise-looking cove wearing a suit and a solar topi together with a couple of youths clad in loincloths. In the background disembodied heads floated through the ether.

Tom knocked on the door of the room where he had been directed. A voice that he recognized told him to enter and he was not surprised to see, sitting cross-legged in a sunny window seat and smoking a cigarette, the troublesome guest from Colt House. An inkling that the man he'd appointed to meet and the man who'd stirred things up the previous evening at Aunt Julia's were one and the same had occurred to him while walking on the riverbank. Standing in the door he gave his name.

'Ah, Mr Ansell,' said Major Sebastian Marmont, untangling himself and coming forward to give Tom a firm handshake. He was formally dressed although he had removed his suit jacket. 'I saw you arrive at the front entrance downstairs and I wondered if you were my midday visitor from Scott, Lye & Mackenzie. But of course we have already met, in a manner of speaking, even if I didn't know who you were yesterday evening.'

'It is strange that no one at Miss Howlett's house recognized you either, sir, since your face is on bills all over town.'

'If you look carefully, Mr Ansell, you'll see it's not a very good likeness on the bills. No doubt some of the people there last night have seen me on stage at the Assembly Rooms but it's extraordinary how different one looks in front of the stage-lights and wearing a bit of slap.'

'Slap, Major Marmont?'

'Face-paint, my dear chap. I darken my phizog so that audiences imagine I've come straight from tropical climes. And Mr Eustace Flask knows who I am, or at least he does now. I have invited him to one of my shows. I thought it only fair to give him the chance to see a real magician. Please sit down, sir. Cigarette?'

'No, thank you.'

'They help me concentrate, I find, when I am mulling over my tricks. Only this brand, mind,' said the Major taking another one from the packet. 'The Luxor, made by the Alexandria Company in Artilley Lane.'

Tom settled in an armchair while Major Marmont returned to the window seat, where he again perched cross-legged and wreathed himself in cigarette smoke, tapping the ash into a bowl of Benares brass next to him. He might have been the Buddha sitting amid clouds of incense; Buddha with an incongruous moustache. Tom glanced round the spacious sitting room which had a fine view of the cathedral beyond Sebastian Marmont's shoulders. It was well furnished with armchairs and an ottoman, a desk and tables including one laid for dining. An internal door led to what must be Marmont's bedroom.

The soldier-magician asked after David Mackenzie in fond terms and enquired how long Tom had been with the law firm. He had discovered somehow that Tom was married to the daughter of Mr Scott, whom he had known. Tom found himself taking a liking to the Major. It was partly on account of the way he had shown up Eustace Flask but there was also an appealing straight-forwardness to the other's manner. Yet he was a professional magician. How straightforward could he be?

'Why did you visit Miss Howlett's yesterday evening, Major Marmont? You must have known that the other guests would not be, ah, sympathetic to what you were doing.'

'Perhaps I went too far. I did not plan it. But there is something very provoking about that Flask. He's an egregious character. I have been tracking his progress round the north-east like a hunter following a spoor. When I discovered that Miss Howlett was keeping

open house for him, as it were, I could not resist the temptation
to go and beard the fellow. Using a little of my own sleight of hand
and the substituted chalk, I was able to show that he must have
written the tablet answers himself.'

'But my wife and her aunt were touching his hands all the
time.'

'Oh they are very clever, these people. I have known a foot
covered with a dummy hand to be thrust up through a hole in
a table. But that wasn't what happened in this case. Did you
observe how Flask gave a start when he was taken over by his
'control', the Indian maid?'

Tom nodded, fascinated but also surprised at the undercurrent
of bitterness in Marmont's words. It was plain that he despised
the spiritualists or at any rate despised Eustace Flask.

'I would wager a whole evening's takings that both your wife
and her aunt lost contact with Flask's hands for an instant when
he pretended to go into his trance. When they felt him again he
was actually offering both of them the *same* hand. So all that time
the other hand was free to scribble his nonsense on the slate.'

'It is easy to see when you explain, sir. And I suppose the arms
of the Indian maid were actually that woman's, Kitty's.'

'Undoubtedly they were. But I could tell from your own attitude last night that you already had your suspicions about the
medium.'

'My wife and I both. Her Aunt Julia has no suspicions, she
believes in Flask absolutely.'

'A pity. Flask is very adept in his dealings with older women.
Individuals like him bring honest, decent magicianship into
disrepute. You should ask yourself why mediums need the para-
phernalia of conjurers, why they require dim lighting and locked
cabinets and rattling tambourines when they are trying to reach
the departed. Isn't it rather undignified of the dead to choose
such ridiculous means to get in touch? We magicians own up to
our tricks – or rather we own up that they *are* tricks. We might
fear the discovery of our secrets but we don't fear the exposure
of our very selves as the mediums do. But I am running on, Mr
Ansell.'

'Not at all. I can see the depth of your feelings.'

'I have good reason for feeling as I do.'

Tom waited attentively. If the Major wanted to give the reason, he would. If not, not. Marmont lit another cigarette and began to speak.

'Some years ago I lost my darling wife. For a time in my grief and despair I believed I might make contact with her again. I consulted mediums, I attended séances, I willed myself to believe that we might still be able to talk to each other, to glimpse each other. But the harder I tried, the more she seemed to recede into the distance. I came to a simple conclusion, Mr Ansell. You know what that was?'

'I can guess.'

'It is that those who profess to put one in touch with the dead are imposters. The best of them do not know that they are imposters and are merely self-deluded. But the majority are out-and-out frauds. They deserve ridicule and shame and exposure, if not the full rigour of the law. And, as I say, Eustace Flask is the worst of a very bad bunch. The world would be a better place without his presence.'

Sebastian Marmont had stubbed out his cigarette even though it wasn't finished. He was clenching his fists. He looked down at them as though they were the hands of another.

'Where was I? Ah yes, my wife. I could not mourn her forever or waste my time and resources sitting in the stuffy parlours of the mediums because I had responsibilities. You see, she left me with three children, good lads all, to remember her by.'

Major Marmont gave a sudden, barking laugh. 'Of course the desire to expose that charlatan Flask was not the only reason why I did what I did yesterday evening. When word gets round that I've invited Flask to attend one of my performances at the Assembly Rooms, you won't be able to get a ticket for love or money. People will come in the hope of seeing a spat.'

It was oddly reassuring that Marmont had a practical or commercial reason for causing a stir, that he wasn't just driven by fury. There were other questions that Tom would have liked to ask – where, for instance, did all the Major's Hindoos stay? Surely they were not lodging in the comfort of the County Hotel? – but the soldier-magician indicated that they ought to get down to business, the reason Tom was visiting him at the hotel. Sebastian Marmont wished to make a formal statement, an affidavit, of how he had come into possession of the Lucknow Dagger.

He asked Tom to explain how an affidavit was prepared. It was fairly simple. Marmont simply had to produce a document with Tom's help, topped and tailed in the appropriate legal fashion, and then the affidavit would have to be sworn to in the presence of a commissioner of oaths. Marmont went to a writing desk and produced an envelope from which he extracted a couple of sheets of paper filled with small, spidery handwriting.

'I have written down the story here. You may read it.'

'It may be necessary to recast it,' said Tom after few minutes. As far as he could decipher it, Major Marmont's account was somewhat disjointed and sensational. There were plenty of exclamation marks and expressions like 'by the skin of our teeth' and 'shake a stick at'. The history of the Dagger seemed to be strange and bloody.

'To recast it? To make it more lawyerly?'

'I'm afraid so. Then you must affirm it as a true account.'

'Perhaps you would like to see the Lucknow Dagger itself, Mr Ansell,' said Marmont.

Major Marmont paused and with a showman's instinct unfastened his cravat. He removed a loop of braided cord which hung around his neck and drew out a leather sheath from within his shirt. From the sheath he produced the very weapon. He handed it to Tom, who wished Helen was here to see this. It would have appealed to her writerly imagination. Now he took the Lucknow Dagger from its owner. He experienced a strange feeling of giddiness and for an instant clutched the edge of the table.

It was a finely worked object. The blade was about four inches long and the handle slightly shorter. The steel of the blade had a heavy bluish sheen to it, as though it had absorbed the lifeblood of its victims. The handle was decorated with ivory carvings. He peered at the largest of them. A figure with many arms was set sideways-on, trampling several much smaller figures underfoot. There were miniature skulls and what appeared to be spears and lances and arrows flying through the air. Tom had expected something conventionally valuable, a knife whose handle was encrusted with precious stones or worked in gold. He looked up to see the Major scrutinizing him.

'Interesting, eh? The figure is Kali, the goddess of death and destruction. She is rightly held in awe.'

This information, together with the dark blade and the pale ivory work of the handle, was somehow unsettling. Not wanting to hold it any longer, he handed it back to Sebastian Marmont.

'You're wondering whether the right place for this is in a museum – or a bank vault?'

'Yes, I was. Or rather I was wondering whether you always carried it about with you, Major Marmont.'

'It was designed to be carried, Mr Ansell. It is for use and adornment. No Indian would dream of locking up such an item so why should I?'

'Do you keep it for good fortune, for luck?'

'Perhaps I keep it so that others should not get their hands on it,' said the Major cryptically. 'For luck, you ask? I am not especially superstitious, although you cannot spend years in the East without suspecting that "there are more things in heaven and earth than are dreamt of in your philosophy", as Hamlet says. Nevertheless, there are scurrilous stories about how I came into possession of this object – that I took it from a dead man when his corpse was still warm, even that I killed him myself – and that is why I have asked to formally swear to the truth.'

'Who's responsible for these stories about you?'

'Rumours, rumours,' said Marmont with a wave of his hand. He got up from his cross-legged position in the window. 'What I would like you to do, Mr Ansell, is to take the key facts in the account I have just given and write them up in the appropriate legal language. We can then proceed to the business of the affidavit.'

'Of course, Major Marmont,' said Tom, wondering whether anyone in the firm of Scott, Lye & Mackenzie had ever overseen a stranger, more exotic affidavit.

'And I would be honoured if you and your wife were to be my guests at my next performance in the Assembly Rooms. It should be interesting because, as I said, I have written to invite that charlatan Eustace Flask. He will see a real magician at work. I may even invite him to assist me in one of my acts.'

The door opened and an Indian strolled into the room. Like the Major he was wearing a suit.

'Ah Dilip,' said Marmont. 'May I present Mr Thomas Ansell.

He comes to visit me from a London firm of lawyers – on that business you know about. Mr Ansell, Mr Dilip Gopal.'

They shook hands. The Indian was a handsome man with dark eyes and an incipient smile.

'I am delighted to make your acquaintance, Mr Ansell.'

'Dilip assists me in some of my performances. He is staying with my Hindoo assistants, the boys, keeping an eye on them.'

'We are in a boarding house close by,' explained Mr Gopal.

So that little mystery was solved. Tom supposed the Indians were lodging elsewhere for reasons of cost, perhaps also because they would not be altogether welcome in the city's best hotel.

'The lads hardly need an eye kept on them,' said Mr Gopal. 'They are very well behaved.'

'I should say,' said the Major, 'that Dilip is also my brother-in-law.'

Tom couldn't hide his surprise and confusion. The Major seemed pleased at the effect he had produced.

'Yes, my wife, my late wife, was Indian. Didn't I say?'

The House in Old Elvet

It was unfortunate that Ambrose Barker came back to the house in Old Elvet when he did. He ought to have stayed in the alehouse growing even more sozzled than he already was. Unfortunate for all three of them, Ambrose and Kitty and Eustace Flask. Ambrose had been drinking in one of the local alehouses and found it hard to align the key with the front-door keyhole. He succeeded at the sixth or seventh attempt and stumbled into the tiny hallway then through the kitchen and, after more fumbling with the back door, out to the privy in the yard. Here he enjoyed a prolonged piss, swaying slightly and clinging on to the rough whitewash of the wall with one hand. Back in the yard he glanced up at the sky. The day had been fine and there were still a few streaks of light in the west.

Having groped his way back into the hallway, he stood at the bottom of the stairs, grasping the banister. It was quite dark indoors. After a time his attention was roused by noises from the floor above. After a bit more time he recognized them. Little groans and squeals and sighs. Kitty, the bitch! His hand tightened round the banister knob. But instead of thundering up the stairs, Ambrose became all calmness and deliberation. He slipped off his shoes. He went back to the kitchen, found a kerosene lamp and lit it, adjusting the wick to reduce the amount of smoke.

He returned to the foot of the stairs and, holding the lamp in one hand, climbed up one tread at a time. He need not have bothered about keeping quiet. The noises from above were growing louder and more oblivious. Mingled with them were the fluting tones of Eustace Flask, uttering meaningless sounds that reminded Ambrose of a bleating goat. Ambrose paused on the cramped landing. There were three doors leading off it, one to the bedroom which he shared with Kitty, one to a space so small that it was more cupboard than boxroom, and one to the chamber which Flask occupied all by his long, lonely, weedy self. That was where the noises were coming from.

104

Standing outside the door, Ambrose took a deep breath. He
had been drunk and now he was sober. Well, fancy that, he
mouthed to himself. He gripped the knob, twisted it and kicked
the door so hard it almost came off its hinges. Then he held the
lamp aloft. It threw an incongruously soft glow across the occupants of the room. Ambrose might have laughed at the absurd
spectacle before him. He might have laughed but he did not.

Kitty Partout was lying beneath Eustace Flask. They were slant-
wise on the medium's spacious bed. Her chemise was bunched
up and her legs splayed out either side of the spiritualist's hindquarters. Those hindquarters had been pumping away like billy-oh
but the crash of the door caused them to freeze like small animals
caught out in lantern-light. Flask was still wearing a shirt but had
gone so far as to remove his trousers. Ambrose saw legs as pale
and thin as pipe cleaners.

Ambrose did not laugh. Neither was he angry, not yet. Instead
he was conscious of an instant of high glee. So this was what the
refined medium got up to when he thought no one was looking,
the dirty bugger. He was no better than all the rest of them. In
the few months since he and Kitty had met Flask he had suffered
from a sense of inferiority. Ambrose was the brawny assistant,
Flask was the one with brains while Kitty provided the ornamental trimmings. Now Ambrose Barker had the upper hand
over both of them.

All this flashed through Ambrose's head in the few moments it
took for Flask and Kitty to jerk their heads round and realize there
was a person standing in the doorway. Instinctively, they flinched
away and blinked, unable to see properly. Then Flask leapt off Kitty,
pulling down his shirt to conceal his member – which was thin
and raw-looking like a dog's – but leaving Miss Partout exposed.
Her hands flew down to cover the black bush between her legs.
Don't bother, I've seen it all before, Ambrose was about to say, but
he stopped himself. The remark did not rise the occasion. He felt
as clear-headed and powerful as he had ever felt in his life, standing
there in the upstairs doorway of the rented house in Durham's
Old Elvet and confronting this pair of . . . this pair of . . .

Something special was required, a remark that would put
Eustace and Kitty in their places for a long time. Something to
show that he too could be clever with words.

'Oh my,' he said, imitating (not very well) the fluting tones of Eustace Flask. 'Oh my, Uncle Eustace. I am *so* sorry to disturb you when you are *so* busy with your *niece.*'

'I'm not his niece, Ambrose,' said Kitty. 'You know that. Don't be silly.'

She spoke quite composedly. Flask, for once, had nothing to say for himself but continued to kneel on the bed, looking absurd as he tugged his shirt down to hide his shrinking pizzle even though the movement served to reveal more of his flat buttocks.

Ambrose Barker revelled in his moment of power. He carefully formed the next sentence in his mind. He ignored the fact that Kitty Partout wasn't Flask's niece – of course she wasn't his niece, Ambrose was making a witty gibe – and said, 'You ought to have the law on you, *uncle* Eustace, the law, I say. You know why? An uncle doing it with his niece. 'S a clear case of incest.'

But Ambrose was not as clear-headed as he imagined. His voice was slurry with all the pints he'd swallowed that evening and he was stumbling over his words. He had difficulty with 'niece' which sounded more like 'nice' and he mangled 'incest' altogether so that what he wanted to say emerged as 'a clear case of insects'.

And then Kitty made the mistake of laughing. It was more of a titter than an outright laugh. She took one hand from between her legs and clapped it over her mouth.

'Oh Ambrose,' she said. 'A case of insects!'

All at once Ambrose's sense of cool superiority drained away. How dare the bitch laugh at him! It was as if he had shifted back from being sober to being drunk again, drunk and raging, although he had really been drunk the whole time. He strode a couple of paces into the bedroom and swung the kerosene lamp at her head. Eustace scrabbled from the bed and cowered on the far side against the wall with his hands covering his head while Kitty screamed and rolled to the edge of the bed.

The glass case of the lamp shattered and within seconds the burning wick had set a pillowcase and top sheet on fire. Flask reacted by huddling further down against the wall while Ambrose glared, stupefied, at what he had done. It was only Kitty's quick response which saved them. There was a china jug and bowl on a side table, used by Flask for his morning ablutions and (luckily) unemptied. Kitty jumped from the bed, seized the jug and bowl from the table, and threw the contents over the flickering flames. Then she smothered the burning linen with a blanket, which she beat down with her hands.

The bedroom was filled with a horrible stench – of kerosene and singed bedclothes and burnt feathers – and the air was already thick with smoke. But Kitty's quickness had doused the fire. At a cost, though. She held up her hands which were bleeding in several places from the glass shards of the shattered lantern.

Ambrose Barker was finally roused from his stupor. He saw Kitty Partout's bloody hands, he saw Eustace Flask rising shakily up from his huddled stance. He was still angry, very angry indeed, but he realized that now was not the right moment to exact his revenge. Instead he shook his fist at the pair – although it's not certain that either of them noticed the gesture – and stalked from the room and down the stairs. Only when he'd slammed the front door to the house and was standing in the street did it occur to him that he had not the faintest idea where to go or what to do next. But that wasn't quite true. He did have an idea. It came to him from nowhere. He'd show her, he'd show them.

Meanwhile, upstairs in the lovers' chamber, Eustace Flask had recovered a little of his composure. He did his best to remove the glass splinters from Kitty's palms and fingers. He created makeshift bandages for her out of torn-up bits of bed-sheet. He tutted and cooed and tried to still his trembling hands. Despite the shock and her injuries, Kitty was the calmer of the two. She was simultaneously tearful and calm. Blinking her eyes, she watched as Eustace fumbled to wrap the linen strips about her hands.

Men were very foolish, she concluded.

Before the Performance

It was an outing to the theatre. Not only the Ansells but Julia Howlett and Septimus Sheridan were going to see the redoubtable magician and his Hindoo troupe. Tom and Helen had been invited to visit Major Marmont in his dressing room at the theatre before the performance. He was curious to meet Helen, since he had known her father.

The Ansells walked to the Assembly Rooms which were not far from Aunt Julia's house in the South Bailey. A dozen yards behind them came Miss Howlett and Mr Sheridan, her arm twined companionably through his. From a distance they had the appearance of an elderly married couple and Helen, looking back, wondered whether she'd been too hasty in dismissing the idea of marriage, even this late.

But Helen had other and more pressing things on her mind. She asked Tom if he remembered the name of the policeman who had attended the séance at Tullis Street.

'It was Seldon. Why do you ask?'

'And his wife's name was Elizabeth?'

'Perhaps. Yes, I think he called her Lizzie. But you said '*was* called', Helen. What's happened? What do you know?'

'I thought so all the time but I was hoping my memory was playing tricks. A Mr and Mrs Seldon, Arthur and Elizabeth, were killed by gas poisoning in Norwood several days ago. He was a policeman. I would not have known of it except that there was an article about the safety of gas supplies in *The Durham Advertiser*—'

'Which you just happened to be reading.'

'You know me, Tom, I am a gannet for any printed matter my eye happens to fall on. What leaped out was the reference to the death of the Seldons, even if the writer mentioned it only to show the risks of piped gas and because it was a recent accident, I suppose.'

'An *accident*, there you are.'

'But it is a strange coincidence, isn't it, that it should happen so soon after that man Smight threw himself off Waterloo Bridge.'

'A coincidence but no more. What could be the connection?'

'I don't know, Tom. If I were more imaginative I'd say that Mr Smight had laid a curse on the Seldons from beyond the grave.'

'Then it's surprising he has more power now he's dead than he ever did when he was alive. He cut a pretty feeble figure while he was threatened with being taken to court.'

'Oh, I am well aware it is a ridiculous idea but, still, it has made me uneasy.'

Tom did his best to reassure Helen in the few minutes it took them to reach the theatre although what she said made him a little uncomfortable. When they arrived, they were directed to a poky room somewhere in the innards of the building. Sebastian Marmont was scrutinizing himself in a mirror, then applying dabs of extra 'slap' to darken his already ruddy complexion. He was wearing the trousers and waistcoat of his white tropical three-piece. A solar topi sat on the table beside him. He smiled to see Tom and Helen reflected in the glass. He stood up and raised Helen's gloved hand to his lips.

'*Enchanté, madame.*'

'I am pleased to meet you, Major Marmont,' said Helen, sounding genuinely pleased, then looking round, she added, 'This is a veritable Aladdin's cave.'

It was the right thing to say. The room was jumbled with costumes and incongruous bits of equipment from a wicker basket to what looked like the trunk of a palm tree. Tom reached out an experimental finger. It felt like papier-maché.

The door to the dressing room suddenly burst open and three lads tumbled into the room. They had not realized that Marmont had visitors. One of them started to say, 'Dad—' and got no further. They were wearing turbans and their faces were neither pale nor dark but in between.

'Boys!' said the Major. 'Manners! Let me introduce you to Mr and Mrs Ansell. Alfred, Arthur and Albert.'

The boys lined up as Sebastian Marmont pointed them out in rapid succession.

'These are my sons, my Hindoos. They assist me in the performance in a variety of guises. The smallest one there, Albert, even dresses up as an ape – as if he wasn't enough of a monkey already! You only have twenty minutes, you three. Go and get ready now.'

And the three tumbled out of the room again, without a word.

'Well, Mr and Mrs Ansell,' said Marmont, 'you have found out one of my secrets. I employ my sons and pass them off as natives. Their mother is, alas, no more and I value their company. Having them with me, I can keep an eye on them.'

As he mentioned the loss of his wife, he looked keenly at Tom. Then he looked back at his reflection in the mirror and tugged his waistcoat down. He settled the topi on his head and gave his moustaches an extra twirl.

'There,' he said. 'I am point-device the very man, even if I do say so myself.'

'Bravo, Major Marmont,' said Helen, giving a little clap.

Act Three

It is the climax of the evening. Major Marmont comes down to the foot-lights and speaks directly to the audience while behind him two of his Hindoos are wheeling on to the stage a cabinet painted in red and gold.

'Ladies and gentlemen, you are about to see a feat which is unique. I have styled this object the Cabinet of Perseus. Let us see what it contains – or rather what it does not contain.'

He nods at the two boys who are standing on either side of the cabinet, which is about four-feet wide and deep and seven-feet high. The boys revolve the cabinet on its castors, pausing when each side is opposite to the audience. Every time, Sebastian Marmont raps the side sharply and several times over with a long stick to show that there is nothing concealed within, no hidden exits. When the cabinet is facing front again the boys open the narrow double doors. The interior walls are covered with the same red and gilt pattern as the outside but the cabinet is empty apart from a wooden post in the centre. This supports a gas lamp which casts such a bright light on the inside that it is impossible to imagine that there is the space for even a mouse to hide itself. The Major walks right up to the cabinet and waggles his stick around the front of the open space.

When the audience have had a good stare, the Major orders the doors to be closed again. He returns to the footlights and says in a confidential style, 'I am sure that, in the presence of such learned inhabitants of so distinguished a city, I do not have to explain why I have selected the name of Perseus. But, for the benefit of any who might have forgotten, I shall inform you that Perseus was presented with the famous helmet of invisibility by the gods when he went to face the terrifying snake-headed Medusa. I hope there are no Medusas here tonight – are there, gentlemen? – but we do require a Perseus. We need a hero who will become invisible, one who will disappear before our very eyes. Will any brave gentleman step forward now?'

The Major waits. He raises his hand to his brow and scans the theatre which is full to capacity. He looks quite threatening, like a general asking for a volunteer for a dangerous mission. Not a person stirs in the house.

Perhaps nobody is sure exactly what the Major wants, perhaps the men in the audience are a little nervous. Then Marmont fixes on an individual in the second row of the stalls. He points to him and in a stentorian voice says, 'You, sir, I can detect in you a desire to show yourself capable of heroic feats. Would you be so kind as to rise from your seat next to that pretty young lady and make your way up here.'

It is as much of a command as an invitation. In any case it is the kind of invitation difficult to turn down if you don't want to be shown up for a wet blanket or, worse, a coward. There is a bustle in the stalls as a lanky man gets up. Those sitting close by look to see if the woman next to him is indeed pretty. She is, although she must have recently suffered some accident for one of her hands is bandaged.

The man climbs a short flight of steps at the side of the stage and comes into the illuminated area. The Major reaches out his hand in a no-nonsense, manly fashion. The newcomer hesitates before taking it. It is evident that he is not pleased to be up on stage in the public eye, and the way he leans towards the Major and whispers something in his ear suggests that he is a reluctant participant. Several in the audience recognize him and a few may be aware that these two men have met before, that there is hostility between them. They are a contrast, the Major is short and deeply tanned while his guest is tall and has the pallor of a candle.

'Now, ladies and gentlemen,' says the Major, 'In a moment I am going to request my friend here to step into the Perseus Cabinet behind us. I shall follow him for an instant into the cabinet and then I shall reappear and then . . . well, we'll see.'

The doors are opened for a second time. Major Marmont ushers the tall gentleman into the cabinet, putting his hand in the small of the other's back to urge him forward. He looks round at the audience briefly before stepping into the cabinet himself. The boys shut the doors without ceremony and then one produces a flute and the other a tabor, and they proceed to make a weird rhythmic sound, the steady beat of the little drum contrasting with the wandering tones of the flute.

It must be an unpleasant fit inside the Perseus Cabinet, two men packed into a little space with the gas lamp hissing above their heads. But not for more than a few seconds because, even while the drum is beating and the flute piping, the doors are opened from within by the Major and he steps out and stands well away from the cabinet. It is empty. The flaring light reflects off the red and gold wallpaper but there is no sign of the Major's guest — or perhaps that should be his victim. The Major steps up to the cabinet and waggles his stick round the interior. It is definitely empty. The lanky man with the reddish hair and the pallor of a candle has disappeared.

After the Trick

Tom and Helen could only admire the way in which Sebastian Marmont inveigled Flask into stepping on to the stage and then entering the Perseus Cabinet. Tom had not taken seriously Marmont's promise – or threat – that he would attempt to involve Flask in one of his acts but evidently the Major had been planning all the time to pick on the medium or at least to show him the superiority of his form of magic. That was why Eustace and Kitty were given complimentary seats near the stage and why Marmont had not allowed much time to pass before he selected Eustace, even though to most of the audience it would have seemed a random choice.

The Ansells were sitting at the back of the stalls with Julia Howlett and Septimus Sheridan. When they saw Flask whispering in Major Marmont's ear, Helen also whispered in Tom's ear, saying, 'That is no love message.'

On Tom's other side, Julia Howlett said rather more loudly, 'I do hope nothing terrible is going to happen.'

Tom thought the magical act was reminiscent of Flask's, except that everyone was aware it was done with the intention of deceiving and so, in a sense, no one could feel cheated. But there was the same role for the performer's assistants: the Hindoos in Marmont's act; Ambrose and Kitty in Flask's. There was a similar introductory speech in which the performer drew attention, whether subtly or boastfully, to what he was going to do. There were invitations to check for fraud by examining clothes or furniture. There was even a comparison between the spirit cabinet used by Flask and the Perseus one belonging to Marmont.

The Ansells watched as the medium was almost pushed into the cabinet by Marmont, and the flute and drum noises started up. The Major duly reappeared and the doors were left open behind him to show that the cupboard was bare.

'What next?' said Helen.

'I expect our friend will turn up through a trapdoor in the floor or something.'

'I wouldn't mind if he vanished for ever,' said Helen but softly so that her aunt should not hear.

But Eustace Flask did not reappear. The performance was, seemingly, concluded even if in a rather unsatisfactory way. Wasn't it part of the unspoken agreement between a magician and his audience that whatever had been done on stage, whether it was a breakage or a dismemberment or a disappearance, should be put right by the end of the show? But not this time. The Major and his Hindoos stepped forward to take the applause of the house and the curtain came down.

As the crowd was filing out, Tom observed Kitty pushing her way through it in an agitated way. It made him wonder exactly what had happened to Eustace Flask.

There were other interested parties in the Assembly Rooms that night. One of them was Frank Harcourt who had brought his wife Rhoda to see the sensational new magician. The couple were sitting in the less expensive seats, which Rhoda complained about from the moment they arrived. But her attention was soon caught by Marmont's act and she forgot to gripe as the evening went on. When Eustace Flask was summoned to the stage she sat up straighter and nudged her husband in the ribs. For his part, Superintendent Harcourt was rather glad to see the medium shown up in the public eye. Perhaps it would hasten his departure from Durham. And he was even more glad when Flask did not emerge from the Perseus Cabinet. In fact, his hope that Flask might never reappear was at that instant being echoed by Helen Ansell.

In the cheapest seating at the top of the house was Ambrose Barker. He had been keeping a covert eye on Flask and Kitty for most of the day and turning over schemes of retribution in his mind without resolving on any firm plan. Ambrose might have wondered how Flask would manage without him but he was no fool and knew that the answer was, he would manage pretty well. Flask's schemes in Durham had almost come to a head. He did not need help any longer putting up his spirit cabinet or taking off his frock-coat. So Ambrose was still undecided on his retaliation. He had not even decided whether Flask alone should feel the full force of his anger or whether Kitty ought to be included.

Seeing the pair heading for the theatre, and following at a distance, Ambrose had bought himself a sixpenny seat. Once the performance was underway he soon realized that the magician and the individual who'd tried to expose the guv'nor a couple of days before were one and the same person. Apart from the voice, there was something about the way the man held himself. When Flask was brought into the act, Ambrose relished his discomfort. And when Flask failed to come out of the Perseus Cabinet, Ambrose wondered how the trick was managed.

There was one other individual who attended the performance at the Assembly Rooms and who took a more than usually close interest in the proceedings. It was the man who had arrived in Durham on the same train as the Ansells, the man in the shabby clothes who had pretended to find Helen's lilac handkerchief on the river path. He too had sat up straight at one point in the performance but it was nothing to do with Eustace Flask. Rather it was connected to the appearance of Major Sebastian Marmont. This individual had noticed the name on the advertisements plastered around town and bought a ticket. When he observed the soldier-turned-magician striding towards the footlights, when he heard the first words out of the performer's mouth, he experienced a shock of recognition. And then he started to think, very hard.

Eustace Flask did not reappear again that evening or in the early part of the night. He failed to return to the house in Old Elvet. Kitty Partout waited up for him. She had already shoved her way backstage at the theatre to confront Major Marmont if necessary, only to find that the magician had departed and that no one seemed able to help her in her quest for the medium. Yes, he had 'disappeared' but it was all part of the show, wasn't it? In real life, people don't simply vanish in front of one's eyes. It's a trick, an illusion.

Kitty eventually dropped off in the small hours of the morning. She had not been sleeping very long when she was wakened by the sound of someone on the stairs. Kitty felt chill. But after a moment she recognized the tread as Eustace's. From her bed she called out drowsily, 'Where you been?'

★   ★   ★

Flask had not of course disappeared for good after his entry into the Perseus Cabinet. He might be physically untouched but he was the humiliated victim of a trick and he was very angry with Sebastian Marmont. Indeed, they had almost come to blows afterwards although, as during the session at Miss Howlett's, the medium had restrained himself. He suspected that the Major would be capable of licking him with one hand tied behind his back. However, he had taken a kind of revenge on the magician and also had the pleasure of insulting his Indian assistant.

He spent at least an hour striding about the old town, feeding his fury against Marmont and contemplating further acts of retribution. It was not so far from midsummer and there was still a tinge of light in the west. Flask was now standing on Framwellgate Bridge looking down at the waters of the Wear. His heart was as dark as the river. Towering above him to his left were the silhouettes of the castle and the cathedral. It was close on midnight and perhaps not very safe for a nervous individual like Eustace Flask to be out and about alone. He started from his reverie when he heard footsteps on the cobbles behind him. He wheeled round. There were gaslights at each end of the bridge but he was standing in the middle in a pool of darkness.

A man was coming in his direction. Flask remembered the item which was tucked in one of his pockets. Too late to get it out now. He might have run but instead he was rooted to the spot, his back against the parapet of the bridge.

'Don't do it,' said the man. 'I have been watching you.'

Flask's first reaction was one of relief. The man had an educated manner. He did not sound like a ruffian or a bludger.

'Do what?' he said, trying to control his voice.

'Throw yourself into the river.'

'It never crossed my mind,' said Flask, truthfully. 'I – I am out for a stroll.'

'I wonder what it would be like to throw oneself from a bridge and plunge into the water,' said the man. He was standing next to Flask by now. Then he turned about to stare down into the river. The medium could not make out much of the other's appearance, except that he was clean-shaven and about Flask's own height.

'What passes through your mind as you plunge through the

dark air? Regret or elation or despair? The fall would not last much more than a second. Is it a long second, I wonder?'

Eustace Flask had relaxed for an instant but now began to think that he might be in the presence of a lunatic.

'No doubt you consider this as idle speculation, sir,' said the man, as if he guessed Flask's thoughts. 'But I have had good cause recently to imagine the last plunge from a bridge – then the immersion in dirty, fast-flowing water – the instinctive struggle to survive – the inexorable way in which one's garments become waterlogged and drag the wearer down. Even if you had willed yourself every step of the way thus far, do you think you would sink without a fight?'

'Probably not,' said Flask.

The man shivered, though whether from the chill of the evening or the thought of a watery death, Flask did not know. He made to move off but the man put out a hand to detain him.

'Not so fast, my friend. I saw you at the theatre this evening.'

'I don't want to talk about that.'

'You are not well disposed towards Major Marmont, I think?'

'No.'

'You would like revenge on him?'

Flask, normally so fluent, said nothing but that was answer enough for the man, 'I could tell you things that might surprise you.'

The man might have been about to say more but they were interrupted by the sight of the beat constable at the eastern end of the bridge. He was standing under the gaslight, clearly visible and presumably a deterrent to any nefarious activity in the area.

'But not now,' said the man. 'Meet me tomorrow morning and I shall tell you more.'

'Where?'

'Here. At ten.'

He spun on his heel and loped across to the western side of the bridge. He passed under the pool of light from the gas lantern on that side and, for an instant, Flask thought of a predatory beast; there was something so silent and purposeful in his movement. Still, there could be no harm in meeting him again, could there?

Something had fluttered to the ground as the other man walked away. Flask picked it up. It felt like a handkerchief. He held it to his nose and detected the faintest trace of a woman's scent.

The Medium Departs

As far as the rest of the world was concerned, Eustace Flask came to light the next day. A band of workers were using saws and axes to cut up a fallen tree on the eastern bank of the river where it doubled back on the far side of the cathedral. Their overseer was alerted by the cries of a woman. With a couple of his companions, he followed the direction of the sounds. The three ran a couple of hundred yards or so along the bank and then up the wooded slope to a small clearing.

There lay the body of a man, face up. He had died violently and blood was welling from a deep wound on his neck. But, more shocking and surprising than this sight, was the presence of a woman standing close to the body. When she saw the men enter the clearing, her cries ceased and she began to shake. The woodman made to go towards her but one of his companions held him back. He said nothing but nodded towards the woman's hands, which she was holding out stiffly in front of her. They were bloody.

The overseer despatched the man to get help while he and the other worker kept a wary watch over the woman. After a time she seemed to realize the oddness of her posture. She let her hands drop to her sides. She made no move to run away but neither did the men come any closer. After a time – which seemed a very long time – there was the sound of whistles and police rattles and a constable came red-faced and panting into the clearing. Within moments others arrived, including a superintendent. Two of them approached the woman warily as if closing in on a wild horse.

'I think you had better come with us, Miss,' said the superintendent.

'It's Mrs,' said the woman. Her voice was high and unsteady.

'You had still better to accompany us,' said the officer. He spoke quite gently. As he and a constable led the woman away out of the clearing, the others clustered about the body which would very soon be identified as that of Mr Eustace Flask.

★　　★　　★

The workmen had not been the only people in the vicinity of Flask's body. There were various other individuals on this eastern portion of the bank of the River Wear who had noted him (when alive), and responded in their various ways.

There was Septimus Sheridan, for example. He was not toiling away in the cathedral library this morning. Rather, he had been so wearied by dear Julia's harping on the subject of Eustace Flask that he decided to get some fresh air before burying himself in his ever-open books. He loved Miss Howlett with an undeclared love but even he could take only so much of her agitation over the wretched medium who had disappeared the previous evening at the Assembly Rooms. Good riddance to him! But from Julia there was a stream of questions and queries. What should they do about poor Mr Flask? Should they go to the police, for instance?

Septimus Sheridan noticed that the nice young couple felt the same way. Helen had become almost impatient with her aunt while her lawyer husband had quit the breakfast table as soon as possible to do some work. Eventually Septimus could stand it no longer. He left the house in South Bailey and rather than go the few hundred yards to the cathedral precincts he walked several times that distance, crossing the Elvet Bridge and turning south towards Church Street.

As he sometimes did when he felt weary or dispirited he went to St Oswald's Church which lay on a wooded bluff overlooking the river. It was not the church where Septimus had served as a curate during his time in Durham many years before but he liked St Oswald's for its extreme antiquity and its slightly forlorn air. He did not always go inside the church but contented himself with wandering off the flagstone paths and into the quiet of the graveyard. This was an overgrown place especially towards its western, river-facing fringe and Sheridan felt the long grass brush his trousers as he ducked under tree boughs and skirted the graves which poked lopsidedly through the soil. There was a ragged line of palings marking the church boundary and an unlocked gate on to a steep path which led to the riverside walk.

Septimus paused here and breathed deeply. The smells and noises of the town were drowned by the sound of birdsong and the scent of blossom. Dominating the tree-line on the far bank was the great eastern tower of the cathedral but from this aspect it was softened and framed by foliage and Septimus imagined that the scene could not have changed very greatly in almost a thousand years.

All those centuries ago an individual like Eustace Flask, with his cheap tricks and his claims to be in touch with the dead, would have been regarded as a witch. A warlock. A heretic. Flask would have been tried, convicted and summarily burnt at the stake. Septimus was not a violent man. He knew that he lived in a kinder, more enlightened age and he was thankful for it. But there was something to be said for those ancient forms of justice.

Septimus attempted to push such thoughts and imaginings out of his head. He distracted himself by listening to the birds. But the place was not so peaceful after all. From the wooded slope below came a crashing sound as of some animal forcing its way through the undergrowth. Septimus thought it must be a deer but a flash of bright, artificial colour – someone's jacket perhaps – showed that it was a person. The colour immediately stirred an unwelcome recollection in Septimus Sheridan and he waited to see the route taken by the intruder in the woods. After a time curiosity got the better of him and he pushed open the gate in the dilapidated fence and started to tread carefully on the downhill path.

Any observer in St Oswald's churchyard about a quarter of an hour later would have seen a rather stout man making his way at quite a lick through the long grass. More than once the man stumbled over a low-lying grave before he reached the flagged path which led to Church Street. An observer would also have heard a woman's screams coming from the river area and rising above the birdsong. If the stout man was aware of them he did not stop, let alone turn back and investigate. Instead he walked as rapidly as decorum and his aching lungs would allow back in the direction of Elvet Bridge.

Another wanderer in the area was Ambrose Barker. He had been following Flask and Kitty for over a day now. He had attended the performance at the Assembly Rooms the previous evening and had been greatly cheered when Flask had been shut up inside that cabinet and made to disappear. Pity it was all a trick. Sure enough Flask had turned up again, like a bad penny. Ambrose was aware of this because he had been on the point of returning to the house in Old Elvet earlier that morning to have it out with Kitty once and for all. But as he was about to turn into the street he saw Flask coming out of the door. Ambrose turned away and waited until the figure in the bright green frock-coat had passed. Ambrose changed his mind about seeing Kitty that instant. His feelings, of resentment and anger, were directed once more towards the guv'nor. If he had disappeared once, surely he might be made to disappear again?

Superintendent Frank Harcourt had left his house earlier that morning. For him it was a brisk walk along Hallgarth Street towards the police-house in Court Lane. As he was approaching New Elvet he was dismayed to see Eustace Flask on the other side of the street, although the medium seemed to have lost something of his usual swagger. Flask was apparently heading for the old part of town. Harcourt would have identified him anywhere by that frock-coat. The Superintendent took advantage of a convenient tree and watched as Flask passed. When the medium had gone a hundred yards or so, Harcourt wondered whether to follow him and see what he was up to.

So the body in the woods was soon identified as that of Eustace Flask. Just as the woman standing over his corpse would soon be identified as Mrs Helen Ansell.

Durham Gaol

'Why has she been brought here? Tell me. I demand to know.'

Tom was beside himself. The sweat was standing out on his forehead and he could not stay still for an instant. He wanted to lash out at something or someone. But the police superintendent standing on the opposite side of the desk kept a stolid calm.

'It is for her own safety, sir. Will you sit down?'

'Safety! In a gaol!'

'You might be surprised, Mr Ansell, but this place behind us is quite salubrious compared to the police-house in Court Lane. We are not adapted for accommodating people of, er, quality in the station-house. And we would have drawn more attention taking your wife there than we did by bringing her here. She is quite comfortable. She will not have to mix with any of the other inmates, yet. I can recognize a lady when I see one. I ask again, sir, will you sit down?'

'Why should I sit down?'

'Then I can sit too.'

'All right,' said Tom, aware that he was only harming his – or rather Helen's – cause by his confusion and anger. 'I must apologize, Superintendent . . . ?'

'Harcourt, sir, Frank Harcourt.'

Tom and Superintendent Harcourt were standing in a plainly furnished office in the Crown Courts behind which stood Durham Gaol. Tom had a view of the prison through a grimy window. There was a vase of wilted flowers on the window ledge. The building beyond was bulky and formidable and somewhere inside it, only a hundred yards distant, his wife was confined. It was almost impossible to believe. Tom took a deep breath and sat on a hard chair. His heart was beating hard, as it had been ever since the message had arrived at Miss Howlett's house in South Bailey that a Mrs Ansell was in the custody of the police. Luckily, the servant had brought the message straight to Tom.

Without telling Aunt Julia or anyone else, without putting on his coat, he ran to the police-house in Court Lane, only to be informed that he should apply to the County Court instead. He gathered no more than that Helen had been apprehended near a dead body which had been discovered in the woods below the cathedral. Tom arrived at the County Court, sweating and furious and fearful. Dashing into the spacious hallway and spotting a superintendent's uniform he had buttonholed the man. By chance he had encountered the very one who could tell him what was happening.

Now Frank Harcourt was settling himself on the far side of the desk and toying with an empty pen holder and a blotter. He picked up a paperweight and looked at it curiously.

'Not my office,' he explained. He eventually found a notepad and a pencil in a drawer. 'A few preliminaries, if you don't mind. You are Mr Thomas Ansell?'

Tom nodded.

'And your profession, sir?'

'I am a solicitor, with a London firm. Scott, Lye & Mackenzie of Furnival Street.'

'Is that L-I-E?'

'With a Y.'

Harcourt bent over the notepad and laboriously wrote all this down, pressing hard on the paper. He stuck out his tongue as he wrote and his face turned more ruddy. The pencil point broke and a couple of minutes passed while Harcourt rummaged in his clothing. He produced a little clasp knife which he snapped open with a grunt of satisfaction. He shaved the tip of the pencil until a decent length of lead was showing. He gave his whole attention to the job. To avoid gazing out of the window and seeing the prison beyond, Tom stared round the room. The walls were bare apart from a framed sampler that bore the embroidered legend: 'Blessed Are They That Hunger And Thirst After Righteousness.'

'And your wife, Mr Ansell?' continued Harcourt, his sharpened pencil poised again. 'She is called Helen?'

'Yes. But she must have told you so already.'

'She did. You are visiting Durham on legal business?'

'Helen's aunt lives here. We are staying with her for a few days. That is, with Miss Julia Howlett in the South Bailey.'

If the name meant anything to Superintendent Harcourt he

didn't show it. He said, 'I gather your wife knew the deceased.'

'This may sound absurd, Superintendent, but then the whole thing is absurd. I do not even know who is dead.'

'You don't know who is dead, Mr Ansell? Well, well. The deceased is a gentleman who has caused a certain stir in this town . . . his name is . . . or was, I should say . . . Eustace Flask.'

'Oh God! How did he die?'

'He was murdered. Stabbed, it seems. A vicious blow to the neck with a sharp knife. May I take it from your response that you were also familiar with Mr Flask?'

'Plenty of people knew him, I imagine,' said Tom, cautiously.

'As a matter of fact, I knew him myself,' said Harcourt. 'A glancing acquaintance only, mind.'

'But he disappeared last night.'

'Last night? Ah, you are referring to the performance at the Assembly Rooms when Mr Flask was invited to enter the magician's booth.'

'If you were there then you must have seen him vanish too.'

'That was a trick, Mr Ansell.'

'But Flask never reappeared.'

'All part of the act, I suppose,' said Harcourt.

'Shouldn't you be talking to the performers on stage, talking to Major Marmont for example, to find out exactly what happened afterwards? Flask could have died last night.'

'The body was still warm, the blood was still flowing, when your wife found him this morning. He had only just been killed.'

Tom noted that the policeman was not implying that it was Helen who had killed Flask.

'So he disappeared temporarily and then popped up again. Someone must have seen him in the in-between.'

'No doubt,' said Harcourt. 'We will talk to the magician and others but in our own good time, Mr Ansell. We must talk to your wife first and find out what she was doing with the deceased.'

'She wasn't doing anything with him. She had the bad luck to find his body, that is all. You have as much as said so.'

'Possibly, sir, possibly. But caution is the watchword in these affairs. You are lucky because I was actually on the scene of the murder.'

'You saw it?' said Tom, not understanding.

'I mean that I arrived shortly afterwards, happening to be in the neighbourhood by chance. Fortunately, several of my men were also in the area. Tell me, Mr Ansell, did your wife ever express an opinion of Mr Eustace Flask?'

Helen had said several things about Flask, all of them unfavourable, so Tom cast around for a neutral way to answer. He certainly wanted to avoid any hint that she had come to Durham with the specific intention of persuading her aunt Howlett away from her infatuation with the medium. He saw Frank Harcourt looking at him, tapping the end of the pencil against his mouth. There was a shrewdness in the policeman's eyes but also something else there which Tom couldn't quite place.

'Neither of us has much time for mediums and séances and that sort of thing,' said Tom eventually. 'We had, both of us, met Mr Flask once – at her aunt's house as it happens.'

There was a double tap on the door and Harcourt went to answer it. A police constable stood outside. Without any preamble, he launched into an urgent explanation. The man's accent was so broad that Tom had difficulty following him but, as far as he could gather, something had occurred which required the Superintendent's immediate attention, something to do with the delivery of a parcel.

Harcourt came back. He said, 'You may see your wife if you wish, Mr Ansell. There has been a development in the case.'

'What is it?'

'I am not at liberty to say. But if you come with me now I shall direct a warder to take you to Mrs Ansell.'

The Crown Court and the prison occupied the same site. Superintendent Harcourt led Tom down some stairs and along increasingly drab passageways until they emerged into a small high-walled yard. He rapped on an iron-barred door on the far side and, when a wooden panel slid back, grunted a few words to the whiskered face on the other side. There was the clank of keys from within.

'I'll leave you with Perkins, Mr Ansell. You are in good hands.'

Tom was thinking not of himself but of poor Helen as the warder escorted him across a chilly vestibule occupied only by a desk, chair and filing cabinet. Half a dozen flat blue caps were hanging from a row of pegs. Perkins took a key from the great

bunch which dangled at his belt and, without looking to check
whether he had the right one, unlocked another reinforced door.
Beyond this was a barred gate which led directly to one of the
prison wings. There was same instinctive procedure with the keys.
Without saying a word, the warder beckoned Tom to follow him
up a spiral metal staircase to the left of the gate and they climbed
to the second tier of the building. A row of doors opened off a
narrow walkway, echoed by a similar arrangement on the other
side.

It was curiously silent, with no sound apart from the thud of
the men's feet. There was an acrid smell, a mixture of food and
carbolic and human waste. Perkins halted at the seventh or eight
door. This time the warder had to search for a specific key. When
he found it, he used it to tap on the door to alert the occupant,
before turning the key and swinging open the door in a single
smooth action.

Helen was sitting on a bench against the far wall. Her head
was bent in concentration and she was scribbling in a notebook.
She looked up, blinking.

'Tom! It's you.'

'Helen. You're all right?'

'Of course I am all right.'

'What are you doing?' said Tom. It was a stupid question but
other words failed him. He was standing just inside the cell door.

''Fraid I'll have to lock you in, sir,' said Perkins, making a show
of drawing a pocket-watch from his uniform jacket and consulting
it. 'I will wait outside on the landing. I can give you ten minutes.'

'I am sure you can give us longer than that,' said Helen. She
glanced at Tom and surreptitiously rubbed her thumb and forefinger together.

Tom gave the man half a sovereign. The coin disappeared like
magic.

'Half an hour, sir, no longer,' said Perkins. He shut the door
and turned the key.

Helen said, 'Well, Tom, in answer to your question I am writing
down the details of my surroundings. An author never knows
when these things will come in useful. I might send one of my
characters to gaol at some point and, when I do, I will need to
know what the inside of a cell looks like.'

Helen spoke more rapidly than usual. Tom noticed that there was some blood on her dress. She snapped the notebook shut – it was her diary, he saw – and placed it neatly beside her. She got up from the bench, came to him and he put his arms around her.

'I don't know how you do it,' he said at last. 'You are so calm, so brave. Oh Helen!'

'Now, Tom. Do not be foolish. This is all a silly mistake. I shall be out of here very soon. After all, you have been in the same plight yourself.'

It was true. The previous year Tom had spent an unhappy night in a cell in the county gaol in Salisbury when he too had fallen under suspicion for a crime he did not commit. Helen had visited him in that place, just as he was now visiting her in this one. Tom wondered if there was some malign or mischievous fate subjecting each of them to a parallel experience of prison.

Tom released his wife and took his first careful look at the cell. With its curved ceiling, it was like a vault or the interior of a compartment in a train carriage. The flaking walls were white-washed. A few feet above the bed there was an unglazed and barred window which allowed in small quantities of light and air. At the moment a stray draught was bringing in the ghost of summer to the cell. In the winter it would be bitterly cold. Apart from the bed, the only covering for which was a coarse blanket, there was a wooden chair and a three-legged stand for a wash-basin, a ewer of water and a thick glass tumbler. A bucket was lodged under the bed.

Helen had gone back to sit on the bed. She saw Tom looking round.

'As you can see, there is not much to note down. Not much to distract the mind or lift the spirits. Thank goodness I had my diary tucked away. They didn't have a searcher to hand and so they did not discover my diary.'

'A searcher?' said Tom.

'A woman who is employed to search female suspects. I already have a grasp of the police jargon, you see. I must say I will be glad to get out of here. I need to change my clothes.'

She glanced at the bloodstains on her dress. She looked at her hands. She shuddered.

'I must have touched him. I got too close to the . . . to the body. I have washed my hands several times over but I have not been able to get my clothes laundered in this place.'

She gave an odd laugh. Tom came to sit beside her and felt the bed give under their weight. He put his arm round her. After a while, he asked Helen to tell him what had happened. Did she want to talk about it? How had she come to find Eustace Flask?

As Tom knew, she had gone out that morning to look at the shops – a rather un-Helen-like thing to do but she needed to get away from Aunt Julia who was preoccupied with the fate of Eustace Flask after his disappearance at the Assembly Rooms. Every few minutes over breakfast it was, 'I wonder what's become of dear Mr Flask?' or 'I do hope he's all right' or 'Do you think we should tell the authorities?' Tom noticed that even Septimus Sheridan's patience was wearing thin. He excused himself to go and look at the notes on the Lucknow Dagger which Sebastian Marmont had written up for him, and to try to make sense of a rambling, disjointed narrative.

Helen described how she had walked to the Market Place and then lingered over the shop windows in Silver Street. It was a fine morning and she wanted to stretch her legs. She walked down the cobbled slope to Framwellgate Bridge, across which they had driven on their arrival in Durham. She paused and looked casually down at the river. Below her was the path where she and Tom had strolled the previous day. She walked to the far side of the bridge, the western end. There was a similar riverside path running below here.

She gave a start to see below the gentleman they had encountered yesterday, the one who had claimed to be returning her handkerchief. It was him, she was sure of it. The same loping stride, the same shabby coat. Perhaps, she thought, he goes up and down the river paths in search of discarded handkerchiefs.

But Helen was much more surprised, even shocked, to see a similarly tall figure emerge from the shadow of the bridge and move off in the same direction keeping the castle and cathedral to his left. There was no doubt in her mind about *his* identity. That stride which was mincing rather than loping, the rather fine attire, the pale red hair escaping from under his hat. It was Eustace Flask.

Her first reaction was, oddly, disappointment. So it was a trick after all, he hadn't been made to disappear in the Perseus Cabinet. Her next was, Aunt Julia will be relieved that he is back. Then curiosity got the better of her. What exactly had happened last night? How had Flask been made to disappear? Why, come to that, had he now chosen to reappear? Where was he going?

Before she was really aware of what she was doing Helen Ansell found herself descending the steep stone steps leading from Framwellgate Bridge down to the river level. By the time she reached the path Eustace Flask was in the far distance. Helen couldn't bring herself to shout or run after him. She set off at a regular pace, now thinking better of the idea of accosting Flask and quizzing him. What business was it of hers? To talk to the medium would give him the idea she was somehow interested in his welfare, whereas she wanted nothing more than that he should stop fleecing her aunt and leave Durham. There were other walkers on the riverbank, and a group of boys was fishing in the dirty water with makeshift rods and lines. She paused for a time to admire the view of the cathedral in its western aspect.

'I decided to walk for a few more minutes and then go back to Framwellgate,' she said to Tom. 'I had almost forgotten about Mr Flask. As I drew nearer to the mill on the other side of the river I heard the thud of the hammers and smelled the stench of the — what is it they use? — yes, of the ammonia. There is a second mill on this side and a couple of workmen outside were unloading sacks of wool from a wagon. The path skirts the mill and I walked further so as get a clear view of that handsome bridge where the river curves round on itself.

'This is quite a deserted stretch of the riverbank, I suppose because it is more distant from the town or because of the noise and smell of the mills. I don't know why, Tom, but I grew suddenly alarmed when I rounded the loop of the river. The sun vanished behind a cloud and it turned gloomy. Even the river seemed to take on a blacker hue. I looked round and saw no one though I could hear the sounds of wood being chopped and sawed. I was about to retrace my steps when a figure burst from the slope of trees ahead of me and ran away. He did not see me. I cannot be sure but I think it might have been the man I noticed earlier, the one who tried to hand me a handkerchief.'

Helen paused at this point in her story. Tom looked up and
saw a whiskery cheek and a single eye staring at them through
the shuttered peephole in the cell door. The half-hour according
to Perkins must be up. Tom mouthed the word 'later' and rubbed
his thumb against his forefinger as Helen had done. The segment
of face withdrew, apparently satisfied. Helen, absorbed in what
she was saying, observed none of this.

'I was foolish, Tom. I should have turned back there and then.
I should have remembered that there is always, always, a penalty
to be paid for curiosity. I suspected something was amiss and I
ought to have summoned help. But I walked on until I came to
the point where I had seen the man running from the shelter of
the trees. I waited, listening to the wind in the branches and the
rushing of the water and the distant sounds of saws and axes. The
sun had come out again, which fortified me. Then I heard a
different sound.

'It was one that made my skin crawl. Something between a
groan and a gurgle and coming from among the trees further up
the slope. More animal than human. There was a kind of track
leading uphill. What drove me to follow it and discover the source
of the sound, I do not know. It is a strange thing but I remembered then what that poor medium, Mr Smight, said to you –
or what your father's spirit said to you – that there was danger
in the woods and near water. It was a warning to me not to you.'

'It must have been,' said Tom, his skin crawling.

'Is it not strange,' persisted Helen, in a musing way, 'strange that
we are not always governed by the instinct for self-preservation
and will run our heads into the noose? The noose? What am I
saying?'

Helen stopped once more and gulped several times. Tom poured
water from the jug into the glass and gave it to her.

'You don't have to say any more, Helen. I heard about what
. . . what happened next. Do not distress yourself by living over
the details again.'

'I cannot escape the details anyway, Tom. Everything is like a
terrible dream – there was Mr Flask – for I recognized him
straightaway – I went close – and there was blood welling from
his neck and he seemed to shake and quiver where he lay on
the leaf-mould – and the sunlight was dappling the ground like

gold coins and the birds were still singing in the trees without a care in the world. I must have shouted and screamed. I know I opened my mouth with the intention of doing so. At last some men in labouring clothes came into the clearing but they would not approach me and one said something under his breath and another ran off and then he returned with a constable and there were whistles blown and other police appeared and one of them who is a superintendent, I think, he spoke quite kindly to me and then they took me away and led me to this place and to this cell and, oh, Tom, what is going to happen to me?'

'Nothing is going to happen to you, my darling. I will do my utmost to protect you.'

'Thank you, Tom.'

They embraced awkwardly on the prison bed. There was the sound of a key being turned in the lock and Tom mentally cursed Perkins for being a greedy, heartless intruder. But it was Superintendent Frank Harcourt who was standing on the threshold of the tiny chamber.

'Mr Ansell and Mrs Ansell, my apologies for disturbing what was obviously a, ah, delicate domestic moment but I would like you to accompany me.'

Tom got up reluctantly. He thought he detected a different tone in the policeman's voice, more deferential, less assured. Helen stayed where she was, sitting on the bed.

'Both of you, if you would be so good. I said that there had been a new development in the case, and I would like to discuss it with you.'

They left the cell. Perkins was standing outside. He had his palm artlessly extended as if to show the way and, as Tom passed, he slipped another half-sovereign into it while the Superintendent's back was turned. Perkins touched his blue cap to Helen.

'A pleasure seeing a real lady in here,' he said.

'Enough of your guff,' said Harcourt over his shoulder.

They retraced their path along the walkway and down the spiral stairs. Perkins unlocked the barred gate and the doors on either side of the bare vestibule. They crossed the walled yard and re-entered the Crown Court and so went along drab passages and up bare stairs until they came once more to the office where Tom had first talked with Harcourt. There was a constable inside, the same one who had knocked while Tom was first with the Superintendent.

'You can go, Humphries,' said Harcourt.

'Very good, sir. I've been keeping a careful watch.'

When the three were alone Harcourt gestured at the single additional feature of the room. This was the item over which Humphries had been keeping his careful watch. A yellow cardboard box about a foot long and six inches wide had been placed in the centre of the desk. Brown paper wrapping and a length of cut twine lay next to Harcourt's clasp-knife. The Superintendent picked up the brown paper and handed it to Tom who showed it to Helen.

'There,' said Harcourt. 'It was sent to me by name at the policehouse. Knowing I was at the court building they brought it straight here.'

Printed in red ink and in rather straggling characters was: 'FRANK HARCORT, POLIS HOUSE, CORT LANE'. Above the address in the same script was a single word: 'URJENT!'

'My name is misspelled as are the words "Police", "Court Lane" and "urgent",' said Harcourt unnecessarily. 'Would you open the box, Mrs Ansell?'

'I will open it,' said Tom.

'No, sir. I would prefer your wife to do the honours. It won't bite. Look at the lid first, Mrs Ansell.'

There was a pale rectangle on the lid where a manufacturer's or shopkeeper's label must have been pasted. The label had been torn off although unidentifiable fragments still adhered to the top of the box.

'Someone didn't want you to know the source of the box,' said Helen.

'Just so,' said Harcourt. 'Now open it if you please.'

Holding the box with one hand, Helen removed the lid with the other. Tom was standing too far away to see what she could see. She gazed at the contents of the box and then her hands flew to her cheeks in horror. Tom was beside her in a second. He looked down. Nestling on a piece of fabric inside the box was a knife. He recognized it as the Lucknow Dagger. The multi-armed figure of Kali, goddess of death and destruction, trampling on the fallen figure and surrounded by skulls, was clearly visible.

But even that sinister image could not distract Tom's eyes from the bluish steel of the blade which seemed to have taken on a yet darker hue.

The last time he had seen the Dagger it had been in the possession of Sebastian Marmont. Should he say so? He was about to speak out but something prevented him. Not yet. Not until he had had the opportunity to confront Marmont who was, after all, a client of his firm. Of course if the Major did not have a credible story then it would be Tom's duty to report what he knew to the Durham police.

While all this was spinning round in Tom's head, Superintendent Harcourt had been watching Helen closely. 'Sit down, Mrs Ansell,' he said. 'I can see the sight of the knife has given you a turn.'

Helen had gone pale. She slumped into the seat by the desk.

'That was deliberate,' said Tom, his anger rising. 'You had no need to subject my wife to this ordeal, Harcourt.'

'On the contrary, sir, it all goes towards confirming her innocence. You should be pleased. Moreover, you should be especially pleased with this.'

He fumbled in his pockets and brought out a folded sheet of white paper which he passed to Tom. There was some writing on it which was in the same red ink, the same style of capital letters, as the address on the brown wrapper. Tom took it round to where Helen was sitting. He placed the paper on the desk and they read it together.

'Oh God,' said Helen.

Tom turned away to look out of the window at the bulk of Durham Gaol. The sun shone on the slate roofs of the prison wings but he felt chilled. He picked up the sheet from the desk.

It read: 'THE LADY DID'NT DO THE DEED COZ I DID THIS HOMISIDE FOR PRUFE PLEASE FIND THE KNYF I USED'

'It's a facer, isn't it,' said Harcourt, pleased at the effect of the knife and the note on the Ansells. 'That appears to be the murder weapon. It does not look English to my eyes.'

'No,' said Tom, 'it is not English.'

'And the note is obviously written by a person of small education because of the spelling.'

'Or by someone who wants you to think he is not educated,'

said Helen. Her initial horror over, she peered again into the box which contained the knife. She pulled out the piece of fabric and dangled it by a corner. It was a handkerchief. Though smeared with blood, the delicate lilac colour showed through. Helen caught Tom's eye but she said nothing and hastily put the cloth back. Something else about the cardboard box must have attracted her attention, though, for she put her face close to the knife and handkerchief as if to scrutinize them even more closely.

'Well,' said Harcourt, 'I think we can say that this exonerates you, Mrs Ansell. These items, taken together, have opened the door of your cell.'

'Who delivered the parcel to the police-house, Superintendent?' said Tom.

'My sergeant says a dirty-faced urchin ran into the station and dropped it like a hot coal before running out again. By the time he got to the door, the boy was nowhere to be seen. Whoever did it probably gave him a couple of pennies for his pains.'

'Wouldn't it be worth trying to find the boy? Whoever paid him those pennies was most likely the murderer. You might get a description of the person.'

'Very true, Mrs Ansell. But there are plenty of scruffy children in this city who'd do more for twopence than deliver a package. I do not propose to go in search of them. Please do not let me detain *you* any longer though.'

Once he'd ascertained that they were staying in town a little longer and that Helen would be available to make a formal statement in the next day or so, he showed them to the door. As he stood there he said, 'I hope you do not think any the worse of me, Mrs Ansell, but you will understand that we had no choice but to apprehend you, given your proximity to the body and the fact that there was no one else in the immediate neighbourhood. No hard feelings, eh?'

'Not at all, Superintendent,' said Helen. 'But I will take more care in future not to be found in the region of the dead.'

When the Ansells had gone, Superintendent Frank Harcourt went to examine once more the items which had been delivered to him. First he picked up the letter and read it for what must have been the tenth time. She was clever, Mrs Ansell, no doubt about it. Clever to have understood that the writer might wish to pass for being only half-educated rather than really being so. Astute in her suggestion that if they could get hold of the boy who'd dropped off the parcel, they might get a description of the person who'd given it to him in the first place. Harcourt hoped that his declared reluctance to go searching for the boy had sounded plausible.

He studied the knife in the box. Yes, it was definitely foreign – and valuable. He would leave it as it was, with its bloodied blade, but place the box in the safe in the police-house. He folded up the brown paper with its crudely written address and rolled up the length of twine. He placed them both inside the cardboard box, along with the letter. He slipped his clasp-knife back into his waistcoat pocket.

Once he had deposited the package in the station at Court Lane, he would set about investigating the murder of Eustace Flask. He would make a show of activity. He would question people and take statements. He would satisfy the Chief Constable, Alfred Huggins, who had so recently been demanding that action be taken against Flask. He would be rigorous, a model of professionalism. Yet, even so, the murderer of Eustace Flask might never be found. It happened from time to time. Despite the best efforts of the police, people occasionally got away with murder, didn't they?

The Perseus Cabinet

It was fortunate in one way that Helen Ansell had been taken to the gaol even if it was only for a few miserable hours. Fortunate because Aunt Julia's distress and outrage at this completely eclipsed any disturbance she might have felt at the news of Eustace Flask's murder.

She said she would speak to the Chief Constable and the Bishop of Durham. She was going to protest to their Member of Parliament. She would write to *The Times*. But before that, she insisted that Helen should bathe, sleep, be seen by a doctor, be dosed up, eat a good meal, imbibe pots of tea, and swallow several cordials, all at the same time. Helen did agree that her dress, which was stained by Flask's blood, ought to be got rid of rather than laundered, but otherwise she distracted herself in the attempt to calm her aunt. Septimus Sheridan too was upset and fussed around in an ineffectual way, muttering about the indignity of incarcerating a lady and the sacrilege of a murder committed a few hundred yards over the river from the cathedral.

Helen put on a good front so it was only Tom who knew how deeply she had been shaken by what happened. She could not sleep that night and, at one o'clock in the morning, they lay side by side talking about the peculiar turn events had taken.

'Thank goodness that parcel was sent to the police-house, Tom. I might be spending my first night in Durham Gaol otherwise.'

'But you are not. Thank God you are here with me. We are together.'

'It is odd though, isn't it? If you had committed a murder and someone else – the wrong person – was apprehended for the crime, what would you do?'

'Nothing, I suppose.'

'Instead you would be pleased that the police were on the wrong scent. You would want them to go on holding that wrong person for a long time, even for the person to be put on trial and . . .'

'And all the rest of it.'

'We know what the 'rest of it' means even if we don't want to spell it out. Why, if you were the real murderer you might even be pleased to see someone sent to the gallows in your place. A scape-goat. Or, if not *pleased*, then at least prepared to have him standing on the trapdoor rather than you. Even to have *her* on the trapdoor.'

'Don't talk in that way, Helen. Your imagination is too vivid.'

'But you see, Tom, what we have here is a murderer with a conscience. He – let us assume it is a he, perhaps the very man I saw running away from the scene – he is capable of killing but he acts quickly when the wrong person is apprehended. He is scrupulous. He doesn't wish to share the blame. He goes so far as to deliver the murder weapon and a helpful note to the police saying that he has done the deed.'

'Helen, I haven't said this yet but I recognized the knife, the one which was sent to Harcourt.'

Helen sat straight up in bed.

'What!'

Tom had kept silent so far about the fact that the knife in the box and the Lucknow Dagger were one and the same. Now he rapidly explained that it was the very implement which Sebastian Marmont had shown to him in the County Hotel.

'My God, Tom, why didn't you tell the superintendent?'

'Because I sense that this business is more complicated than we realize, Helen. How do we know what passed between Flask and the magician last night after the performance? He made the medium disappear but what happened next? I must speak to the Major before doing anything. He is a client of Scott, Lye & Mackenzie, after all.'

'Oh, so anything he says or does is privileged?'

'Not exactly,' said Tom, 'but—'

'You could not protect Major Marmont if he was the murderer.'

'Of course not. I will go and see him tomorrow.'

'You will not go alone. I have a stake in this now.'

'Then both of us together will lay things out as fairly as we can to Marmont, mentioning the murder weapon and so on. If he cannot explain himself, then we will hand him over to Superintendent Harcourt. And, Helen, it's not only me . . . you too have held back a piece of information.'

140

'Me?'

'I could see that you recognized the bit of material in the box with the knife. I recognized it too. It was the same as the hand-kerchief which that man tried to give you on the riverbank.'

'The very same. It was a woman's handkerchief although it was not mine. I suppose I was afraid that, if I drew attention to it in the Court office, then the Superintendent might have looked at me with even more suspicion.'

'But you said nothing about the man either. You didn't even mention you saw someone running from the woods.'

'I know.'

Tom waited. Eventually Helen said, 'There was something rather . . . frightening about that man. Can you remember what he looked like?'

Tom struggled to recall the encounter on the river path the other morning. The man had been tall, dressed in a shabby coat and hat. He had deep furrows on his face and a thin mouth. Helen had said he reminded her of someone. Would Tom recognize him if he saw him again? Probably. Was he the murderer of Eustace Flask? Possibly.

'I can remember enough to give a description to the police if we need to.'

'Can we leave it for a time, Tom? Just as you are going to leave informing on Major Marmont. There's something else about the murder of Mr Flask, you see.'

'What is it?'

'It is rather shameful to confess.'

'Even to me?'

'I cannot be altogether sorry that Mr Flask is dead. I had rather he had never arrived in Durham. I had rather my aunt had never taken such a shine to him. But he did arrive and she did take a shine and we cannot alter that. Now he is dead and, however it occurred and whoever did the deed, I cannot be wholly sorry. There, is that not a terrible thing to say?'

'You want me to show you how it works? Nothing could be easier.'

Major Sebastian Marmont did not have the look or manner of a murderer. He welcomed Tom and Helen like old friends.

He expressed his regret at the death of Eustace Flask even if he did so in a somewhat perfunctory manner. He explained that Superintendent Harcourt had already visited him. According to the magician, the policeman asked only a few questions and was soon satisfied by his answers. Marmont did not seem to be aware of the details of how Flask had died, the fatal wound to the throat, and the use of the Lucknow Dagger as a murder weapon. Either that or he was a good actor; not implausible considering that he performed on the stage for a living.

The magician was candid about the sequence of events on the evening when Flask had been made to disappear. In fact he was willing to demonstrate the mechanism of the disappearance to the Ansells.

'But I thought all your tricks were secret,' said Helen.

'We magicians do our best to keep them secret from each other but there are methods of finding out. Every fresh magic invention has to be patented, you see, otherwise any Tom, Dick or Harry could steal it. But the moment a patent is applied for, details must be provided and when those details are provided the secret is available to the same Tom, Dick & Co at the Patent Office. We magicians are caught in a bind. Which is my long-winded way of saying, Mrs Ansell, that I've no objection to showing you and your husband the secret of the Perseus Cabinet. Or may I call you Helen? I knew your father, you remember.'

'Of course you may. But I shall continue to call you Major if you don't mind. I like the sound of it.'

Major Marmont and the Ansells were standing on the stage of the Assembly Rooms. According to Marmont, they were lucky to find him there since he did most of his magical rehearsals at a variety hall he was renting elsewhere in the city. It was mid-morning. The auditorium was empty and, in the absence of an audience and the full panoply of flaring gaslights, the place looked smaller but more ornate because the fine plasterwork was evident. By contrast, the stage was plain and workaday. The Perseus Cabinet stood in the centre, its double doors shut. The Hindoo servants, otherwise Marmont's three sons named after English kings and consorts, were busying themselves on the fringes of the stage.

'Which of you is to disappear?'

'I will,' said Helen promptly.

'No you won't,' said Tom.

'Thomas, entering a cupboard holds no terrors for me. I trust the Major.'

'Thank you, my dear.'

'Then it's settled.'

'Have a look at it first of all, Mr Ansell. Walk round it. Reassure yourself.'

Tom did so. Apart from the doors at the front, there was no other way out, no flaps or little exits he could detect. He returned to stand by the magician who had been in deep conversation with his wife.

Now Sebastian Marmont clapped his hands and pointed to the cabinet. Arthur and Alfred ran to their positions on either side of it. Tom watched, more than slightly apprehensive, as the Major clasped Helen's arm and walked her towards the cabinet. He whispered something else in her ear and Helen laughed. He left her standing a few feet in front of the doors. Marmont came back to where Tom was standing. Now he took Tom by the elbow.

'If you'd just shift here, my dear chap, you'll get a better view, you know.'

Tom couldn't argue with that for he was now standing directly facing Helen who looked over her shoulder and smiled at him. Marmont nodded at the two boys who reached for the doors and swung them open with a simultaneous flourish. The interior of the Perseus Cabinet was just as it had been on the night of Flask's disappearance. There was the empty space within, apart from the vertical wooden pole in the centre supporting a gas lamp which threw a clear illumination on to the red and gold paper of the internal walls.

Tom recalled that the magician had accompanied Eustace Flask into the cabinet but this time it was enough for Marmont to say, 'Please step forward, my dear. Remember what I said.'

What was it the Major had said, Tom wondered, while he watched his wife step up and into the Perseus Cabinet. The 'Hindoos' promptly closed the doors after her and began to play on the flute and tambour.

Tom felt his mouth go dry. The Major continued to hold him

by the upper arm. Was he doing that to show that he could not possibly be interfering with whatever was going on in the cabinet?

A few seconds went by. Without a word being said but as if at some unseen signal, the boy players put down their instruments and unfolded the doors once more. Tom saw the pole holding the gaslight, he saw the bright colours of the wallpaper. But of Helen there was no sign. He was standing about fifteen feet from the cabinet. He made to move forward, his unease turning to genuine anxiety. But the Major restrained him. He said, 'Wait. All shall be well.'

The process was repeated. The doors closed, the monotonously hypnotic music was replayed, the instruments laid down again, the doors opened once more. And out stepped Helen Ansell.

Tom laughed in relief. Not that he thought anything had really happened to his wife. But she had definitely disappeared. And hadn't they been toying with the possibility that the magician might also be a murderer?

'How is it done?' he said.

Marmont, all smiles and affability, tugged his moustaches.

'I'll let your wife explain. She is in on the secret now.'

Helen drew Tom right to one side so that they were almost in the wings. She told him to look at the cabinet from this angle. Did he notice anything odd about it? Yes, there was something he couldn't quite put his finger on, an irregularity in the patterning of the wallpaper inside the booth. They walked back towards it at a diagonal. Helen said Tom should keep his eyes on the interior. There was an unexpected flicker of movement, a glimpse of a sleeve. When Tom stopped and stepped back a pace, the sleeve reappeared. It was his own sleeve, his own arm.

Light started to dawn. He went right up to the cabinet and, with Helen's encouragement, stepped inside. He saw now that there were two full-length, hinged panels on the interior which could be swung in and out from the back corners of the cabinet and which met at the central point provided by the pole. The panels were mirrored on one side and covered with the red and gilt paper on the other. When the the mirror-faces of the panels were flush against the side walls they were indistinguishable from them because the back 'wallpaper' side was revealed. When they were opened at a diagonal angle the mirrors reflected the actual side walls, covered in the same paper.

He realized that the pole was necessary for the illusion. Its function was not to support the gaslight, which could have been suspended from the ceiling, but to hide the meeting point of the mirrored panels. If you looked at the Perseus Cabinet directly from the front or from any angle except the most oblique ones in the wings, the mirrored panels when in place gave viewers the illusion that they were looking at the *back* wall, patterned in identical red and gold swirls.

Behind the reflecting panels was a fairly confined area in the shape of a wide-angled V. It was big enough though to take one person. It was where Helen had been instructed to hide herself while the doors were shut, a process that would take only a matter of seconds, just as it would take only a fraction of a minute to make a reappearance.

'Like all the best tricks it is clever and simple at the same time. But now I am working on a new disappearing cabinet to beat all disappearing cabinets, something which will be superior even to the Perseus.'

This was Major Marmont who had come to stand next to Helen. Both were peering at Tom as he put his fingertips to the mirrors and admired the neat way in which each panel fitted snugly against the central pole.

'Don't touch the mirrors,' said Marmont. 'They have to be absolutely clean. Any smudges or smears will catch the light and the audience might notice.'

Tom stepped down from the Perseus Cabinet. Both Helen and Major Marmont were smiling, not exactly at Tom but at the cleverness of the deception.

'You would make an accomplished performer on stage, my dear,' said the magician to Helen. 'Perhaps you would be willing to help me prepare my tricks another time?'

'I would be delighted,' said Helen.

'How did you persuade Eustace Flask to hide himself behind the mirrors?' cut in Tom. 'Why should he want to help you of all people, Major Marmont?'

'He did not want to help me, not at all. But once I had him

up on stage he couldn't back out without looking like a spoil-sport or a milksop, though in my view he was both.'

'He said something to you,' said Helen. 'Everybody in the audience saw him whispering to you.'

'Oh,' said the Major airily, 'it was nothing, a threat, a warning which I dismissed. I couldn't tell him how the trick worked of course, otherwise he would probably have revealed it to the audience there and then. You'll remember that I accompanied him inside the Perseus Cabinet, something I did not have to do with you, dear lady, because you already knew what to do. When the outer doors were closed upon Flask and me, it was the work of an instant to give him a hearty shove into the area at the back and fasten the panels to the pole. If you look carefully you'll see that there are little catches at top and bottom to secure the panels. It wouldn't take much to break them down but usually, of course, we are dealing with those who are willing to disappear, those who are in on the secret. I counted on Flask being sufficiently confused not to kick up a fuss – or to try and kick his way out. The boys were playing their drum and flute, and the purpose of the music is not merely to set the scene but to conceal any untoward noises which may be emerging from the Perseus Cabinet. There, I think you have it all now.'

'Not really, Major,' said Tom. 'I understand the trick but what happened to Flask afterwards?'

'Nothing whatsoever. We came forward to take a bow, I and my Hindoo lads, and the sound of applause must have been gall to Flask's ears even while it was masking any fuss he was making. Then we wheeled the Perseus off stage in double-quick time and I personally released Flask from his captivity. He was looking mighty peeved, I can tell you, but slightly shamefaced as well. I'd certainly paid him back for his earlier deception at Miss Howlett's and he knew it. But what was he going to do? Announce how a magician had tricked him into disappearing? Lay a complaint that I had manhandled him and show himself up for a milksop in the process. He followed me back to the dressing room and judging by his expression he would have liked to make a scene. He might even have thought of raising his fist at me. But he saw the folly of it and he scarcely opened his mouth. In fact, he couldn't get out of the theatre fast enough.'

Tom had more to ask. The three of them were alone, Marmont's boys having made themselves scarce. Even so he was conscious that they were standing on a stage in a public place. He gazed out at the auditorium and thought he detected a movement near the seats at the back. He called out, 'Is anybody there?' but there was no answer.

Nevertheless he lowered his voice as he said to Marmont, 'Did your hear how Flask was killed?'

'Superintendent Harcourt said he was stabbed. I read an account in the paper this morning. I was sorry to read it, believe it or not.'

The Durham Advertiser had carried a vague and sensationalized story, referring to a murderous frenzy and speculating that there might be a madman on the loose in the city. It seemed to Tom unduly alarmist and, oddly, the source of the story appeared to be the police themselves. Despite this, it did not give any reliable detail about the murder. Fortunately, Helen's brief incarceration had not been mentioned, nor the delivery of the mysterious package to the police-house.

'Major Marmont, you showed me the Lucknow Dagger a day or so ago. You have given me some notes on how you acquired it and you are going to swear an affidavit.'

'That won't be necessary now,' said the Major to Tom. For the first time that morning his friendly tone was replaced by something more guarded, even hostile.

'It won't. Why not?'

'I am sorry you have had a wasted journey to Durham, Mr Ansell. I no longer wish to swear an affidavit. Of course, I will expect to be billed by Scott, Lye & Mackenzie for your time and trouble so far but . . . no more is required of you.'

'I am afraid that we cannot leave it there,' said Tom, glancing at Helen.

'I would like to see the Lucknow Dagger again.'

'You saw it yesterday.'

'Even so,' said Helen, speaking more gently than Tom and not giving the slightest hint that she had already seen the Dagger in the court house office, '*I* would appreciate a glimpse of it. Tom has described it to me. It is such a fine piece of work, he says.'

'It is certainly that.'

'We must see it,' repeated Tom.

There was a pause. A lot hinged on Sebastian Marmont's reply. He could not still be in possession of the Dagger which was currently locked up in a police safe. But what he said next would determine how much he knew of the weapon which was responsible for a murder, possibly even whether he had committed it himself.

The Major sighed. He seemed to come to a decision.

'I cannot show the Lucknow Dagger to you, dear lady and gentleman, for the simple reason that I no longer have it. It was stolen from me on the evening of the performance. As I said, Eustace Flask came storming after me into the dressing room. I turned my back on him for a moment – I wasn't afraid of him and his tantrums! – and when I looked round again his expression had changed. He had obviously thought better of starting a set-to. He stalked out. It was only later that I realized that the Dagger had gone. I had taken it off and laid it down as I was changing. He must have removed it as a form of revenge. Like the sneaking opportunistic thief he was.'

'Why didn't you go after him?'

'I decided to leave it until the next day. I knew where he lived, Flask and the man and woman who share a house with him.'

'Yes, you must have known,' said Tom, 'because you wrote a letter to him inviting him to take part in the performance. How did you know that, Major Marmont?'

'You are very suspicious, Mr Ansell. You ought to be a detective.'

'I – both Helen and I – have cause for suspicion, sir. Believe me, the police might have cause for suspicion too.'

'I sense there is something you're not telling me. Very well, yes, I did know Flask's address in the city. I told one of my lads to follow him and his little entourage after that business at Miss Howlett's. It was easy to do. Flask and the woman were sauntering through the old town with that bruiser of a fellow pushing a hand-cart containing all Flask's tawdry props behind them. They finished up at a house in Old Elvet. My lad noted the street and the number, then came back and gave me the information after which I wrote to the medium requesting his presence at the Assembly Rooms. He duly came as a member of the audience and the rest followed.'

'Did you go to get the Dagger back?'

'I went the next morning, only to be told by the woman – Kitty's her name, I think – that Flask had returned to the house very late the previous night, in fact in the early hours of the morning. But by that stage he'd vanished once more, she said, gone to meet someone. She did not say who he was meeting.'

'You asked her about the Dagger?'

'I did not mention it. The matter of the Dagger was between Flask and me. If I encountered him again I was going to call him a thief to his face and demand its return.'

'*If* you encountered him. You don't sound very concerned about the loss of the Dagger.'

'The Dagger has a strange and violent history which I have only hinted at in the notes I have given you. If I'm honest I had mixed feelings about its loss. I suspected that it would bring no good to Eustace Flask.'

'It did not,' said Helen. 'The Dagger was the implement which was used to kill him.'

'Was it now?' said the Major with surprising equanimity, though his face grew more ruddy. 'Well, that is an example of poetic justice, since Flask took the Dagger from me.'

'You did not tell any of this to Superintendent Harcourt?' said Tom.

'As I say, the taking of the Dagger was a matter between me and Flask so, no, I did not mention it. Besides, Superintendent Harcourt did not seem very interested by what I said. He was easily satisfied. I gathered from something he let slip that he was familiar with this man Flask and didn't much like him either. Without giving a demonstration, I merely informed Harcourt of how I first caused Flask to disappear from the Perseus Cabinet and then let him out again five minutes or so later. So where is the Lucknow Dagger now, Mr Ansell? I ask, because you seem to be so well informed.'

'It's in the hands of the police,' said Tom.

Helen told of the strange parcel which had been forwarded to the Crown Court and the yet stranger note which had exonerated her of blame for the murder. She could even recite it word for word – 'THE LADY DID'NT DO THE DEED' and so on – as though it were imprinted on her brain. It was imprinted on Tom's too. Now Marmont looked truly shocked.

'You don't mean that you have come under suspicion yourself, Helen? That is terrible, terrible. Thank God for the anonymous letter-writer.'

'Whoever he was,' she said.

'Major, you will have to go to the police and give a statement about how Flask took the knife and so on. Now that you know it was the murder weapon.'

'Is that the advice of a lawyer, Mr Ansell?'

'It is.'

'Very well. But before that I should like *you* – both of you – to hear the full story of the Dagger's provenance. The notes I have given you, Mr Ansell, only hint at it. A day or so's delay in informing the Durham Constabulary cannot make much difference.'

Tom agreed since he had little choice. Dilip Gopal, Marmont's assistant, appeared at this point. The Major introduced him to Helen and he bowed slightly.

'Mr and Mrs Ansell are curious about the disappearance of Eustace Flask. I have told them that no harm came to him here.'

'That is the case,' said the Indian. 'I saw him go. But not before he had roundly insulted me as he left the theatre. It is fortunate that I am a forgiving fellow.'

He uttered the remark in a light spirit but his mouth was grim.

'Oh I don't think anyone would suspect you, my dear fellow,' said Marmont. 'But I have some bad news, Dilip. The implement which was used to murder Flask was the Lucknow Dagger. It is at present in the hands of the police.'

'I hope that they will return it, Major,' said Dilip Gopal.

'No doubt, but they must retain it as evidence for a time.'

An odd look passed between Marmont and Dilip Gopal. Tom could not interpret it. A warning? A sign of collusion? He felt more than ever out of his depth.

The Police-House

Miss Kitty Partout was visiting Superintendent Frank Harcourt at the station-house. She said that she had come to clear her name because of whisperings and rumours over the murder of Eustace Flask. He was the one to speak to, wasn't he?

'That's right, Miss Partout,' said Harcourt. 'I am in charge of the investigation.'

Harcourt was the natural choice to take charge of the inquiry into Flask's murder. He had practically volunteered himself. Hadn't he been ordered by Chief Constable Huggins to deal with Flask when the medium was alive? Therefore he was the one to handle him when dead.

Normally Frank Harcourt would have enjoyed sitting in his cramped little office in the company of an attractive woman like Kitty. She was slight and dark-haired with a plump figure and quite a forward manner. But he was uneasily aware that Kitty was probably familiar with his own links to Eustace. Although his own early dealings with Flask – when he attempted to make contact with Florry – had been while the medium was operating alone in Durham, Harcourt knew of Kitty and Barker. Therefore she might know of him. Had the medium boasted of having one of the town officers under his thumb?

He wondered if he could discover how much she knew. Before he could utter a word, however, she began to tumble out her own story. He shushed her and said they would do things in the proper, orderly style. He started with a benign query.

'I am sorry to see you have hurt your hand, Miss Partout. I hope it is not your good hand.'

'It's nothing,' said Kitty, tucking the bandaged hand in her lap without answering the question directly. 'I cut it on some glass is all. But thank you for asking. My name is pronounced "Partoo", by the way.'

Harcourt fussed over his pad and pencil as he usually did so

that he could make a covert assessment of those he was inter-
viewing. Eventually he was ready.

'Some preliminaries first, Miss Partout,' he said, taking care to
pronounce her name as instructed. 'What was the nature of your
connection with Mr Flask? I heard tell he was your uncle.'

Kitty might have been about to agree to that but she picked
up on the sceptical, even slightly sneering tone in the
Superintendent's voice so she said, 'He was not my uncle, no. I
don't know how that story got about. But we was as respectable
as brother and sister. I helped him in his séances.'

'And the other gentleman, the other helper. Ambrose Barker.
Is *he* like a brother to you?'

'Sometimes,' said Kitty shifting on her seat, '"cept he's no
gentleman.'

'Where is he now?'

'Dunno. We had a quarrel and he walked out a couple of days
ago.'

'What was the quarrel about?'

Kitty thought for a time. 'Nothing much. A bit of property,
you might say.'

'You haven't seen him since?'

'No.'

'You said just now that Mr Flask returned to the house which
you shared on the evening after the performance in the Assembly
Rooms.'

'He came back very late. I was worried after that magician
disappeared him. But Eustace, Mr Flask, came back late, yes, he
came back in the small hours. He was angry coz he thought he'd
been made a fool of. You ought to talk to that magician.'

'I have talked to Major Marmont,' said Harcourt, beginning
to feel more confident. Perhaps this woman knew nothing at all
of his own dealings with the dead man. 'What you are saying
confirms what *he* says, that Mr Flask left the theatre after the
show.'

'He didn't come straight back, he must have been wandering
round the town.'

'Possibly. But Eustace Flask did come back, that's the main
point. And the next morning, the morning of his, er, death . . .
what happened then?'

'He left the house again.'

'When did he leave?'

''Bout nine o'clock it must have been. Said he had a meeting with someone.'

'Did he say who he was meeting?'

'No.'

'Or where?'

'No.'

'Did you see which direction he took?'

'No.'

Harcourt's hand was gripping the pencil tightly. His confidence had gone again when Kitty referred to Flask's meeting 'someone'. He realized he hadn't yet made a single note of any of Kitty's answers. He didn't need to, of course, because he had himself seen Flask on the morning of the medium's death and she was telling him nothing he was not already aware of. But, for the sake of form, he automatically scribbled down some words on his pad. The little display wasn't necessary because Kitty suddenly sunk her head in her hands, one gloved, one bandaged. She said, between gulps, 'I didn't see him again and now I won't coz he's gone.'

'There, there,' said Harcourt. 'We will catch the person who did this.'

'Will you?' said Kitty. She seemed to recover all at once. She gave him a curious look from beneath her lowered lashes, half flirtatious, half tearful. 'Will you now? You really ought to talk to that magician again. He came round to the house too.'

'Marmont did? I didn't know that. When did he appear?'

'That Major Marmont, he turned up on the doorstep shortly after Eustace, Mr Flask, had left. He asked where he'd gone as well. Like I just said, I didn't know.'

'So what did he do?'

'Took off himself.'

'In pursuit of Mr Flask?'

'Dunno.'

Harcourt gave up the pretence of writing. He leaned back in his chair. It was baffling. Why had Marmont gone to visit Flask? Wasn't he satisfied with having humiliated the medium on the previous evening? Had he come to inflict more pain? Or to apologize?

'What was his manner, Major Marmont's manner? How was he behaving?'

'He wasn't best pleased about something, I can tell you.'

'This is significant information, Miss Partout,' said the Superintendent. 'I will certainly be talking to the Major again.'

There was little more to say after that. Harcourt indicated to Miss Partout that she could leave. Although he was still curious enough to ask her what she planned to do now that her employer – or protector – or brother – but not uncle – was gone.

Kitty stood up. She shrugged her pretty shoulders.

'Dunno,' she said for at least the third time, ''spect I'll make my way. I usually do.'

When she had gone, Harcourt sat in thought. Did the unexpected appearance of Major Sebastian Marmont at the house on the morning of the murder help to clarify or muddy the waters? It muddied them, he concluded. Which was a state of affairs that suited him. Also, he might now add the name of Ambrose Barker to those who could plausibly be suspected of wanting to see Flask dead. The more potential murderers, the merrier. Harcourt would have bet a week's salary that the quarrel that Kitty mentioned had involved a dispute between Ambrose and Flask. Perhaps the injury to her hand was related to it as well.

Even Kitty herself might be viewed in a suspicious light, as one of the last people to see Flask alive and someone whose relations with him were murky rather than uncle-like or brother-and-sisterly. The Superintendent, in his detective role, had tried to establish whether Kitty was right-handed (it was the right which was bandaged) by asking whether it was her good one but she hadn't responded to his hint. If she happened to be a southpaw, she might have wielded the knife against Flask herself. At least that's what a detective might think!

Harcourt was interrupted by a knock on the door. It was Constable Humphries. He was carrying a telegram form. He most probably knew its contents since there was a telegraph wire direct to the police-house where messages were transcribed by a clerk. Nevertheless the excitement of its arrival caused Humphries to hover by Harcourt's desk. The Superintendent waved him away

and the constable went to the window and blocked the light
while pretending to examine the view.

Harcourt unfolded the telegram and read:

> *Arriving Durham by 2.30 from London. Please arrange for*
> *someone to meet at railway station and escort to police-horse.*
> *Urgent and confidential business. Inspector William Traynor, Great*
> *Scotland Yard.*

Harcourt was baffled, even after he had substituted 'police-
house' for 'police-horse'. But, more than being baffled, he was
deeply worried. Why should a London police inspector be
travelling – urgently, confidentially travelling – to Durham? He
thought of the murder of Eustace Flask. But that had occurred
yesterday and, even in the Durham paper, news of it was being
circulated only this morning. Too soon, surely, for Scotland Yard
to be alerted to take action? What was it to do with them anyway?
This was Durham business.

Harcourt took out his watch. It was dinner time. An hour or so
until Traynor was due in. Humphries cleared his throat. Harcourt
looked up, he'd almost forgotten the constable's presence. He
needed some time alone, time for reflection. He ordered
Humphries to go to the railway station and collect Inspector
William Traynor of Great Scotland Yard. He laid emphasis on the
last words and was gratified to see the expression of alarm, almost
panic, on Humphries' stolid face.

The constable bustled for the door and fumbled with the
handle.

'Beg pardon, sir.'

'Yes.'

'How'm I go'in to reckernise him?'

Harcourt thought. Would Traynor be wearing a uniform? He
didn't know how they did things in London. It was all a mystery.
He said, 'He'll be wearing a – an air of authority. Anyway, you
will be wearing a uniform and he will recognize *you*.'

When Constable Humphries had left, Harcourt tried to gather
up his thoughts. But, since he had no idea why Traynor was
visiting Durham, he did not get very far. He would find out soon
enough. He remembered the recent interview with Kitty Partout

and the one piece of fresh information which she had given him.

There was another knock at the door. For an instant he thought it was Humphries returning with Inspector Traynor before realizing that the constable would not even have reached the railway station yet.

'Yes.'

The door opened timorously. A man in a shovel-hat which barely suppressed an unruly thatch of white hair poked his head round.

'Superintendent Harcourt?'

'What is it?'

'I was directed to your office by the sergeant. May I come in?'

'Who are you, sir?'

'My name is Septimus Sheridan.'

Septimus Sheridan? Harcourt struggled to place the name. The face was vaguely familiar. Couldn't he be left in peace?

'Why do you want to see me, Mr Sheridan?'

'It is to do with the . . . the murder of Eustace Flask.'

At once Harcourt was alert.

'You have some information about Mr Flask?'

'I do, yes I do.'

'You had better come in and sit down, sir. Make yourself comfortable. If you'll just wait while I get my pad and pencil. Oh dear, I see it needs sharpening.'

Harcourt fiddled with his clasp-knife and honed the pencil to a dagger-sharp tip. All the time he was studying the gent on the other side of his desk. He looked like a reverend, except that he was not wearing a collar. What connection could he possibly have to Flask? Eventually he was ready.

'Tell me, Mr Sheridan,' said Frank Harcourt. 'Tell me everything.'

The Return

Kitty went straight from the police station back to the house in Old Elvet. She had said to Harcourt that she would 'make her way' but in truth she had no idea what to do next. She thought the rent on the house was paid for another week or so and she had a few pounds in hand but, for the first time in months, she was without a male protector. Eustace was dead – she went cold as she recalled the fact of his murder – and Ambrose Barker was gone. At least she hoped he was. She had known Ambrose for nearly two years and this was not how she had felt about him at first.

She had fallen head-over-heels for Barker when she had glimpsed him, battered and bleeding, as he was being helped from the sparring ring in the Black Lion near Drury Lane. There was something game about the man even though he couldn't walk straight and blood was pouring from his cheek. Then she had been literally swept away when he seized her hand outside the pub and the next few days and nights passed in a physical oblivion.

The couple had thought they might make a go of it like respectable folk. They found jobs that didn't pay much but were sufficient to provide food and shelter that was superior to the Hackney nethersken where they first lodged. But Ambrose still had his connections to the boxing underworld and he felt the lure of that kind of life. Somebody had called in a debt – Kitty didn't know the details – and Ambrose was invited to use his fists and brawn in a robbery. Kitty refused to play her part and, at that stage, she had enough sway over Ambrose to make him think twice. They had to quit London though.

When they arrived by chance in Durham they were at their wits' end. All Kitty's scruples were vanishing fast and the attempt to rob Eustace Flask was a desperate throw. After they were taken up by the medium and trained in some of his arts, Kitty felt as happy as she had ever been. She knew from the off that Flask was a conman but he did it with such style! By comparison,

Ambrose was not much more than a bruiser. She wasn't exactly drawn to Flask, not in that way, but he was more entertaining company than Ambrose and he had been responsible for giving Kitty a whole new view of the world and herself.

They had not planned to fall into bed together but Kitty had been teasing him for days and letting him feel her tits in a companionable way until late one evening, when Ambrose was out drinking, it just happened. Kitty had not been much impressed by Flask's efforts – in fact she wondered whether he was a virgin in the female department – but she had played along. It was unfortunate Ambrose picked that moment to make his drunken return and burst in on them. Kitty almost laughed when she remembered his remark about a 'case of insects'. But the consequences had not been funny, not at all. The bedroom still smelled of singed feathers and burnt linen from the spilled oil-lamp. Her hand was still bandaged from the glass cuts.

From that instant everything had gone wrong. They had attended the performance at the Assembly Rooms and Eustace had been persuaded to go up on stage. Kitty had been genuinely worried because she recognized the magician as the man who caused such a stir at Miss Howlett's house. After Eustace failed to emerge from the Perseus Cabinet she thought that Marmont had somehow done away with him. That was why she had pushed her way backstage, only to be told that it was all a trick. Even so . . .

When Flask returned to the house late that night, he was in a queer mood, half angry, half gleeful. She was almost asleep. He mentioned that he had got hold of something of Marmont's, some item the magician would regret losing. He did not tell Kitty what it was and she had not passed on this particular bit of information to the police. Perhaps the item was what Major Marmont was looking for when he arrived at the house on the morning of Eustace's death.

Otherwise she had told Harcourt everything she knew, which was not much. Eustace had left saying he was going to meet someone. Then, minutes later, Major Marmont had tipped up. If she was the police, she would have questioned the magician very closely. But that Superintendent had not seemed to be very concerned. He had asked her nothing much about Ambrose. In her book, they should be looking for Ambrose as well. Was he a murderer? Kitty didn't believe it although he'd certainly looked capable of the deed when he burst into the bedroom. Was he still in Durham? Kitty thought she'd caught a glimpse of him over her shoulder once or twice. Was he still consumed with anger? Enough to commit murder? Had he followed Eustace yesterday morning, got him on his own and done for him? If so, would he come after her next? Strange to say, these ideas had not occurred to Kitty before. She knew that Ambrose was not so hard underneath, for all his fighting airs.

Now, alone in the rented house in the early afternoon, she grew frightened. She went round drawing the thin curtains and bolting the front and back doors. Ambrose had a key but he could not get past a bolt. She was standing in the kitchen when out of the corner of her eye she suddenly noticed a shadowy movement in the tiny backyard. Heart in mouth, she crouched down below the sink. There was a tap at the back door.

'Kitty, are you there? I know someone's there. Kitty, open up.'

It was Ambrose.

Later, when they'd made everything up, Kitty ventured to ask a question. *The* only question that mattered. She and Ambrose were lying in their bed, the one in the back room with its view of the gaol. Not so spacious or comfortable as the mahogany one in the better bedroom but that was associated with Flask and, besides, there was still the stench of burnt feathers in the room. It was late afternoon. Kitty stretched. She felt warm and relaxed – and hungry. She'd hardly eaten that day, what with her visit to the police station (which she was tactful enough not to mention). In a moment she'd go down to the kitchen and see if there was anything to cook.

It was strange, she reflected, that a few hours before she had been hoping never to see Ambrose again. It was good riddance as far as she was concerned. Yet here they were, snugged up tight together, like nothing had happened. Except something had happened. Eustace Flask was dead. Hence *the* question.

'Ambrose, did you do it?'

'Do what?'

'You know. Did you do Eustace?'

'What do you think, Kitty?'

'I don't know. That's why I'm asking.'

'You think I'm a murderer,' said Ambrose, gripping her throat not hard but not so playfully either.

'Leave off, Ambrose. 'Course I don't. Otherwise I'd hardly be lying here with you, would I? I'm not stupid.'

'I don't know 'bout that. It takes someone pretty stupid to think they could get away with lying with a molly like Flask.'

'Oh that. That was just a – ' Kitty searched for a word that would not offend him ' – a 'speriment. I was curious.'

'You know what they say about curiosity and the cat. The cat, remember, Kitty Kitty.'

Ambrose was sufficiently amused by his own joke to move his hand from the area of Kitty's throat and to start stroking the inside of her thigh instead. She was encouraged. She ran her own hand – her left one, not the bandaged one – down his body and said, 'If I'm a cat, Ambrose, look at what I've found here. Why, it's a mouse, a very large mouse. Don't you worry your head about Eustace. He couldn't even get it up.'

'Not true from what I saw.'

'Not properly up anyway, not for more than a mo. It was all I could do not to laugh out loud. Not like you, Ambrose. You can always get it up. But, serious, where've you been the last few days? Have you been sleeping rough?'

'What's it to you?'

'I missed you.'

Ambrose pulled away from her hand. He looked slightly uneasy. Not really guilty but a bit uncomfortable.

'Where've I been? Here and there. But not sleeping rough, no.'

In fact, Ambrose had prudently invested in a widow, not too old a widow, who lived in a neighbouring street. His investment had taken the form of a few knowing words and suggestive grins over the last couple of months and she was more than receptive when he went knocking on her door round the corner. It was the night when he'd stormed out the house after discovering Kitty in bed with Flask. Being round the corner had been convenient too since he was determined to keep a close eye on Flask and Kitty. On the subject of the widow, he might have said to

Kitty that a wise mouse needed more than one hole to creep
into but the thought did not occur to him. He was split between
wanting to boast about the other woman to Kitty – except that
the widow would lose a few years in the telling – and wanting
to keep quiet. Truth was, he was a little bit nervous of Kitty's
reaction. So he said nothing except to repeat that he had not
been sleeping rough.

Kitty had a fair idea that something of the widow-variety
might have occurred. It didn't bother her. They were quits in a
way. But Ambrose still hadn't answered the question about the
murder of Flask, not right out. She had to know. So she approached
the problem less directly.

'What were you up to while I was missing you? You with
someone?'

'You sound like a police jack with all this quizzing. No, I
wasn't. If you want to know, I was keeping an eye on you and
Eustace. I went to that theatre like you did. I saw Flask vanish.
That was a good trick. Take my hat off to the magician.'

'He came back afterwards,' said Kitty.

'I know he came back, more's the pity,' said Ambrose. He hesitated for a moment before continuing. 'I had a glimpse of him,
didn't I? He was a long way off. I recognized his coat.'

Kitty stiffened. Was Ambrose saying that he had been following
Flask on the morning of his death? Was this his way of edging
towards a confession? As though he could read her mind he said,
'But I didn't get no closer to Flask. I kept my distance. Next I
knew there was some big kerfuffle, the crushers coming and blowing
their whistles and shaking their rattles and all that. I made meself
scarce.'

She wasn't sure whether to believe him. Not the bit about
making himself scarce but whether he really hadn't got close to
Flask, close enough to kill him.

'Tell you who I did see, though,' said Ambrose suddenly. 'That
old fellow who was at Miss Howlett's. He passed me in a right
state. If he weren't so old I'd say he'd been running.'

Teatime Confession

Septimus was not usually at Colt House at teatime since he tried to put in a full working day in the cathedral library. But he had not been back to the library for two days now. Like the rest of the household, he had been unsettled by the murder of Eustace Flask and so these two old friends, Septimus and Julia, naturally turned to each other for comfort. Septimus had something else on his mind which he had yet to reveal to his landlady. First, though, he had to establish how Miss Howlett was bearing up. He commiserated with her on the death of the medium.

'Oh, it is terrible, Septimus, terrible. But I have hardly given the unfortunate Eustace a thought because I have been so worried about Helen. What happened to my niece is a disgrace, it is an outrage.'

'I expect the police thought they were acting for the best. Perhaps they had no choice in the matter because Mrs Ansell was found near the . . . because she was . . .'

'How dare they arrest my niece! How dare they suspect her of having a hand in Mr Flask's demise! Helen would not hurt a fly. She is not robust, you know.'

'I never like to disagree with you, Miss Howlett, but from what little I have seen of Mrs Ansell she strikes me as being quite the opposite. She is robust, she is capable. She even hinted to me that her experience might be useful to her in her writing. For she is writing a novel, one of those novels they call a three-decker.'

'I know, I know,' said Julia, 'but there are some experiences which a lady ought never to have, whatever the length of the novel she is writing.'

'I was there,' said Septimus, putting his teacup down in the saucer with particular care.

'Where? Where were you, Septimus?'

'I was near the river when Eustace Flask was . . . was murdered. I saw him.'

'You saw him what, Septimus? You saw him alive, you saw him dead?'

At once Julia Howlett looked very alert, especially bird-like. 'Both.'

'I am afraid I do not quite follow you.'

'I was visiting St Oswald's. I do sometimes, when I want peace and quiet to think. I was walking in the graveyard and looking at the view of the cathedral over the river and through the trees. All at once, I heard a noise below me, from among the trees. And I saw someone making his way in haste through the branches and the undergrowth . . .'

'Really, Septimus, *you* are not writing a three-decker novel. Less circumstantial detail, if you please. Who did you see?'

'It was Flask. I recognized him by his coat, the bright green coat, like a peacock's I have always thought. I was curious to see what he was up to. There is a path from the St Oswald's graveyard leading to the river. I began to go down it. I am not sure what happened next but I rather think I stumbled over a tree root. Anyway I lost my footing and I fell over, and was badly winded and confused. I must have lain on the ground for some time. When I came to myself again, I was aware of strange noises from a spot further down. I went to investigate and I saw . . . oh, Miss Howlett, I saw a body lying there which I think was that of Mr Flask . . . I think he might have still been alive.'

'*Think*, Septimus. Aren't you sure?'

'It must have been him.'

'What did you do?'

'Nothing, I did nothing. I am ashamed to say that I was frozen with fear. And then I heard the sounds of someone coming from the other direction, from the river, and I responded by moving as fast as I could upwards, back to the graveyard of St Oswald's. I suppose I was fearful that I too would be attacked. It was not my most glorious hour.'

'It was not,' Julia agreed.

'My life has not been very full of glorious hours, Miss Howlett.'

In his distraction Septimus ruffled his hair so that it was more straggly than ever. He looked so woebegone that Julia reached across and patted his knee.

'But I suspect many men, younger and fitter men, would have done just the same.'

'Your niece did not, she was brave, she went to investigate. It may have been her who I heard coming.'

Septimus did not mention that he had also heard distant screams as he was stumbling through the graveyard, the screams of a woman. That would have been an admission too far. Miss Howlett would think even worse of him if he revealed that he had not gone back to assist.

'Perhaps you are right in saying Helen is a robust girl,' said Julia. 'A little foolhardy too. But, Septimus, there is one thing which you can do – one thing which you must do – to make amends. You must tell the police everything which you have told me.'

'I already have. I visited the police-house earlier today. I spoke to Superintendent Harcourt.'

'Good, good. Your account is useful because it helps to exonerate Helen even more. Since you saw poor Mr Flask when he was already dead or dying and then heard a person approaching, a person who was most likely my niece, it confirms she cannot possibly be considered responsible for this heinous crime.'

'That is what Harcourt said although he didn't put it quite like that. The trouble is—'

'What is the trouble now, Septimus?'

'The Superintendent seemed to think I might have done the deed.'

'You! That is as ridiculous as imagining that Helen did it. Almost as ridiculous.'

'He established that I lodged with you, Miss Howlett. He was already aware of your, ah, friendship with Mr Flask. He asked whether I like the medium, whether I approved of him.'

'Which you did not.'

'Was it so obvious?'

'You never said much but I could see from your expressions, even from your silences, that you were a sceptic.'

'A sceptic not so much on my own account but on yours, Miss Howlett. I did not like to see Eustace Flask practising on you.'

'I can look after myself,' said Julia firmly. 'But if you related all this to the policeman, I can see that you might have made him suspicious. But not so suspicious that he locked you up, like poor Helen.'

'Perhaps I should have been locked up. It would be a fitting punishment, Miss Howlett, for my many failures. But I did not lay a hand on Mr Flask. And I do not believe that Superintendent Harcourt really thought I might have done. Instead he said something rather odd.'

'Well?'

'He said, "The more the merrier".'

The Visitor from the Yard

Earlier that afternoon, a mystery had been solved. Detectives from Great Scotland Yard did not wear uniforms. The individual sitting in Superintendent Frank Harcourt's room was wearing an ordinary suit, and if Harcourt had passed him in the street he would not have given him a second glance. He'd scarcely have looked more than twice if they were sharing a railway compartment. Inspector William Traynor, with his round face and bland gaze, was average in every respect. Harcourt began to relax slightly.

'Welcome to Durham, Inspector. I do not think we have been privileged to receive a visit from Scotland Yard before. You have had something to eat, I hope.'

'I bought a meat pie when I changed at Derby. But I would appreciate it if you could recommend a place where I might stay in the city for a day or two.'

The Inspector had come straight from the station. He travelled light, his only luggage a small portmanteau by his chair. Harcourt was about to suggest a couple of places when a better idea occurred to him.

'We have some good hotels and lodging houses in Durham but it would be a pleasure if you would stay with us, Inspector. My wife would be delighted to meet a detective from Scotland Yard.'

Traynor nodded and was, in his quiet way, effusive in his thanks.

'Although I am a bachelor, Superintendent, there is nothing that pleases me more than the sight of domestic felicity. Your invitation is appreciated.'

Harcourt was thinking such a guest would impress Rhoda. It will do my career no harm either when the Chief Constable gets to hear of it. And it would be better to have this stranger from the Yard in a place where I can keep an eye on him. But, on the heels of these thoughts, it occurred to him that he had yet to discover exactly what Traynor was doing in Durham. What was the urgent and confidential business that had brought him all the way from London?

Harcourt decided to grasp the nettle. 'You're here about the Flask business, I expect.'

'The Flask business?'

'A well-known local . . .' Harcourt hesitated. How to describe Eustace Flask, since he was reluctant for some reason to say 'medium'? He settled lamely for '. . . a local character.'

Inspector Traynor looked even blanker and Harcourt relaxed even more.

'Mr Flask had the misfortune to be murdered yesterday. The crime was perpetrated near the river.'

'I know nothing about that.'

'Well, that's a – that's not surprising. I mean, it *would* be surprising if the news had already reached the London papers.'

'I dare say the news will eventually,' said Traynor. 'An interesting case? You have apprehended someone?'

'Only a matter of time,' said Harcourt. 'So, if it isn't to do with this murder, why are you here, Inspector?'

'Just as I am unaware of your man Flask, Superintendent Harcourt, I don't suppose you have heard of a recent accident in London. It occurred in the suburb of Norwood. A married couple died because one of them had carelessly left the gas jets open. It was fortunate there was no explosion. A neighbour caught a whiff of gas, and smashed a window. She alerted the constable on the beat and together they ensured that no one caused a spark in the vicinity, until the supply could be turned off at the mains and the house thoroughly ventilated. But it was far too late. The man and his wife were found upstairs, asphyxiated in their bed.'

Now it was Harcourt's turn to put on a blank face. Had the Inspector travelled all the way from Great Scotland Yard to give him a first-hand account of an accident in a London suburb? He wondered how to respond.

'A sad story. I hadn't heard it. To be frank, Inspector, an accident such as this – a London accident – is unlikely to feature in *The Durham Advertiser.*'

Harcourt spoke not knowing of the article which Helen Ansell had mentioned to Tom.

'I suppose not,' said Traynor. 'The name of the couple was Seldon. He was a policeman. And you are also a policeman, Superintendent, like me. Anything about the story strike you as odd?'

Now Frank Harcourt put on his thinking face. A dead policeman. That explained the Inspector's interest. Mentally, he ran over what he'd just heard about the gas mains in the Norwood house but without result. Was this a Scotland Yard test? Why didn't the fellow on the other side of his desk get to the point? Harcourt shrugged and Traynor said, 'You see, you might be careless enough to go to bed leaving the gas lamps on but only after you had cut off the supply at the mains. Alternatively you might leave the mains supply on but only if you ensured that all the jets in the house were turned off.'

'Yes, I see,' said Harcourt, glimpsing what Traynor might be on about.

'This was a murder, a double murder. Someone had broken into the house via a back window to a privy. We know that because one of the window bars was prised away. The same someone went round turning on the gas taps and, after that, the supply from the mains. He was careless. He left his coat on the floor of the privy.'

'And you've traced the owner of the coat, Inspector?'

'No such luck. The burglar – the murderer, I should say – did not leave his name with the coat. It was an old, battered item, impossible to trace back to a shop or manufacturer, let alone an owner. Just the kind of thing you might be glad to discard. But a day or two later we received a note at the Yard. It was anonymous, scrawled.'

'Ah,' said Harcourt, thinking of the note, also an anonymous scrawl, which he had received with the knife in the box.

'I have it here,' said Traynor, taking a folded piece of paper from his pocket. He passed it to Harcourt. The Superintendent read: 'LOOK TO DOCTER TONY HE MURDERED THOSE 2 IN NORWOOD'. Harcourt returned the paper and looked enquiringly at Traynor.

'Interesting, eh? Now usually such a note – and we get them from time to time at the Yard – would not take us much further. Who is to say that this is not simply a malicious or mischievous communication? But the writer of it knew something. He knew that this was a case of murder even though the deaths had initially been reported as a household accident. And then we had a stroke of luck. One of our detectives on the metropolitan force makes it his business to be familiar with the area of London round Rosemary Street. He knows its courts and alleys, he knows many of its disreputable inhabitants. He knows too of a gentleman called Tony, Doctor Tony, who lodges in the vicinity. No last name at that stage but it appears he might have been a genuine medical man once. Of him we could find no trace. But we did lay our hands on an individual called George Forester of the Old Mint, which is near Rosemary Street. It did not take long to break Forester. It turned out that he was the writer of the note. He confessed soon enough. He said he felt under some sort of obligation to this Tony, claimed that the doctor had saved the life of one of his children and that ever since he, George, had run the odd errand on the doctor's behalf.'

'I see.'

'One of the things he had done recently was to spy on a couple of dwellings, one of which belonged to the Seldons. Doctor Tony had requested this and George did it without thinking very much about the reasons. When he heard about the death of the Seldons he put two and two together. George is not a bad fellow even if he has had the odd brush with the law in his younger days. He didn't want to sing out direct to us so he wrote that note, hoping we'd nab Tony without involving him. Fact is, though, I think he was relieved when we hauled him in. Said it had been weighing on his conscience. He told us everything. We didn't even have to threaten him with being an accessory.'

'So this doctor – this Tony – turned on the gas taps in the policeman's house. Do you know why, Inspector?'

'We've been doing a bit of deep digging, which is our method at the Yard. We reviewed all the arrests which Seldon had been present at. We looked at cases where he had given testimony in court. And we discovered that Seldon had recently been involved in a case against a medium – what's the matter?'

Traynor hesitated. At the mention of the word 'medium', Harcourt had given a start.

'It's nothing,' said the Superintendent. 'A coincidence perhaps. I'll explain in a moment.'

'Well, there was to be a prosecution against the medium under the Vagrancy Act. Seldon had attended a séance at which a man called Ernest Smight accepted money in exchange for his predictions. No great crime perhaps but it is still an offence. We don't always concern ourselves with such matters but someone high-up had laid a complaint against Smight, and we were obliged to investigate. Ernest Smight was due to appear before the magistrates. It wasn't the first offence either so he might have served a few months inside.'

'But something happened?'

'You might say so, Superintendent. Smight threw himself off Waterloo Bridge. Obviously he thought he was facing financial ruin and penury. He preferred the cold waters of the Thames to prison gruel. He has a sister who assisted him in his presentations and she as good as accused the police of bringing about his demise. He also has a brother who has gone much further than words. By a combination of close questioning of Miss Smight and keeping our ear to the ground, we have established that George's friend Tony is Doctor Anthony Smight. He has assorted letters after his name and might once have enjoyed a respectable practice. But he allowed himself to sink in the world. He haunts an opium den near the London docks, having acquired a taste for it out in the East. He consorts with dubious men and loose women. He occasionally does a good turn, as he did when he attended that child of George's, but in general his life is one of indolence and vice. However, he has never committed murder – until now!'

Inspector Traynor paused in his recital. In his quiet way he had been leading up to this climax. Only he wasn't quite done.

'We believe that Tony – Doctor Smight – with his brains addled by years of dope-smoking and moral turpitude has embarked on a reckless homicidal course. He may not even care if he is caught provided he has accomplished his grim task. He is determined to revenge himself on those he regards as responsible for his brother's suicide. There were six people at the séance in Tullis Street. Two of them are believers and played no part in the unmasking of Ernest. Two more are already dead, Mr and Mrs Seldon, the policeman and his wife. And there is a third couple whose lives, we consider, are in real danger. And they are currently in Durham.'

Finally, thought Harcourt as he struggled to keep his head in this whirlwind of explanation, we have arrived at the reason for Traynor's presence.

'We have made discreet enquiries – which is also our method at the Yard – and have found that they are here on a visit. The lady has an aunt who lives in the city and they are staying with her.'

This time Harcourt didn't give a start. But he was pretty certain he knew who the aunt was, and the couple too. Nevertheless he asked Traynor for their names.

'The aunt is called Miss Julia Howlett,' said the Inspector. 'Helen Ansell is her niece. She and her husband Thomas were the others present at that fateful séance. Mr Ansell is a lawyer and it seems as though he may have helped to expose Smight. He and his wife would have been called as witnesses if the affair had gone before the bench. Miss Smight, the sister, gave these names to her doctor brother – she says now she had no idea of his murderous purpose, although I am not sure that I believe her. The danger to the Ansells is plain as day. We have reason to believe that Anthony Smight is also in the city. An individual of his description was seen boarding the northbound train from the London terminal at about the time the Ansells left the city.'

Frank Harcourt said, 'I have met Mr and Mrs Ansell in some-what unfortunate circumstances. It may be hard to believe but Mrs Ansell was briefly suspected of an involvement in our murder, I mean the murder of Eustace Flask.'

Now it was Traynor's turn to look both baffled and curious, insofar as his bland face could register those reactions. Frank Harcourt gave a brief account of Flask's death and the reason for the apprehending of Helen Ansell. He described the strange delivery of the cardboard box with the knife to the police station. He hinted at a plethora of suspects but also that an arrest could not be far off. Then he mentioned that Flask was a medium.

'What! Why didn't you say so at first, Superintendent?'

'It did not seem relevant, Inspector. I was not aware that your own case was connected to a medium. Besides, yours took his own life while Flask had his taken from him.'

'A coincidence, no doubt,' said William Traynor, 'but unsettling as coincidences may sometimes be.'

'What are you going to do? Do you intend to alert the Ansells to their danger?'

'Yes. I will require you to call on the resources of the Durham force to, ah, keep an eye on them. And we will need to be on the lookout for Dr Tony. I have a likeness of him.'

Traynor unfastened his portmanteau and drew out a sheaf of papers, one of which he passed to Harcourt. The Superintendent looked at a drawing of a thin-faced man in late middle-age. His face was creased with lines and the police artist had put a malicious glint in his eyes.

'It was George Forester who provided most of the detail for that,' said Traynor, 'but we also called on Smight's sister for confirmation. Her position is more serious than Forester's and we may charge her as an accessory. Doctor Smight has a sallow complexion to the point of yellowness. He is about six feet tall and he is thin. Few of these addicts waste their time in eating, you know, Superintendent. You must distribute that picture and the other facts I've mentioned to all the men in the city force. How many constables have you?'

'Sixty-five for the city and the surrounding area.'

'Good. You should take personal charge of passing on these details, although I would like to be able to attend when you do. But every constable should know that this is a dangerous man, one we suspect is already responsible for two deaths and one who is on a quest for more victims in Durham.'

'Of course,' said Harcourt, slightly irritated that the Yard man was telling him how to do his job. He said, 'Shouldn't we be distributing this picture to the newspapers.'

'No,' said Traynor firmly. 'I do not want Smight alerted to the fact that we are looking for him. He will only go to ground. Besides, in my experience, if you provide a picture of a wanted man for the public to pore over, you receive a hundred false sightings for anything genuine.'

'Very well.'

'Next we should call on Mr and Mrs Ansell and alert them to their, ah, predicament. And tonight I will take up your most kind offer of accommodation.'

Harcourt summoned Humphries to take Traynor's portmanteau direct to his house in Hallgarth Street. He instructed the constable to inform his wife that they were expecting an important visitor from Great Scotland Yard. Then he and Traynor went to Julia Howlett's house in the South Bailey, only to find that neither Tom nor Helen was there. They had apparently gone to the County Hotel.

The police officers did not want to cause alarm by mentioning the reason for their visit or even hinting at the existence of 'Doctor Tony', but Harcourt – prompted by the Inspector – did tell the housekeeper to check on the locks and bolts and shutters. He said that there was a particularly skilful housebreaker at large. This was the story the men had agreed on beforehand.

The Lucknow Dagger

Helen and Tom were having an early supper in Major Marmont's room at the County Hotel. He said that he could not appear on stage unless he had eaten beforehand. He welcomed their company – the slight prickliness of their earlier discussion in the Assembly Rooms had disappeared – and he wanted to give them his personal account of the Lucknow Dagger.

'You've got my notes, Mr Ansell, though as I said I don't require an affidavit now. But I feel I owe it to you to tell you both how I came by the wretched thing.'

So over cold pork, chicken and hard-boiled eggs together with pickles and warm potatoes and a bottle of Sauternes, Major Marmont related how he had been a junior officer in the Native Infantry at the time of the Mutiny less than twenty years before. Efficiently, he sketched out the circumstances leading to the Lucknow siege. The attack on Meerut, the terrible massacre at Cawnpore which filled every true-born Englishman with horror and fury, and then nearer to Lucknow the rebellions at Sitapur and Faizabad. Fortunately the quick action of Sir Henry Lawrence, the Commissioner at Lucknow, resulted in the higher parts of the town around the Residency being fortified or at least made defendable.

'But we must come to the immediate reason you are here, Mr and Mrs Ansell. It is to hear how I acquired the Dagger of Lucknow. We hung on by our fingertips, as I say, but we hung on. We had a great piece of good fortune when we discovered more stores hidden beneath the Residency. Good old Lawrence had had them put there but he had neglected to tell anyone – his death got in the way of imparting the information, you see. But what we found in the cellars was enough to provision us for a couple more months and the relief parties were starting to get through. One of them had secured a place called Alum Bagh about four miles south of the city. It wasn't a town or settlement, more of what they sometimes call a *pleasaunce* in that part of the world, a kind of park. But it had walls and was capable of being defended. More importantly, messages could be got through from Alum Bagh to Cawnpore, which had been retaken by this stage. Of course someone first had to cover the ground between Lucknow and Alum Bagh. Later they worked out a system of signalling by semaphore but before that they depended on fool-hardy volunteers to carry messages.'

As he was speaking, Major Marmont laid out a salt cellar and pepper pot close together and put a knife-rest on Tom and Helen's side of the table to show the relative position of the three places. This was hardly necessary but Tom supposed it was a habit acquired from years in the army. Given his other trade, perhaps Marmont would shortly make the salt cellar disappear.

'I was young and reckless enough to volunteer to deliver a message to Alum Bagh, information which had to be carried forward to Cawnpore. Also someone was required to guide the next relief column into Lucknow. We were surrounded by rebels and, poorly organized though they were, the sepoys were scat-tered at points around the city which were known only to the defenders. Having volunteered myself and received a pat on the back from Colonel Sir John Inglis, I decided that I would carry out my mission in native disguise as a sepoy. It was a foolish thing to volunteer, no doubt. I had every reason to live, even though all our lives were in peril. But I had found a girl, you see. An Indian girl. I suppose I wanted to show off.

'You may not think it, but I was once a lithe young man, quick and nimble. Months in the sun had darkened my complexion but I darkened it further by the application of walnut dye, not forgetting arms and legs, and I clad myself in native garb. I must have had the desire to dress up even then. I was accompanied by a local man called Lal. He was a little younger than me, almost a boy in fact, and although a fairly recent arrival in Lucknow he was familiar with every inch of the ground.

'The distance between the Residency and Alum Bagh was only a few miles as the crow flies but we decided not to go through the city which lies to the south of the Residency compound – it was too full of rebel sepoys and dark alleys where any peril or patrol might be lurking. For safety's sake we would take the longer route through the open country in the east and past the entrenchments before we circled back to the west and so towards Alum Bagh. It was a night with a crescent moon and a few stars. Although the rains had started it was very hot and humid.

'I remember sitting with Lal while we waited for it to grow dark enough for us to get started. I hadn't eaten. I couldn't have kept anything down. Concealed under my shirt was a pouch containing various letters from Inglis which were to be forwarded to Cawnpore. They were to do with the number of soldiers and civilians left in the Residency, our dwindling stock of ammunition and so on. I also carried hastily drawn maps showing the best routes into Lucknow, although these might change from day to day. The pouch was secured by a cord about my neck. In the event of danger I was to dispose of the maps and letters, although no one told me exactly how. Eat them perhaps.

'I noticed that Lal also had an object secured by a cord about his neck and, seeing my gaze, he drew out a sheath attached to the cord, withdrew a dagger from the sheath and handed it to me. It was one of those fine Hindoo artefacts, half for use and half for ornament. It sat nicely in my hand but I felt very uneasy holding it. There were ivory designs on the handle. We were sitting in the half-dark but the ivory gleamed like a skull. I was surprised that an ordinary young man should be carrying something so apparently precious – and indeed he had shown it to me with an odd sort of reluctance – but I said nothing and handed back the dagger. Seeing the weapon made me think that I should equip myself with a knife or a pistol. But I had no knife handy, and I thought that if I took my pistol it would conflict with my disguise. I was setting out, unarmed.

'Anyway, to distract ourselves we talked a lot, talked about anything and everything. Lal had pretty good English. I didn't know much about him before except that he was an admirer of the British. Turned out that he'd been born outside Lucknow and that he was much grander than I thought. He was the son of some prince in those parts. There are more Badshahs and Rajas and Nawabs and Nizams up there than you can shake a stick at. That no doubt explained how he came by the dagger.

'Anyway I suppose I spoke to Lal with a touch more respect than I would have done otherwise but I didn't spend much time

thinking of his lineage. You don't when you might be walking
to your imminent death.'

Marmont paused for a mouthful of food and half a glass of
Sauternes and to catch his breath. Tom thought, old Mackenzie
said I'd enjoy meeting the Major and listening to his tales and
he was right.

'The going was straightforward at first,' resumed Marmont. 'We
had to cross a canal at the point where it met the Gumti River
but we already knew that the sepoys had damned the canal so
that a stretch to the south would flood and make it harder for
any relief to get across with their heavy guns. We crept across the
nullah – that's their word for the canal – which was little more
than a dried-out depression in the earth at that point. It was
eerie. There was no one about but we imagined sepoys waiting
to jump out at us from behind every palm or pepul tree. They
weren't expecting any trouble in the eastern quarter but only
from the south, you see, which was why they'd flooded the canal
down there.

'Anyway, Lal and I made our slow progress to east and south.
When we began to go parallel to the line of the nullah between
Dilksuka and Char Bagh Bridges, which were half submerged,
we could see what little moonlight there was glinting on the
flooded plain. There was the occasional spark of a campfire on
the far side. Eventually we arrived at Char Bagh itself, which was
a kind of landmark no more than a couple of miles from our
destination. Char Bagh was another walled-off area. That part of
northern India is full of gardens and secluded areas. This one,
though, was in a dilapidated state, its walls broken down in places
because of the fighting which had already occurred there.

'Lal and I had been on the move for about three hours now
and I suppose we were growing a little tired and careless. Because
we had so far encountered no trouble, we'd forgotten that we
were crossing what was literally enemy territory. I was even regretting that I hadn't had anything to eat before we started. I spotted
a gap in a wall and, with gestures, indicated that we might rest
up for a few moments. I scrambled through the gap. Lal followed,
only more quietly. I walked forward and stepped on something
soft, something that squealed. At first I thought it was an animal
but the squeals were soon followed by curses and a man rose up

before us in the open space beyond the wall. He must have been sleeping and was as surprised to see us as we were to see him.

'I was frozen not with fear exactly but with uncertainty. I did not know what to do next. But Lal did. The moment he heard the noises he'd started to circle round the man and was now on his far side. The man opened his mouth – he was about to shout, to scream, to call for help – I could distinctly see the black hole of his mouth and a raggedy circle of teeth, dark as it was. He was about to shout, I say, and bring down ruin on both of us, when Lal clapped one hand over his gaping mouth and with the other seemed to punch the unfortunate fellow between the ribs. The man arched forward and toppled on to the ground, and Lal almost fell on top of him. He continued to strike at him and I realized that he was using not his fists but the dagger. The dagger with the ivory handle.

'After a time the man lay still and Lal scrambled to his feet, though not before he'd wiped the blade on the dry grass. He was panting hard and muttering some words I couldn't make out. I sensed rather than saw the fresh blood on his garments. We looked down at the prone body. I said something like "Well done." He said that he had not meant to kill the man but that the dagger had a mind of its own. That's how he expressed it, a mind of its own.

'I glanced at the corpse. It crossed my mind that this might have been not one of the rebel sepoys neglecting his duties as a sentry but an innocent who'd lain down to sleep in the wrong place – a peasant or what they call a *ryot* over there.

'But he was no innocent. From the far side of the wall there came cries of alarm and within moments we saw shapes on the other side of the gap. Lal and I took to our heels, dodging among the trees and looking for another way out of this enclosure. I risked a glance back and saw a few of them, now equipped with flaming torches, gathered about the fallen body of the sentry. There was a collective cry of rage and grief. We knew that if we were taken by the sepoys they'd show no mercy, particularly as my companion, a fellow Indian, was covered in the blood of the one he'd killed.

'As I've said, the Char Bagh wall was pierced in plenty of places and we slithered through the next gap we came to, fast as rabbits. I'd lost my bearings by now, as you tend to if you're being pursued by a crowd with murderous intentions. In fact the only idea in my head, apart from not falling into the hands of the sepoys, was to get rid of the pouch containing the letters and maps which I could feel knocking against my own ribs as I ran. Before we knew it we'd reached the edge of the area that had been flooded by the damning of the canal. Unawares we'd turned back in a northerly direction, the opposite one to the Alum Bagh route. Too late now!

'The water stretched in front of us for several hundred yards. By luck, there were no signs of sepoys on the far side of the floodwater, or at least no camp fires. Behind us were our pursuers, their torches like angry fireflies. We could hear them crashing through the grass and brush. There was a crack as one of them loosed off a rifle shot. We didn't need any more encouragement to wade out into the floodwater. It was no more than knee-high at first and very spongy underfoot. Altogether I thought it would not prove much of a deterrent to those behind us.

'But of course we were soon out of our depth. While we'd been wading in I unfastened my pouch and I half scattered, half thrust the documents into the water as soon as it got deep enough. I reckoned whatever was on 'em would soon be erased by the water – which by the way was turbid and foul-smelling. The sheets of paper floated away under the stars. But by that stage I had other things to worry about. Lal was floundering, his head bobbing on the surface. He couldn't swim of course and he was in a muck-sweat. The only mercy was that our pursuers weren't minded to follow us into the water. I could see them clustering on the edge. I'm no mean swimmer myself but it was a struggle to get hold of Lal and avoid being dragged down with him. I managed it, though, after swallowing and spluttering out mouthfuls of filthy water while I was ordering him to keep still and allow himself to be saved – if I could do it!

'As long as we'd been in difficulties, the watchers on the bank had done nothing, neither shouted, nor loosed off any shots. Perhaps they could see the shape of our heads regularly dipping underneath the water and must have been expecting us not to reappear. But when I started to pull strongly with one arm, cradling Lal with the other, they realized we might get away.

They began to shoot and run up and down, shouting to attract attention on the side we were heading for. It was our great good fortune that their shots went wide and that we were opposite a vacant stretch of ground. The only way across was to swim since the bridge at Char Bagh was impassable. Lal and I struggled out, dripping and exhausted, and crawled into the shelter of some trees.

'We couldn't stay there. It would be getting light in two or three hours. We retraced our steps although this time on the inner side of the flooded canal. Again we were lucky because it was that point in the night when everyone is least alert, even those who have been tasked with keeping watch. We reached the half submerged Dilksuka Bridge and then made a sweep north and west, skirting Lucknow. It might have been a dead city, there was no movement, no sound except for the barking of the pye-dogs. Just as the first streaks of light were creeping into the eastern sky, the two of us were also creeping under the steep embankment by Secunder Bagh, knowing that the sepoys had fortified that area.

'We nearly got ourselves shot on the edge of the stronghold around the Residency. Each corner of the defended area had a battery dug-in. By now there was enough light for the guard to see two bedraggled figures in native costume staggering towards his battery. He raised his rifle and shouted out to his sleeping companions and if I hadn't called out in English, giving my name and rank, we might have fallen to a bullet from our own side. Anyway we were welcomed back and were soon fed, washed and changed as best as our straitened circumstances would allow.

'Our mission had been a failure, a complete failure. I must say that Inglis was very decent about it. He patted me on the back just as he'd done before I set out, and praised me for having the presence of mind to destroy the documents I was carrying. "No harm done," he said. "No good either," I might have replied. And within a day or so, a second volunteer did manage to reach Alum Bagh to guide in the next relief column. He was a civilian although a soldier's son, a fellow by the name of Thomas Kavanagh. He received a medal for his achievement, and well deserved it was too. The relief column broke through to Lucknow under Campbell and then the Residency was finally abandoned.'

Here Major Marmont paused and his expression took on the
introspective look of earlier. Tom wondered whether he was
thinking that that medal might have been his, if the mission had
turned out right. But there was something else on his mind.

'Before any of this happened, the relief and so on, I was back
on my feet and ready to do my part in defending the depleted
population in the Residency. But Lal was not so fortunate. He
was a fit young man but he must have picked up something in
that filthy canal as we were floundering across it in our escape
from Char Bagh. I went to see him in the makeshift infirmary
on the first floor of the Residency. I felt an obligation to him –
I might have saved his life in the water, even if only for a brief
time, but he had preserved mine first of all by killing the sentry.
It was the end of the day when I visited the infirmary and the
sun was a great ball of red above the horizon. The light burned
through the tattered muslin screen over the window which was
meant to keep out the bugs.

'Lal was lying on a narrow cot, shaking and sweating profusely.
His skin was a queer greenish tint and his eyes were wild. The
doctor shook his head at me as I looked towards him. The doctor
was a civilian but could have passed for a soldier for he had a
brisk, clipped manner and used as few words as possible. Mind
you, we never said much to each other. This doctor was no friend
of mine. I mentioned to you, Mr Ansell, that my wife Padma was
Indian. She was the girl I met in Lucknow. The doctor fancied
himself a rival to me for the hand of this beautiful girl. Padma
means lotus flower, you know. Thank God, she chose me – but
that was later.

'Anyway, on this occasion the doctor didn't have to speak.
Anyone would have known what that head-shake meant. It might
have been different in a well-appointed hospital but here we were,
under siege, without medicines.

'I bent over Lal to offer him some words of comfort. He didn't
recognize me at first but then he seized my wrist and gabbled
some words I couldn't understand. Eventually I made them out.
"It is fate," he was saying. "It is deserved."

'At the same time he was struggling to untie the cord which
secured the sheath and dagger that still hung about his neck. It
might seem strange that no one had removed – or stolen – the

dagger with its strange ivory handle but it is a measure of those desperate days that we all had other more important things on our minds. He pressed sheath and dagger into my hand. I thought he wanted me to examine them again and reluctantly I withdrew the weapon from its sheath. It's not fanciful to say that the blade seemed to gather to itself the furious red light of the setting sun, as if it was once more steeped in blood. I made to return it to Lal but, no, he wanted me to have the dagger. He pushed it back with all his strength. It was a gift, a dying gift if you like. He whispered, "It is yours. May it bring you better fortune, Lieutenant Marmont."

'Naturally I didn't know what he was talking about and nor was I to find out because he was seized with a worse bout of shaking, amounting almost to a convulsion. I stood there, helpless. At length the doctor more or less ordered me from the room. Lal had subsided into an exhausted sleep or something deeper.

'When I had a moment to myself I looked more carefully at the dagger. It was a fine piece of work, no doubt, but I would have been glad to return it to Lal. I don't know why, but there was some quality to it which made me uneasy. It had been used recently to kill a man, and had very likely despatched other men in the past. But it wasn't that exactly. After all, we were surrounded by carnage in Lucknow and any weapon you touched might have been used to kill and maim.

'But I was the possessor of the dagger whether I liked it or not, Mr and Mrs Ansell. Lal died a few hours later, and his last words to me had been a request, a command even, that I should take the thing. There was a witness too in the shape of the doctor. He had some more unwelcome information, which was probably why this medical man took pleasure in passing it on to me. It seemed that Lal had been talking half lucidly during his brief sickness, and that he had referred to having left his father's house in disgrace. In fact, he appeared to be some kind of fugitive. I remembered that he had mentioned his background before we set off on our mission and that I'd been surprised he came of princely stock. Perhaps it wasn't true, perhaps it was all fantasy. But plainly there was some sinister association with the dagger. Why else should he have said, "May it bring you better fortune"?

'I learned later that the dagger was indeed cursed. One of Lal's brothers had died while he, Lal that is, was wielding it in what was supposed to be a playful tussle and the young man had fled his family home in shame. Hearing all this, I examined the dagger carefully and, imagination or not, it took on a very malevolent aspect. A weapon with a mind of its own, Lal had said, as if the spirit of Kali dwelt within the thing.'

Major Marmont might have had more to say but he was interrupted by Dilip Gopal and his nephews, the Major's sons, arriving from their lodging-house nearby. It was time to go to the Assembly Rooms for that evening's performance.

Visiting the Chemist

As Inspector Traynor and Superintendent Harcourt were returning from the South Bailey and on their way to the County Hotel, the London policeman surprised the Durham one by turning aside when they were nearing the market square. Harcourt suggested they might get a carriage but Traynor insisted on walking everywhere. The only true method, he said, of getting the feel of a place was from the feet upwards. It took him back to his days on the beat in Finchley.

Then without a word of explanation Traynor suddenly entered a chemist's. Brought to an abrupt stop and standing next to the plate-glass, Harcourt pretended to study the curling gilt script which announced the proprietor as FRED'K W. PASCAL. Then he fixed his attention on a poster for fresh leeches next to one extolling the virtues of arrowroot from Bermuda. Perhaps Traynor had been stricken with a sudden attack of something. Perhaps he had forgotten to pack some necessary medicine.

Harcourt turned his back on the window and scanned the shoppers and idlers and passers-by. He was looking for a man fitting the artist's image which was folded in his pocket. Doctor Anthony Smight should not be too hard to pick out from the mass of people, given his yellowish skin, his lined face and above-average height. Nor, presumably, would he speak with the local accent. It would be a coup if he, Frank Harcourt, was the one to detect him in the crowd. One in the eye for the representative of Great Scotland Yard.

Privately, Harcourt thought it unlikely that this so-called Doctor was still in Durham, assuming he had ever been here in the first place. Neither did Harcourt consider that the danger to the Ansells was as great as Traynor had made out. The story of a man seeking vengeance for the suicide of a brother seemed too far-fetched and melodramatic. And those deaths of the London policeman and his wife, might they not have been an accident after all? Harcourt remembered witnessing the aftermath of a gas poisoning in a house over in Allergate, deaths which had been caused not by malice but by carelessness.

Someone tapped him on the shoulder. It was Traynor.

'How many chemists are there in the city?'

Unlike the question about the number of constables, this was not one that the Inspector could answer straightaway. 'Four or five, I believe. Are you in urgent need of some remedy, Inspector?'

'No, no. I was showing the chemist the drawing of Anthony Smight. I asked if anybody resembling the picture had called in during the last few days – without result. Will you detail one of your men to make a round of the other chemists in the city with the picture? It is a long shot but one worth trying. You recall that Doctor Smight is in thrall to opium. Your man is to ask if anyone of that description has lately purchased laudanum or opium pills.'

'Very well.'

'This is your town, Superintendent—'

'Durham is a city.'

'Of course. But like any town or city it must have its less salubrious quarters. To your knowledge are there places where opium is regularly smoked?'

The two men had strolled down into the market square. For answer Harcourt halted and gestured at the market scene.

'This is a respectable town – ah, city – Inspector. We may be built on coal but we have an ancient cathedral and now we have a university too. What with the men of the cloth at one end or those who toil away underground at the other, I do not think that Durham would provide fertile soil for *that* kind of activity. We are not a port city.'

In his mind Harcourt associated opium dens with Chinese men in pigtails and white females who were either haggard or seductive. But Traynor was already thinking in a different direction.

'How far is Newcastle from here?'

'About twenty minutes by train. There is a regular service.'

Traynor said nothing for a time. When he did speak, Harcourt was baffled by his words.

'If I am pursuing a villain, Superintendent, I sometimes put myself into his shoes. I reach a fork in the road and, knowing that the person I seek has travelled this route before me, I do not choose for myself but ask which path *he* would take.'

Harcourt turned to look at the stolid, average figure beside him. He was surprised that such a bland man as Traynor could display any power of imagination.

'You think this man, Doctor Tony, is staying in Newcastle?'

'Newcastle is larger than Durham, is it not? Besides, it is a port city and ports are more easy-going than inland places. Newcastle offers greater opportunities for anonymity, no doubt. Yes, if I were Anthony Smight I might well make Newcastle my base. So there is one more request I must make of you, Superintendent. Choose a group of your most reliable men. Put them on a rota watch at the railway station but not in uniform. Let the man on duty keep particular note of travellers between Durham and Newcastle, one for each platform. If he sees someone fitting Smight's description either boarding the Newcastle train or alighting from one here, he should follow him to see where he goes – but always exercising the utmost caution since I believe we are dealing with a ruthless murderer. Have you got men up to the task?'

'Of course I have,' said Harcourt, divided between wanting to show willing and at the same time assert his own interests, or rather those of the Durham force. 'But, Inspector, you are aware we are dealing with our own murder. This man Flask.'

'Yes. In my experience, though, heightened police activity directed towards one purpose sometimes uncovers other criminals along the way. Give me more details of your affair this evening when we are snug in the bosom of your family. The murder of this Eustace Flask might after all be connected with the arrival of Doctor Smight.'

'Which you have already called coincidence.'

'A coincidence is only so until it is proved otherwise.'

He is quite the police philosopher, this William Traynor, thought Harcourt as they strolled through the old town and across the river to the County Hotel. But naturally he said nothing of his annoyance and contented himself with pointing out some more of the sights of Durham.

By good fortune they encountered Tom and Helen in the lobby of the hotel as they were leaving after their meeting with Major

Marmont. Neither of the Ansells was exactly pleased to see Superintendent Harcourt again but he was quick to reassure Helen that their call was nothing to do with the Flask business. He introduced Inspector Traynor, explaining that the detective from Great Scotland Yard had significant information which concerned the couple.

William Traynor spoke to the hotel porter. He required somewhere quiet where they might chat. The four were directed to an empty snug next to the hotel dining room. Tom and Helen sat together on an old ottoman, the two policemen in armchairs opposite with a low table between them. The smell of food together with the distant chink of plates and cutlery reminded Harcourt that he hadn't eaten since breakfast. The London detective seemed tireless, unaffected by hunger. Fuelled only by the meat pie from Derby station, he had already spent a lengthy period in the police-house, visited Miss Howlett's house and questioned a chemist, besides suggesting a couple of investigative lines. Harcourt thought this must be the pace at which police business was conducted in a big city. He wondered whether to send a message to Rhoda that he and his special guest would be late for supper.

It took some time for even an abbreviated form of the story which Inspector Traynor had to tell. First, he checked that the Ansells had indeed attended the séance in Tullis Street at which Seldon, a policeman in civilian clothes, exposed Ernest Smight.

'But Mr and Mrs Seldon are dead,' interrupted Helen. 'I saw it in the paper. I mentioned it to you, Tom. An accidental gas leak, wasn't it, Inspector?'

'It was no accident, Mrs Ansell,' said Traynor, observing the I-told-you-so look which passed between wife and husband. Swiftly he outlined his reasons for concluding that the death of the Seldons was an ill-disguised murder. He explained the part played by Doctor Anthony Smight, his motive being revenge for the suicide of his brother, Ernest. He said he believed that the Ansells were next on Smight's list.

'That is hard to believe,' said Tom. 'I admit I would have been ready to testify against Ernest Smight if I had been summoned, and I can't say I had any sympathy with the man in the first place. But I – we – were sorry to hear of his death, even if it was by his own hand. Surely this involvement of ours is too small and insignificant for his brother to want to . . . harm us as you've described? It's not rational.'

'Mr Ansell,' said Inspector Traynor, allowing the smallest of smiles to creep across his face, 'you're a lawyer, as I understand it. You are surely aware of just how irrational people can be. That is why the law was invented.'

Then, as he had at the chemist's, he produced the police artist's sketch of Doctor Tony. A less impassive man than Traynor might have been gratified by the effect the picture produced on the couple.

'My God,' said Tom. 'It is the man on the riverbank.'

'Which man is that, Mr Ansell?'

'A few days ago we were out for a walk and the person in this picture tried to return a handkerchief which he said my wife had dropped.'

'It wasn't my handkerchief,' said Helen. 'I told him so quite clearly. At the time I thought he was being very insistent. It was as if he wanted to find some excuse to speak with us, to see us face to face.'

'That's probably what he did want,' said Traynor.

'There is more,' said Helen, taking the picture from Tom and studying it carefully. 'I knew that this individual reminded me of someone. There is a likeness between him and the unfortunate medium, the one from Tullis Street. See, Tom.'

'I do now,' said Tom. 'Something about the eyes and forehead. Not surprising if they are brothers.'

'In one way, this is good news,' said Traynor. 'It confirms, Harcourt, that the man we are seeking is in Durham. But it also underlines the threat facing Mr and Mrs Ansell. Doctor Anthony Smight is on your trail. Do not be afraid, though, for we are on his.'

Despite the reassurance, Tom and Helen automatically glanced round as if the murderer might be lurking in a corner of the oak-panelled snug.

'I cannot help being a little afraid,' said Helen. 'Fear seems justified on this occasion.'

'You really think we are in danger, Inspector?' said Tom.

'We shall act as if the danger to you and your wife is real, Mr Ansell,' said Traynor.

'It is real,' said Helen firmly. 'Before we left London there was a person keeping watch on our house. Remember, Tom, I told you that as well. He was asking questions about us at the grocer's.'

'That was most likely George Forester,' said Traynor. 'It was lucky that the two of you left London for Durham when you did. You might have ended up like the Seldons otherwise.'

Tom put his hand over Helen's. He said. 'We will be all right. At least we know the danger now.'

He spoke with more confidence than he felt. He was conscious of the need to keep his voice steady. He was conscious, too, that Helen had been correct in every one of her fears and forebodings. She thought they were partly responsible for the suicide of Smight, although she had nothing to do with it. She'd been alerted by the snooper asking questions about them and uneasy over the deaths of the Seldons. She sensed something odd about the man on the riverbank – Doctor Anthony Smight – and now she was being proved right on all counts.

'I will have my men keep watch over you,' said Harcourt. 'A discreet watch when you are out and about in the city and there will be a police presence in your aunt's house too.'

'Could not this man Smight have been responsible for the murder of Eustace Flask also?' said Helen. 'Or are there *two* murderers at large in Durham?'

'Either of those things is possible,' said Traynor. 'The Superintendent here has given me an outline of the local murder. I understand from him, Mrs Ansell, that you were unlucky enough to discover Flask's body and even more unlucky to be held in custody for several hours, although anyone meeting you could see that you were no more capable of committing a murder than Harcourt or I.'

Frank Harcourt looked shamefaced, and Helen let him stew in his own discomfort for a few moments before saying, 'I saw the man in the picture on a second occasion. He was walking on the riverbank at around the time Mr Flask was killed. I even saw him near the scene of the murder.'

'Why didn't you say so before, Mrs Ansell?' said Traynor. He spoke mildly.

'The circumstances were not . . . propitious. At the time I was more concerned with establishing my own innocence.'

'Of course,' said Traynor, with a glance at Harcourt who refused to meet his eye. 'I'd have reacted in the same way myself.'

'But what would be Smight's motive for killing Eustace Flask?' said Tom. 'Flask was a medium, like Smight's brother.'

'Who can tell? We won't know until we have Anthony Smight safely under lock and key. But it is my view that this doctor is unhinged. He has gone bad, and when a doctor goes bad he is more dangerous than almost anybody else. He has nerve and experience. Furthermore Smight is an opium addict, a habit which we believe he first acquired in the East. Prolonged indulgence in the drug quite saps the moral sense and sweeps away all inhibitions. Once embarked on a course of murder, such a man will find it very hard to stop.'

'There is another mystery,' said Helen. 'According to you, Inspector, this Anthony Smight is determined to do us harm because we were present at the séance after which his brother killed himself. If that was the case, he ought to have been pleased when I was under suspicion for the death of Eustace Flask. He might have been happy if things had gone much further and I had been put on trial—'

'That never would have happened, dear lady,' said Traynor.

'I am glad to hear it. But, if you accept what I've just said, then explain why Smight took the extraordinary step of sending the murder weapon and a note to the police announcing that I did *not* do it.'

Tom wondered why Helen was so troubled by this question. She'd already raised it with him. What did it matter who had sent the mysterious box with the dagger as long as it exonerated her? But Traynor had an answer, one which was disquieting.

'As I've said already, there is no accounting for human behaviour, Mrs Ansell. It is possible that Anthony Smight did not want you to face the rigour of the law. He wanted you released so that he could . . . well, I shall say no more.'

'You don't need to,' said Helen. 'Your meaning is all too clear.'

'You should talk with Major Marmont, the magician,' said Tom. 'We have just been to see him. He is a client of my firm.'

'I have already spoken with him but I intend to interview him again,' said Harcourt, then under his breath, 'And look who is here . . .'

There was the sound of the door to the snug opening. Tom and Helen were sitting with their backs to the door but Harcourt, who was facing it, raised his eyebrows while even Traynor's impassive expression was replaced by a look of curiosity. Five people entered the snug. They were the magician and his Indian assistant, Dilip Gopal, together with Marmont's three sons. They were on their way to the Assembly Rooms for that evening's performance. Marmont conferred briefly with his entourage then indicated that they should leave without him. He walked briskly to where the others were sitting.

'Superintendent Harcourt, I didn't expect to see you so soon but this is a timely meeting. I have only a few minutes to spare and will give you a full statement later. But you should know that I possess some information about the weapon which was apparently used to kill Eustace Flask.'

'Information which you have withheld from me, Major Marmont?'

'Not deliberately withheld. I did not know it was relevant.'

The Major remained standing. He glanced at Traynor and Harcourt made a show of introducing him as a detective from Great Scotland Yard.

'Give us the facts, sir, the bare facts if you please,' said Traynor.

Rapidly Marmont explained how Flask had stolen the Dagger on the night during which he had disappeared from the Perseus Cabinet. He made no reference to the Dagger's chequered history. Regarding the theft as an act of opportunistic revenge, Marmont had gone to see Flask the following morning only to find that the medium had left the house in Old Elvet.

'Flask's companion, the woman called Kitty, will confirm that I came calling. Also that Flask had departed by then.'

'We are one step ahead of you,' said Harcourt. 'She has already given me her story.'

'You went on looking for Flask after you called at the house?' said Traynor.

'I didn't know where to look. Kitty said he had gone to meet someone but she couldn't say who it was or where they were meeting.'

'Well, it would hardly have been *you* he was meeting,' said Traynor. 'From what you are saying he would have been glad to get away from you. No, our thoughts are turning in a different direction.'

The Inspector glanced automatically at the drawing of Anthony Smight which lay on the table. Marmont appeared to notice it for the first time. He picked up the drawing and studied it carefully. He even ran his fingers lightly across the picture. He nodded once, then again, a gesture more for himself than the others.

'This is the man you are looking for?'

'Yes sir,' said Traynor.

'Is he in Durham?'

'We believe so. I could say we are almost certain of it. You have seen him, Major Marmont?'

'Not in Durham, not at all. I would take an oath on that.'

'But from your expression you seem to know him.'

'It is many years since I have seen this gentleman. It is a very odd coincidence and I have not spared him a thought, let alone referred to him, for ages and yet . . .'

Sebastian Marmont seemed undecided whether to say more. He looked towards Tom and Helen.

'Out with it, sir. We are used to coincidences by now,' said Traynor.

'When I was in India in the army, I was caught up in the Siege of Lucknow during the Mutiny. I have only just now described my experiences to Mr and Mrs Ansell here. Well, there was a doctor in the infirmary in the city. There are more lines on the face in the picture and altogether a changed cast to his features, but this is the man from the infirmary.'

'What was his name?'

'Smight,' said Major Marmont. 'Doctor Anthony Smight.'

Act Four

The Major says, 'Tonight, ladies and gentlemen, you will witness something quite unprecedented. As you can see, I am not equipped with any
props except for this simple kitchen chair and this −'

   He draws from his pocket a silk handkerchief. He sits in the chair
which is positioned to face the audience. He claps his hands. One of his
Hindoo assistants answers the summons. The Major hands the handkerchief to the boy and sits, arms folded, while the boy ties it over his
eyes. When the Major is blindfolded, the boy leaves.

   The Major's colleague, Mr Dilip Gopal, now enters. He is immaculate.
He looks at the magician and shakes his head. Evidently he is not satisfied with something. He takes another handkerchief from his pocket and
proceeds to bind that one too about the head of Sebastian Marmont so
that the unfortunate Major looks like a casualty of battle. But it is surely
impossible for the Major to see a thing.

   'Now,' says the Major, 'my associate Mr Gopal will pass among you,
the audience. Any one of you is at liberty to hand him an object which
you have about your person. Any object, I say. Mr Gopal will hold the
said object in his hands before returning it to you. Using his mind, he
will transmit through the ether an image of that object, a mental image.
I will receive the image as it is borne through the ether and I will tell
you, ladies and gentleman, what it is that Mr Gopal is holding.

   'To avoid any imputation of trickery or collusion, Mr Gopal will say
nothing, not a word, as he receives the objects from you. Not a word
beyond the normal courtesies of course. I am not permitted to ask him
questions nor would he be allowed to answer them. Mr Gopal, if you
please . . .'

   Mr Dilip Gopal descends into the audience. He looks to the right
and left and at first no one meets his eye. Then a fellow at the end of
the stalls beckons to the Indian as if he were a servant. Mr Gopal goes
towards him and executes an almost military salute, bringing his heels
together and inclining his head. The fellow in the stalls slips something
into his hand. Mr Gopal examines it. Apart from the little matter of
the double blindfold, there is no possibility that the Major can see what

he is holding – nor can most of the audience, come to that – since Gopal's back is to the stage. Marmont keeps his swathed head fixed forward, his arms now resting on his knees.

'I thank you, sir,' says Dilip Gopal.

'Mr Gopal, I am receiving an image of what is in your hands. Concentrate on it if you please. Just a little more concentration. Yes, I have it. A cigarette case, a silver cigarette case. It is inscribed, I believe, but the image is not clear enough for me to decipher the message. There is a slight disturbance in the ether tonight.'

Dilip Gopal holds up the item. It glints. It is a cigarette case. He returns it to the owner and a ripple of applause spreads round the auditorium. The besuited Indian moves down the aisle. A woman catches his attention. She has something for him. Mr Gopal comes to another smart halt, clicking his heels. He takes the item and looks at it. He says in his formal manner, 'Thank you, Madam,' but nothing further.

'Let me see, Mr Gopal,' says the Major, 'or rather let me not see. I think that what you have in your hand is – yes, a picture is being transmitted to me even now – it is a purse, a small and delicate purse.'

Dilip Gopal duly holds up a purse to the admiring audience. Now he moves towards the back of the stalls. A sallow-faced man is holding out an item. The Indian takes it, with thanks.

'Now concentrate, Mr Gopal—'

Suddenly Major Marmont breaks off. Those in the front rows notice that his posture stiffens. After a moment the magician and mind-reader seems to recover his poise.

'I have a distinct impression of this item as it crosses the ether between Mr Gopal's mind and my own. It is, yes it is a cravat pin, a stickpin.'

Dilip Gopal again holds up the object to the audience, most of whom have to twist in their seats or crane forward to have a glimpse. But it does indeed appear to be a cravat pin, a rather fine one topped with a pearl. The Indian returns it to the man in the stalls. They look at each other. The man smiles in a way that Mr Gopal could only describe as mirthless.

The Railway Station

For at least the tenth time that morning Constable Bert Humphries completed a casual patrol along the down-line platform of Durham Station. He paused at the southern end and stared at the graceful curve of the double lines as they crossed the Flass Vale viaduct. It was a fine June morning and the sun was gleaming on the tracks. Humphries glanced across the valley separating the railway line from the peninsula dominated by castle and cathedral. A light breeze had blown away the haze that usually hung over the city.

Like a sentry at the end of the platform, Humphries performed an about-turn in a military fashion before remembering that this was not the way he was meant to be doing things. Fortunately there was no one to watch him.

Constable Humphries was wearing not his uniform but civilian clothes. He did not mind much the fact that he had been deprived of his police helmet or his brass-buttoned dark blue greatcoat – since these were the obvious and visible signs of his office – but he missed the comfort of the truncheon and rattle. Lacking these made him feel naked. If the fellow they were after was half as dangerous as old Harcourt and the Scotland Yard man had claimed during the briefing at the police-house, then he might well need to summon help with the rattle. But Harcourt insisted that none of them should carry any item which might give away who they were.

Furthermore, Humphries and the rest had been instructed to forget their training and years of experience. They were not to behave like policemen on the beat. Not to stride along with authority. Not to gaze around with suspicion nor to act as if they had the weight of the law behind them. Altogether, Constable Bert Humphries felt like a truanting schoolboy while he mingled with the ordinary travelling folk who were waiting for trains or getting off them.

Humphries took out his watch. Nearly half an hour until Constable Makepiece replaced him at midday. A Newcastle train was due in ten minutes. Humphries had been on duty since the first train at five o'clock that morning, and the mere thought of the early hour caused him to yawn. He glanced at the opposite platform, the up-line, and saw his counterpart, Constable Atkins, avoiding his eye while trying to look inconspicuous. Did he, Atkins, have the appearance of a policeman in his civvy garb? Humphries thought not. But then he'd never thought Atkins had the appearance of a policeman even when he was wearing the uniform.

Bert Humphries was growing increasingly dubious about this business. Inside his jacket was a picture of the man they were searching for, Doctor Anthony Smight. He looked a bit of a villain, true enough, and was supposed to have committed a couple of murders in London and was presently under suspicion for what the local papers were calling 'The Riverbank Murder'. And they said he was looking to carry out a spot more homicide. Beyond that, Humphries had not been told very much. Why this doctor should be travelling by train to or from Newcastle to commit his murders in Durham had not been explained. Seemed it was some theory of the Great Scotland Yard fellow. Still, theirs not to reason why. Simply do what you're told.

It took a lot of manpower though. Two police on duty, one per platform, to check the trains arriving in both directions. Inspector Traynor must have plenty of pull to demand the services of half a dozen men a day. Humphries worked out the figures. Six men amounted to about a tenth of the entire City of Durham force. Yes, that represented a lot of pull from the Great Scotland Yard man.

The southbound train appeared in the distance, announced by a smudge of dark smoke and the sudden arrival of a knot of porters and a general air of renewed alertness among the passengers on the platform. The rails quivered and sang as the 11.45 from Newcastle slid into the station and slowed before jerking to an abrupt halt, trailing smoke and steam. Constable Humphries rubbed his eyes and positioned himself at the rear of a group of travellers waiting to board the second-class carriages.

Rapidly the constable dismissed most of the new arrivals. Two ladies descended gracefully from first-class, ready for a day's shopping or sightseeing in the city. A trio of clergymen from the same section helped each other to clamber arthritically on to the platform. Some unaccompanied children got out of second-class and a gaggle of labourers together with some women who looked like factory-hands swept from the third. The women were talking loudly, the men were silent. Shift-workers, Humphries guessed. There was a rotund person with a bag who looked like a salesman. A well-dressed gent was loudly requiring two porters to manhandle his luggage from a first-class compartment. Humphries wondered why anyone would need to travel with so much gear.

Then he saw him! A man was coming from the tail-end of the train. Tall but stooping slightly, shabbily dressed, his face largely obscured by a wide-brimmed hat but sallowish. He was carrying a small bag. It must be Anthony Smight! Humphries felt a tremor of intuition. The constable automatically turned his gaze away but kept the newcomer in the corner of his eye as he headed for the booking-hall and station exit. His heart beating fast, Humphries recalled what he'd been told. 'If you see this man do not accost him. Follow him discreetly and keep your distance. Do not arouse his suspicions. Mark where he goes. As soon as he is established somewhere – be it at a lodging-house or a chop-house or a pub – report at once to the police station.'

Humphries decided to give the man half a minute to clear the station. He risked a single look and saw the back of the tall stranger disappearing into the booking-hall. He took a couple of steps in the same direction. He was so absorbed that he collided with another alighting passenger, a second man.

'Pardon,' he said instinctively.

The man glanced at him but said nothing and swept past. Bert Humphries' heart thudded even louder. My God! This individual too had the appearance of the wanted person. *He* was of more than average height, *he* had a creased, jaundiced-looking face and *he* too was moving with a determined air.

Resisting the temptation to get the artist's impression of Smight from his pocket, Humphries counted to ten and then followed this second individual through the booking-hall and station entrance. On the forecourt were several carriages waiting for fares. The two elegant ladies were boarding one and the trio of clergy-men another. The artisans and the factory hands were walking in separate groups away from the station area. As were the two men.

From the back they looked quite similar, although the second –
the one Humphries had bumped into – wasn't wearing a hat nor
was he carrying anything. The two had nothing to do with each
other but were walking separately, yards apart.

The railway station was set high on a hill. The area beyond
the forecourt, on which Humphries now stood facing the city,
fell away steeply. Any traveller to the centre of Durham who
could not afford a cab or who preferred Shanks's pony had two
choices. Either he followed the main road as it looped down-
ward, echoing the path of the railway overhead, or he took a
short cut which branched off this road from a kind of lookout
point about two hundred yards to the left. This path made a
zigzag course down several flights of steps overshadowed by trees
and shrubs. An individual walking from the station at night might
prefer to take the better lit route by the road but the stepped
path was safe enough by day.

Constable Humphries moved off, watching the two men as
they headed down the road, each of them keeping to a stretch
of pavement in a law-abiding manner. The group of artisans and
the female hands were straggling across the road, the women
noisily oblivious to the carriages which would shortly be rolling
downhill. Humphries was very glad that there were other people
on foot. They helped to hide his presence.

The first man he'd seen, the one with the hat, was in advance
of the hatless one. Neither looked behind him. Both were walking
with a sense of purpose. And, as Humphries had half feared and
expected, each proceeded to pick a different path towards Durham.
The individual with hat and bag didn't hesitate but turned off at
the lookout point and went down the steeper route. A few seconds
after him the other man, the hatless and bagless one, continued
down the curve of the roadside with scarcely a glance at the first
who was already out of sight down the steps. This split seemed
to confirm that neither had anything to do with the other.

But it presented Constable Humphries with an acute dilemma.
Which should he follow? The one who'd chosen the short cut
or the one who was taking the road? He had only a matter of
seconds to resolve the problem or face the possibility of losing
both of them.

Humphries put on speed to overtake the working men and

women who were dawdling on foot. He attempted to put himself in the mind of a detective like Great Scotland Yard's Inspector Traynor. How would a proper detective think this through?

Both suspects had alighted from the Newcastle train, both fitted the description of Anthony Smight. It was the first, though, who had given Humphries that tell-tale tremor of intuition. He was wearing a wide-brimmed hat as if he felt the need to conceal his face. He was carrying an anonymous little bag, which somehow added to his suspicious air. And, most conclusive of all, he had turned aside for the short cut into Durham, down a path that wasn't signposted or named in any way. That decision indicated a familiarity with the city, which was certainly what Smight had.

All this passed through Humphries' mind during the brief time it took him to reach the lookout point and the beginning of the stepped descent. Taking a final view of the back of the second man, who was striding round the curve of the road, the policeman thudded down the first flight of steps. Behind him he heard the chatter and laughter of the women as they too chose this shorter route.

Constable Humphries estimated that his quarry was only a matter of seconds in front of him but, because of the zigzag nature of the steps and the overhanging tree branches, it was possible to see no more than a few yards ahead. He was conscious too that he was in pursuit of a very dangerous individual – 'If you see this man do not accost him' – one who might lash out if he believed someone was after him. So Humphries kept darting his eyes among the shadows on either side of the path. He was quite reassured to hear the women clattering down behind him.

But he saw no one until he emerged at the bottom of the final flight of steps and into a jumbled area of terraced housing dominated by the new church of St Godric's. There, about a hundred and fifty yards ahead of Humphries, was his man! Unmistakable in the wide-brimmed hat, the little bag swinging at his side, the purposeful stride.

Anthony Smight turned into North Road and Humphries' task became both easier and more difficult. Easier because there was less likelihood of Smight spotting anyone on his tail, more difficult because it was by now midday and, North Road being a main thoroughfare, it was full of carts and carriages and passers-by.

Humphries had to get closer to his quarry or run the risk of losing him in the crowd. He walked faster, keeping his gaze fixed on the top of Smight's hat. Fortunately the murderous doctor was so intent on his own purposes that, without looking back once, he passed among the idling window-gazers and the shop-workers buying their dinner from the costers' barrows. He smoothly skirted draymen sliding barrels into the vault of a pub and avoided a cluster of argumentative, besuited men coming down the steps of the Miners' Institute.

Humphries wished that he could lay eyes on a uniformed policeman. He felt isolated in his pursuit of Smight and, had he seen one of his fellows, he would have alerted him. It would have taken only a moment of explanation since the whole force had been shown the picture of Smight and knew what was what. The uniform could have reported back to the police-house while Humphries continued his chase. But there was not a police uniform in the entire stretch of North Road.

So the constable in civvy clothing pursued the tall man with his bag and hat into the start of Silver Street and across the river by Framwellgate. This was a smarter part of town. Humphries began to wonder where his quarry was going. Surely a fugitive like Anthony Smight should be haunting the less reputable areas of the city? And Humphries suffered his first twinge of doubt. Was he on the trail of the right man? What had happened to the other one, the one who went walking on down the station road?

Then Humphries was reassured when he saw Smight turn aside and enter a chemist's near the marketplace. Reassured, because he knew that Smight might be seeking to purchase supplies of opium or laudanum. This area of the city was sometimes allotted as his beat and Constable Humphries was on nodding terms with the chemist, whose name FRED'K W. PASCAL was emblazoned in a gilded arc across the plate-glass window. Humphries kept his distance, looking in a ladies' dress-shop before he realized the incongruity of standing before a golden sign for WOMENSWEAR. So he shifted a few yards further to study a gentleman's outfitter's. All the time, though, he kept his eyes on the door to Pascal's.

He waited a long time, almost a quarter of an hour by his pocket-watch. Bert Humphries wondered whether Smight was

committing some outrage inside the chemist's. Had he attacked
Frederick W. Pascal in his frantic search for drugs? Had he left
the unfortunate apothecary bleeding behind his counter while
he made his escape through a back door? But that could hardly
be, because during this anxious quarter of an hour several other
customers had come and gone through the door of FRED'K W.
PASCAL. None of them appeared to have been witness to any
horrors.

Unable to stand the suspense any longer, Humphries was on
the point of going into Pascal's himself, when the tall man emerged.
He was still wearing his hat and carrying his little bag. He turned,
not down towards where Humphries was standing outside the
outfitter's, but up along Saddler Street.

Humphries moved fast. He darted into the chemist's. Frederick
Pascal was not lying bleeding or dead on the floor. He was up
on tiptoe replacing a jar on an upper shelf. He finished what he
was doing and turned round with a what-can-I-do-for-you-sir?
air.

'Mr Pascal, it's me. Constable Humphries.'

'So it is, Constable. I didn't recognize you out of uniform. Day
off?'

'No. I am on duty,' said Humphries, conscious that with every
passing second his quarry was striding further up Saddler Street.
'The man who just left, the one with the hat, what did he buy?'

The chemist, a short man with deep-set eyes, scratched his
head.

'He didn't buy anything.'

'What was he doing here then? Tell me, for heaven's sake.'

'He was selling not buying.'

Seeing the baffled, almost panicky expression on Humphries'
face, Pascal said, 'That was Mr Fish. I know him.'

'Fish? Yer sure his name ain't Smight.'

'As sure as I am that your name is Albert Humphries. Fish
visits the chemists in Durham every month or so to peddle his
cod-liver oil. Not his, of course. He represents the manufacturer.
The quality of the oil from North Sea cod is second to none. I
have just taken four bottles from him and he will be on his way
to sell some to Bennet's up the road. I've always thought it
humorous that a man with the name of Fish should find himself

selling cod-liver oil. Yet we always pass the time pleasantly and the subject of his name has never been mentioned. Are you all right, Constable?'

Humphries had gone to the door. He was gazing up Saddler Street. The tall man with the hat and bag was still in sight. If he'd run Humphries could have caught up with him. But there was no point now.

Humphries wondered about the other man who had alighted from the Newcastle train. Had he made the wrong choice, or was the whole thing a wild goose chase?

Constable Humphries had made the wrong choice. The *other* man who'd alighted from the 11.45 from Newcastle, the one whom Humphries had bumped into, was Doctor Anthony Smight. The murderer had no inkling that the stolid individual on the platform was a policeman in civvy clothes. He barely glanced at Humphries or at a man of about his own height and build who had got off the train ahead of him. Smight was too intent on the next stage of his plans to pay much attention to others. He walked down the curving road away from Durham station and then, by the arches of the Flass Vale viaduct, turned towards the centre of the city.

It was extraordinary, he reflected, how fate had brought him to the same northern place as Sebastian Marmont, the soldier turned magician. Smight had reason to resent Marmont – what he saw as the theft of the girl Padma from him – but it was a resentment which had burned low over the years although he had tried to cause mischief once by spreading the story in London that Marmont had stolen the Lucknow Dagger. His old antipathy to Marmont only flared again when he'd glimpsed the very man on the stage of the Assembly Rooms. Then he encountered Eustace Flask after his humiliating disappearance and saw a way to achieve a small retaliation against Marmont by enlisting the medium's help. It had not quite worked out. Smight remembered the sight of Flask's body, still twitching and bleeding in the wooded glade by the River Wear.

But the death of Flask or Smight's hostility towards Marmont were less significant than his campaign of revenge against all those who had a share in the suicide of Ernest Smight. Anthony was the younger brother to Ernest. He had revered his brother. Ernest had looked after him and their sister Ethel, who was between them in age. Many years before as children, at the beginning of Victoria's reign, they had played in the grounds of the large family house in Mortlake. Once, Ernest had saved Anthony's life by wading into a pond and freeing the drowning six-year-old from the weeds in which he was entangled. Anthony remembered lying on the grass beside the pond with Ernest kneeling beside him, love and distress etched into his face.

They enjoyed an idyllic childhood, the three of them, untroubled by their mother and father, unrebuked by the servants. Then something had gone wrong. The family's money had vanished, almost overnight. Anthony – Tony to his brother and sister – was too young to understand, too young even to be told anything. But he overheard incomprehensible talk of investments on the other side of the world, of minerals in South America, of returns which had not materialized, of more investments and bigger losses. He remembered his father talking about throwing good money after bad, and young Tony visualized a pit in which banknotes fell like leaves to join piles of others which were slowly decaying.

They lost the house at Mortlake and moved to Orpington. Somewhere around that time, they lost their father too. He did not die, he simply disappeared. And, whenever their mother mentioned him again, it was through pursed lips. A few years later their mother died too, and the two brothers and the sister were thrown upon each other even more.

They did go their separate ways eventually, or rather Anthony did by training as a physician and travelling thousands of miles to India. During that time he was caught up in the Lucknow siege, and the rivalry with Lieutenant Marmont over the Indian girl. It was almost a quarter of a century before he returned to England and, when he did see his siblings again, they thought him the shell of the man he had once been. Ernest and Ethel kept house together. They had not exactly prospered either, although the medium enjoyed a brief period of popularity after being taken up by a peer of the realm.

Doctor Tony settled himself in Rosemary Street. He found himself a comfortable niche among the opium-smokers in Penharbour Lane. He did a good deed occasionally, as when he attended to the sick child in George Forester's family. He did no great harm otherwise. Or no more than the odd spot of criminality. But everything changed when he heard the news of brother Ernest's death. The thought of Ernest sliding beneath the cold, dark waters of the Thames – as he, Tony, had once almost slid beneath the weed-infested waters of the Mortlake pond – roused in the doctor a raging pity.

The more he turned over his brother's fate, the more passionate Anthony Smight became in his determination to extract every last drop of vengeance. There were four people he considered guilty. He had set George Forester to spy on the Seldons and the Ansells, and to find out details of their households. He had dealt with the Seldons, not crudely by bludgeoning them over the head or shooting them through the heart with the gun which he kept about his person. Instead he had performed the task in a subtle, almost tortuous style, choking them to death by opening the gas valves in the house in Norwood. There was satisfaction in knowing that the Seldons had perished by drawing poisonous fumes into their lungs just as Ernest had died through absorbing water into his.

Doctor Tony was satisfied to read the account in the papers of the accident although later reports hinted at further police investigations. Smight did not care what they found. He did not even care if they found him eventually, as long as he fulfilled his mission. By now, he had travelled north in pursuit of Mr and Mrs Ansell, the other couple who were going to pay for what they had done to Ernest. As Inspector Traynor correctly surmised, Smight decided to base himself in Newcastle rather than Durham. He preferred the anonymity of a larger city and he felt at home in the area by the docks. But he spent lengthy periods in Durham, tracking his next victims. They were not so accessible as the Seldons and action against them required more thought. Besides, Smight took pleasure in concocting an elaborate plan. As he was doing now.

He was not aware of all the police activity. If he had been, he would still have believed himself capable of outwitting the whole pack of them. Although years of opium-taking might have sapped his moral sense, as Traynor claimed, it had not undermined his sense of superiority. Indeed, at times, he felt invulnerable. He suffered from bad dreams, though.

The Palace of Varieties

Tom and Helen Ansell were chafing under their near confine-
ment in Colt House. Inspector Traynor had suggested that they
would be safer if they spent most of their time at Miss Howlett's.
A policeman, equipped with truncheon and rattle, was stationed
inside the house and occupied himself bantering with the servants
in the back quarters. Another constable was keeping a watch over
the front by making regular patrols along the South Bailey. Aunt
Julia was strangely excited by all the police activity but Septimus
Sheridan seemed terrified, whether of the police or the threat of
a murderer at large. He had stopped going to the cathedral library
and spent most of the time shut up in his room.

If Tom and Helen went out it was with a uniform for company,
which was irritating. They both took the threat from Smight seriously but having a policeman over your shoulder whenever you
wanted to go out was like a form of open arrest. Tom wondered
how long the Durham force could sustain the search for Doctor
Anthony Smight. There were police detailed to cover the railway
station as well as the ones concentrating on Colt House.

He had told Inspector Traynor that he and Helen would soon
be returning to London, and the Great Scotland Yard man looked
unhappy, saying something about the need for material witnesses
in the murder of Eustace Flask. But Tom had the uneasy feeling
that what he really required was for the two of them to remain
in Durham as a lure for Smight. The image of a tethered goat
or lamb left out for a lion flashed through Tom's normally unimag-
inative mind. And when he suggested that it might be a good
idea to publicize the search for Smight in the local newspaper,
Traynor said with great authority that that would merely drive
their quarry underground.

Then everything changed. Traynor came by the house a couple
of mornings later.

'We've got him,' he said without preliminary. His voice was
curiously flat.

'Doctor Smight?' said Helen, shutting the book she was reading.

'Yes, we have the doctor. When I say *we*, I mean that the police in Newcastle have apprehended him. We sent them the picture and other facts. I believe that they caught up with Smight in some low dive by the docks. It all fits.'

Tom, who'd been gazing out of the window, heard the hint of disappointment in Traynor's voice. Of course, the London man wanted to be the one to make the arrest. He'd been beaten to it.

'But my original hunch was correct,' continued the Inspector. 'Smight must have been staying in Newcastle and coming down by train to Durham to do his nefarious work. We had a possible sighting of him at the station yesterday morning but it was a case of mistaken identity, it seems.'

'Could the Newcastle police be wrong?' said Tom.

'Not a chance. I have it here in black and white, just received at the police-house,' said Traynor, producing a white telegraphic form. He walked over to where Tom was standing and showed the message to him, as if to prove his words. 'They have laid hands on Smight. His name is established. I am catching the next train to Newcastle. I have already telegraphed ahead. They are expecting us. Superintendent Harcourt will accompany me. Smight will be closely questioned and then brought back here under heavy escort.'

'Well, that's a relief,' said Helen. She stood up. 'We can get back to leading a normal life.'

'I will ask Superintendent Harcourt to withdraw his men from inside the house and outside,' said Traynor. 'You will not be surprised to hear that this manhunt has stretched the Durham force to the limit. And, yes, Mrs Ansell, you may rest easy.'

When they were alone, Helen said, 'I am tired of being cooped up here. I am going for a walk.'

'I'll come with you.'

'You don't need to, Tom. As the Inspector said, there is no danger now.'

There was something in Helen's manner that made Tom uneasy. Helen seemed uncomfortable too. After a moment she said, 'Oh very well. If you must know, Major Marmont has requested my assistance in rehearsing a trick that he wishes to put on stage soon.'

'Helen, surely you are not going to appear in public?'

The trouble was that Tom could see his wife stepping out on the stage, in a reckless moment. Helen was quick to reassure him.

'No, no, don't worry, I won't embarrass you. But I did receive a note this morning from the Major.'

'A note?'

'Yes, a note, Tom, on County Hotel paper. There are some pieces of apparatus which he needs to refine, and he says I can help. I enjoyed being made to disappear in the Perseus Cabinet.'

'All right,' said Tom. He knew that Major Marmont had taken a shine to Helen so the request was not so surprising. 'But I'll accompany you to the theatre.'

They set off through the older part of town, without a police escort. All the time there was something nagging at Tom, something about the telegram which Harcourt had shown him, briefly. Tom struggled to recall the wording. What was it now? Something along the lines of 'Newcastle force in port arrest Smight. Have your man verify and collect.'

It sounded odd. He mentioned it to Helen, repeating the words as far as he remembered them. She said, 'Telegrams have a special, contorted language all their own.'

'There has been a mistake, I think,' said Tom suddenly, stopping in the street. Helen looked at him. He was gazing fixedly at a shop window, a ladies' dress shop.

'Are you all right, Tom?'

'I must see Traynor or Harcourt.'

'They will surely have left for Newcastle by now.'

'I might be able to catch them at the police-house.'

But Tom was undecided. He didn't want to leave Helen. She saw this and said, 'I'll be safe, Tom. No harm can come to me with Major Marmont.'

'No, it can't, can it? I will join you at the theatre. I will only be a moment.'

He almost ran down the street towards the marketplace. It would take him only a few minutes to reach the police station in New Elvet. He would find Traynor or Harcourt and tell them that they were, almost certainly, on the wrong scent. He was excited by his discovery and wanted to pass it on.

For what Tom had suddenly understood was that the telegraphic message had been wrongly transcribed at the police station. He'd realized it when staring at the window sign. WOMENSWEAR, the dress-shop said in close-packed gilt letters. The apostrophe had been lost and so the two words read as one. 'Women's Wear', of course. But also, and more mischievously, it might be read as 'Women Swear'.

So it was with the telegram from the Newcastle police. It did not read 'Newcastle force in port arrest Smight. Have your man verify and collect.' but 'Newcastle force in port arrests. Might have your man. Verify and collect.'

From his work, Tom was familiar with the way in which telegraphic messages could get mangled, not so much in transmission but in transcription when the clerk at the receiving end wrote down the wrong letter or misplaced a full stop. If the message had come direct to the police-house, where everybody knew they were searching for an individual called Smight, then it was very natural that 'might' could be transformed into 'Smight'. Natural but careless. And enough to send Traynor and Harcourt off to Newcastle on a potential wild-goose chase.

Did it matter? thought Tom, as he walked rapidly across the river and towards the police-house in New Elvet. The policemen would discover soon enough that they were on a false errand and come back, tails between their legs. He slowed down. He considered going back to rejoin Helen. It was more the fear of looking a fool in her eyes than anything else that made him go on.

So he arrived at the police-house, identified himself and told the sergeant on duty he wanted to speak to Frank Harcourt or the detective from Scotland Yard. Too late. As Helen had predicted, they were already on their way to Newcastle. The sergeant said there were other superintendents in the building. Did he wish to speak with one of them? Tom said no. He was starting to regret his eagerness to share his discovery about the telegram. Was he doing anything except proving his own cleverness? Perhaps he was wrong. Perhaps the Newcastle police had detained Smight after all. He hoped so.

Tom retraced his steps to the Assembly Rooms by a route which was now thoroughly familiar. Entering the ornate auditorium, he was relieved to hear from the stage the voice of Major Sebastian Marmont who was, indeed, presiding over arrangements for that evening's performance, his last in Durham. With him were his three sons and Dilip Gopal. But there was no sign of Helen. Tom felt a chill which turned to deep unease when Marmont said he had not seen her.

'But you wrote her a note asking for help in some trick.'

'I haven't written any note. Are you sure, Mr Ansell?'

Tom realized that Helen had not shown him the letter from the County Hotel. If he had seen it he might have recognized the writing, or at least recognized that it wasn't from the magician. He cursed himself for his carelessness. He cursed himself for leaving her and racing to the police station to share his discovery about the telegram. So where was Helen? What in God's name had happened to her?

When Tom set off at a brisk pace for the police-house, Helen Ansell had debated for a moment whether to follow him. But she was rather irritated that he had insisted on accompanying her in the first place and she was baffled by his talk of telegrams. He'd got some hold of some silly notion which he had not troubled to explain to her. She hardly listened to his promise to join her later.

Of course it was safe for her to call on Major Marmont. She did not have to be escorted everywhere by her husband, especially now they had Inspector Traynor's assurance that the danger from Anthony Smight was over. Helen had the magician's letter with her. She retrieved it from her purse and read it again, standing in the street. Marmont was requesting her assistance. In a letter on notepaper headed with the name of the County Hotel, he asked her to come not to the Assembly Rooms but to the Palace of Varieties behind the Court Inn. She knew this was where he stored his conjuring apparatus and where he prepared some of his acts.

The Palace of Varieties did not live up to its palatial name. It was a simple wooden building not far from the court house and the gaol, and a venue for acts such as trick cyclists or hypnotists, judging by the faded and torn bills displayed outside. Its audience would be drawn from the less prosperous areas of the city or the mining communities roundabout.

The outer doors were locked. Helen walked down the alley to one side of the building. There was another entrance here on which was painted 'Performers Only'. This door was ajar. She pushed at it and then hesitated, suddenly not so sure of herself. It opened on to a narrow passage. Helen walked a few feet inside. There was a single gas-jet burning in the passage. She turned a corner and came to a short flight of wooden stairs. It was dim at the top but a draught of cooler air suggested she was somewhere backstage.

She listened hard but heard nothing except the hiss of the gas-jet. She trod softly up the steps. She would just make sure that Major Marmont was not here, and then she would go back. She came to a high-ceilinged but cramped area at the top of the stairs. She picked her way between wicker hampers and wooden crates and mounds of fabric, and pushed at some heavy drapes. At once Helen found herself standing on the stage of the Palace of Varieties. The light here was subdued but better than in the off-stage area. The footlights burned low, giving an effect of an autumn evening.

Near the front of the stage was a queer piece of apparatus. It was a quilted platform, with the dimensions of a very narrow single bed, and it seemed to be floating unsupported about four feet off the ground. As Helen moved towards it the light above the floating platform grew hazier and broke up, almost dissolving into splinters before her eyes. She reached out an experimental hand to touch the object. Her fingers struck against something as taut and metallic as a piano wire. She started back. Then she realized that there was a cluster of wires, very thin strands which held up the platform. The hazy effect was caused by the wires blocking and diffusing the light from the front of the stage.

She stretched out her hand again. The wires were coated in some substance which made them dull, almost invisible. Close to, though, she could see that they converged and ran through multiple points on the 'floating' board. Underneath they were attached to blocks on the stage floor. Overhead the wires fanned out and ran upwards into the dark space within the proscenium arch. Helen saw in the dimness above a device like a great roller suspended out of sight of the audience together with some sort of crank or winch which gleamed faintly in the light. So this was how the floating man trick was achieved!

She passed to one side of the hanging board and, holding her arm below her eyes to reduce the glare from the footlights, she looked out into the auditorium. This was a plainer space than the Assembly Rooms and the seating had a makeshift appearance. But where was Major Marmont? The levitation trick was set up and the footlights were burning low but there was no magician to perform it.

Helen felt a draught on the back of her neck. Her skin prickled and she understood in an instant how foolish she had been to come to the Palace of Varieties, how foolish to come here alone. She was almost too terrified to turn round but, as she was nerving herself to do so, an arm snaked about her neck and a rough cloth was clamped to her nose and mouth. She struggled to remove the hand but the person behind her was taller and stronger, and after a moment she felt her flailing arms grow feeble. Fearing she was about to suffocate, Helen instinctively concentrated on drawing breath through the prickly, strange-smelling fabric fastened across her mouth and nostrils. The footlights wavered and grew dimmer in front of her vision while the man's fingers were hard and rigid, like the legs of an iron spider, and that was the last impression in her mind.

Levitation

There was a terrible burning sensation in her throat and Helen thought she was about to be sick. But the burning sensation subsided and the moment passed. Some time went by without any thoughts at all. Later on – it might have been two hours or two minutes later – she wondered whether she had her eyes shut. If she did it was odd because she was definitely awake. Yet all she was able to see was a black space interspersed with darting yellow streaks. So was she really awake or was she dreaming?

She was lying on her back, resting against a surface that was quite uncomfortable. Where was the iron spider that had leaped on to her face? She could still feel the impress of its horrible legs digging into her cheeks. And there was an unfamiliar, pungent scent in her nostrils and a sweetish taste in her mouth. Not an unpleasant taste or an unpleasant smell but not comforting ones either.

Now, were her eyes properly open or were they closed? It might be absurd but the only way to make sure was by the sense of touch. She went to raise her arm so as to feel her own face, but the arm did not respond even though it wanted to, she knew it wanted to. She was able to wiggle her fingers but not to move her hand. She made the same experiment with her other arm and that too she could not budge. Her arms seemed to be tethered.

With a rising sense of panic, Helen struggled back to what was almost full consciousness. She blinked rapidly but the scene before her eyes stayed the same, a deep well of darkness broken by some yellowish gleams. The gleams were easy to understand, they were caused by lights somewhere below her but reflecting off things *above* her. Machinery of some sort, metal handles and cogs. And at once Helen Ansell remembered where she was, in the Palace of Varieties, and why she had come here, to help Major Sebastian Marmont, and how foolish she had been to come alone.

She knew too that she was lying on the quilted platform used in Marmont's levitation act. Not only lying on the platform but secured to it, tied to it. There was an array of fine wires next to her head. She could see them out of the corner of her eye. She made to raise her head, trying to guess how far she was above the stage, but an abrupt sensation of tightness round her throat made her lie back again. She sensed rather than saw that the plat-form was in the position where she'd first seen it on the stage, hovering about four feet above the ground. There would be no great harm in falling four feet, no danger if she had to tumble off her perch once she was free to move. The platform was stable too. She could not feel it giving or swaying beneath her.

Helen hoped Major Sebastian Marmont would soon come along to release her. She was willing to take part in his magic rehearsals and willing to help him refine his new tricks, but she really had had enough of lying here, had enough of feeling nauseous and terrified.

Then she heard his footsteps echoing on the bare boards.

A head appeared in her line of vision. But it was not Sebastian Marmont's.

She recognized the man from a drawing that she'd seen some-where recently. The lined, thin features, the malicious glint in the eyes. But what was his name? She couldn't remember it, not for the moment.

'Mrs Ansell, you are finally awake. Good.'

Helen wanted to say something but her tongue was thick and cumbersome in her mouth and she thought again that she was about to be sick. She concentrated on swallowing, on repressing the feeling.

'Chloroform doses are tricky things,' said the man, hanging over her. His voice was deep. He spoke like a gentleman. 'Even a doctor or man of science may make a mistake with chloro-form. It depends on the size and weight of the individual, and on the sex of course. Too little and no effect is produced, too much and death may result. Perhaps I administered more than I intended since you have been asleep a long time.'

Helen tried to raise her head once more and experienced the same tight sensation round her neck. A look of genuine concern passed across the face of the gentleman.

'Please don't move your head, Mrs Ansell. There is a wire cord fastened around your throat and it is secured to this floating bed.

The wire is part of the magical apparatus belonging to Major Marmont which I have put to my own use. If you tug against it, you will do yourself no good.'

Helen fought to control her terror. She was in the hands of a madman and although every nerve in her body was screaming at her to flee she could not move. Yet, even in the middle of her terror, she understood she was being kept alive for a reason. This man, this Doctor Anthony Smight, had not killed her – if it was his intention to kill. It must be. She was familiar with his other crimes. But he had not killed her yet even though he might easily have delivered a fatal dose of chloroform or suffocated her or done some other dreadful thing while she was unconscious. She had to remain alive for as long as possible. Every saved moment meant that someone might find her. How to distract him? How to prevent him putting some final, terrible intention into effect?

'You do not know who am I am, do you?' said Smight, almost gently.

Helen was about to make the slightest nodding motion with her head, about to croak out that, yes, she did know his identity and that the police knew it too, when denial suddenly seemed the safer course.

So she whispered, 'No. Who are you? Why are you holding me prisoner?'

'Let me explain, Mrs Ansell. A few weeks ago you and your husband were present at a séance in London as a result of which a man died. He killed himself because he was afraid of persecution despite being an honest medium. Your evidence would have sentenced him to shame and disgrace so he took his own life. Do you know what I am talking about now?'

'Ernest Smight,' said Helen, surprised at the steadiness of her voice. 'I read that he had drowned himself. I was sorry to read it.'

'Your sorrow comes too late to help. Ernest was my beloved brother. I am Doctor Anthony Smight. It was your actions and the trickery of a policeman in disguise that caused Ernest to do away with himself. The coroner's inquest pronounced that he had taken his life while the balance of his mind was disturbed, but I say, Mrs Ansell, that it is you and the others who are truly responsible for his death. As responsible as if you had personally seized him and bundled him beneath the waters of the Thames.'

Helen was gripped by a mixture of fury and indignation. She felt her face grow hot and tears sprang to her eyes. It is absurd, she wanted to scream at this lunatic. Nobody wanted your brother to die. He committed a small crime and he would have served a few weeks in prison, at the very worst. I even felt some pity for your brother. If it had been left to me, there would have been no case to answer. But she said not a word and Smight interpreted the furious workings of her face as more signs of fear. He reached out a hand and patted her shoulder. He was almost smiling. At least his thin mouth lengthened in a kind of grimace.

'Do not worry, Mrs Ansell,' said Doctor Anthony Smight. 'Your suffering will not be as great as my brother's. It will certainly be much shorter since you have not so much leisure to ponder your death. There, I can see that I have shaken you by referring to death. But there are two already dead, the policeman and his wife. Two more must die, you and your husband. Then justice will be done.'

Where was Tom? thought Helen. She'd last seen him sprinting off towards the police-house. But he did not know that she was coming here, to the Palace of Varieties. She hadn't mentioned it to him, annoyed that he insisted on accompanying her in the first place. Tom would assume she had gone to the Assembly Rooms. When he didn't find her there, what would he do? Did Anthony Smight know that the police were on his tail? He was behaving in a strangely relaxed and confident way, just as if he was a family doctor giving some consultation to an old friend. No, he must be surely unaware that the police had his picture and were searching for him. This gave her a little burst of hope. Then she remembered that Harcourt and Traynor had left for Newcastle.

'Wait, wait,' she said. 'How did you know that I would be willing to help Major Marmont with his magic tricks? How did you manage to write to me on paper from his hotel?'

'It's easy enough to get hold of a sheet of hotel writing paper,' said Smight. 'And I was in the Assembly Rooms the other morning when the good Major was demonstrating the operation of the – what is it called? – the Perseus Cabinet. I was at the back of the auditorium, lurking in the shadows you would probably say. I saw how ready you were to enter into the spirit of things and what a nice understanding you had with the military magician. I thought it would not be so difficult to entice you here, where Marmont keeps some of his apparatus. I have been keeping watch on you, on all of you, keeping watch with my invisible eye. I have been planning this for many days.'

'And what are you planning for my husband? Why don't you content yourself with . . . with whatever you intend to do to me?'

'Mrs Ansell, if you weren't such an evident lady, I would be tempted to call you by male terms such as gallant or chivalrous. But your selflessness will not protect your husband. If I choose to dispose of you first it is because I consider that it will add to Mr Ansell's own grief and distress. He will know something of what I have known. He must love you. I can see that you are lovable. Besides that, you are recently married, aren't you, Helen?'

'Married this year,' said Helen. Smight's use of her first name was intimate and horrible. She felt the tears flowing again, and this time her weakness served only to irritate her. If she could have torn herself free from this floating platform, she would not have attempted to run away. She would have battled for her life against Doctor Anthony Smight. She would have bitten and scratched and gouged him like a wild animal. She would have left her marks all over him.

But she had no weapon except time. Time, she told herself, keep playing for time.

'What about Eustace Flask?' she said. 'He was a medium like your brother. And yet you . . .'

'I killed him?' said Smight. 'Is that what you were going to say, Mrs Ansell?'

Helen gulped. It was foolish perhaps to talk about this man's past murders. Smight stroked his jaw. He said, 'Well, there is no harm in explaining, I suppose. You see, I had appointed to meet Mr Eustace Flask down by the river that morning . . .'

He carried on talking but Helen was listening with only half an ear for she thought she had detected some sound from the backstage area of the theatre, a shuffling sound. Her heart leaped. There was someone here with them in the theatre! She strained to hear more while keeping her expression absolutely fixed. Fortunately Smight was still speaking, oblivious to everything else.

But Helen heard no further noises and she grew very afraid.

Afraid that she was imagining the sounds, afraid that it was no more than a draught of air pushing at a curtain. Afraid that she could not keep Smight distracted for much longer. His voice had now descended into a queer monotone and his eyes which had previously been lively had acquired a sort of stillness. She recalled that he took opium, and wondered whether she was witnessing some effect of the drug – or of its absence.

At once, Smight stopped whatever it was he'd been saying. He clapped his hands together in a soft, dismissive gesture.

'Enough of this, Mrs Ansell. Time presses on me as it presses on you. As you are aware, you are secured to this platform by wire cords. Using the ingenuity of Major Marmont's apparatus, I intend to raise the platform by a winching device which is to the side of the stage. The wires run over the rollers which are hanging above our heads. They are covered in felt so as to muffle sounds. It is an ingenious trick and I am sorry I shall never see it employed for the diversion of an audience. While you were asleep, I made some adjustments to the wiring. The cord round your neck is secured to the stage floor and will gradually tighten as I turn the winch. It is a modified form of the garrotte. They used it in Spain, they used it in India. So now I shall disappear from before your very eyes now, just like a magician, except that you will never see me again. Do not worry, Mrs Ansell, the process of being deprived of air will be brief. Briefer than drowning, I dare say.'

Helen surprised herself by laughing out loud. It might have been hysteria, she couldn't have sworn she was not hysterical, but it sounded like genuine laughter in her own ears. The eyes in Doctor Smight's elongated face stared at her in surprise. He patted her shoulder for one last time and then, as promised, he vanished.

She heard the doctor's steps crossing the stage and after that there were no more sounds until a soft click as of some gear or ratchet being engaged. She closed her eyes tight when she felt an almost imperceptible shift in the platform on which she was lying. It was inching upwards. The pressure round her neck grew tighter, and she prayed that it would be quick.

All at once there were the noises of stamping feet and shouts and cursing and scuffling. A shot rang out and her ears rang. There was the bitter smell of cordite. The pressure around her neck did not relent but it did not grow any worse. She did not dare to open her eyes even when she felt a hand again on her shoulder. Someone said something but she couldn't make out the words because her ears were still ringing. It was Doctor Smight come back again. Something must have gone wrong with the apparatus and he had returned to comfort her and to taunt her once more and it was too horrible to be endured any longer. Someone grasped her hand.

Helen Ansell opened her eyes.

Her husband Thomas was standing over her. Other faces crowded round. Some of the faces she recognized. Then the faces swam together in a kind of dancing frieze before fading away altogether into a blessed darkness.

The Trial

The jury was out for less than half an hour. The shortness of the time they had been deliberating, the sombre expression on their faces as they filed back in, the clear-cut nature of the crime committed, all of this meant that the verdict could hardly be in doubt. But the formalities had to be gone through.

The clerk of the court addressed the jury but looked steadily at the foreman.

'Gentlemen, have you agreed upon your verdict?'

'We have.'

'Do you find the prisoner guilty or not guilty of wilful murder?'

'Guilty.'

There was a sigh of satisfaction and a few whispered comments from the people crowded in the gallery, as if they had just witnessed some particularly successful trick on stage.

'And is that the verdict of you all?'

'It is.'

Turning towards the man in the dock, the clerk said, 'Prisoner at the bar, you stand convicted of the crime of wilful murder. Have you anything to say why this court should not give you the judgement according to law?'

'There is nothing to say.'

This prompted a fresh outbreak of whispering in the gallery for these were almost the only words which the prisoner had uttered during his brief trial. A court usher called for silence before going to stand next to Mr Justice Barnes. He placed a black cloth over the judge's wig.

'Anthony Smight,' said the judge, 'you have been found guilty of the heinous crime of murder upon evidence which is as stark and indubitable as any I have ever encountered in many years of passing judgement. You shot and killed a representative of the law as he was going about his duties. It was only the intervention of Superintendent Frank Harcourt and others that prevented you carrying out the wickedly planned murder of a lady, and we may say that Superintendent Harcourt gave his own life in the attempt to apprehend you. On the dreadful and abhorrent nature of the crime which you were about to commit and of other crimes which you have almost certainly committed in the recent past, I shall not dwell. I will only say that it must be particularly shocking to all honest men and women when a doctor who, by his oath, his training and, one would hope, his temperament, ought to be dedicated to the saving of life, turns to the destroying of it. Your counsel has done his best in your defence against almost impossible odds while you have chosen not to explain yourself in this court of law and instead maintained an almost Iago-like silence. I cannot but feel that your silence has been a mercy to us all since any attempt at explanation or mitigation would have been a further outrage to all decent feeling.

'I tell you now, Anthony Smight, that you can and should entertain no expectations of evading the consequences of your actions. The sentence of this court is that you be taken from hence to a lawful prison and from thence to a place of execution, and that you be there hanged by the neck until you are dead, and that your body be buried in the prison where you shall last have been confined. And may the Lord have mercy on your soul.'

Anthony Smight bowed his head slightly before he was led out of the dock by two uniformed constables. The public craned to get their last look at him. What was his expression? Was he distressed, angry, remorseful? They could tell nothing from those lined, sallow features. But Smight did glance upwards for a moment to where Tom and Helen Ansell were sitting. Was that a tiny nod he gave them, a sign of acknowledgement?

Helen gripped Tom's arm but when she rose to her feet with the rest of the court as the judge departed, she was quite composed and steady. As soon as Mr Justice Barnes had left, there was an outbreak of chatter, even some subdued laughter. Several gentlemen of the press pushed their way through the door to be first in telegraphing news of the verdict to their papers.

The same reporters had already called at Julia Howlett's house wanting to speak with Helen and get her side of the story, the sensational account of her suffering and near-death at the hands of the 'Demon Doctor', as he had been christened in the headlines. The first reporter wormed his way into Colt House on false pretences and when Tom found out who he was he wanted to punch him in the face. It was fortunate that Aunt Julia was on hand to restrain Tom and turn the reporter out, saying firmly that Mrs Ansell required rest after her dreadful ordeal, and giving orders that no one else except the police was to be admitted under any circumstances.

This did not stop the press speculating or publishing quite unfounded stories. The death of the Seldons in Norwood was laid firmly at the doctor's door, as was the murder of Eustace Flask in Durham, as well as various unsolved crimes in other cities which had no connection to him. The London journalists hared round to see Miss Ethel Smight – 'the well-known phrenologist' – in Tullis Street but they found her and her pinched-faced maid gone. The house was rented and Miss Smight had speedily decamped once her brother was arrested. Either she feared more attention from the police, who had threatened to charge her with being Doctor Tony's accomplice, or she wanted to avoid the intrusions of the press. Nevertheless the pressmen talked to a client who had had his scalp felt by her and who claimed to have experienced 'strange and sinister emanations' coming from Miss Smight's fingertips, but beyond that they discovered little.

Letters and telegrams were flying to and fro between Colt House and Helen's mother in Highbury. Mrs Scott had read, with mounting horror, the earliest accounts in the papers and had only been prevented from getting the first train north by Aunt Julia's assurances that her daughter was coping well and needed fewer, not more, visitors.

In the event, the fatal shooting of Frank Harcourt was the only charge brought against Smight and it was this which dominated the proceedings. Smight's twisted programme of revenge against those whom he believed to be responsible for his brother's suicide was scarcely referred to. He was painted by the prosecuting counsel and by the press as a clever man whose mind had been turned by vindictiveness and whose moral sense had been sapped by his opium addiction. 'For it has been well established by the leading authorities,' said the prosecution, 'that prolonged indulgence in opiates can lead to a monomaniacal state of mind in which the subject feels compelled to satisfy his desires, however bizarre, vicious or degenerate.'

Smight's counsel tried to show that his client was not fit to plead because his sanity was in doubt, but the lawyer's heart did not seem to be in the attempt. Nor was he helped by Smight's demeanour in the dock. The doctor said almost nothing and seemed impassive, even indifferent to his fate. The public and the reporters scrutinized him for traces of remorse or moral degeneracy and, although they failed to find any sign of penitence, everyone agreed that he looked evil.

So when the guilty verdict and the sentence arrived they were regarded as a formality. But a very satisfying formality.

Meanwhile Helen was indeed coping well, remarkably well, with the aftermath of her experiences and it was she who sometimes had to soothe Tom, who was full of anger at Anthony Smight as well as blaming himself for having let Helen slip away from him.

Once he had discovered that Helen was not at the Assembly Rooms with Major Marmont, he had been plunged into a near panic. Sebastian Marmont had been nearly as concerned and once they established that Helen must have been tricked by a counter-feit letter, they asked each other where she had gone. Where had she been enticed to? Marmont mentioned the Palace of Varieties behind the Court Inn. It was where some of his magical equip-ment was stored. He was renting the place while he was performing in Durham and using it as a convenient space to refine his tricks. Anyone who was familiar with his movements might be aware of that.

He'd scarcely finished explaining this when Tom demanded that Marmont take him there, this instant. By now almost two hours had passed since he had last seen Helen. Marmont instructed his three sons to remain where they were but Dilip Gopal accom-panied them as they ran through the streets of Durham and over the Elvet Bridge. A carriage pulled up by them on the bridge and Tom was relieved to see Harcourt and Traynor in the back.

Rapidly, all was made clear. The two policemen had arrived at the central station in Newcastle to be met by an officer of the city force, and informed that they were on a futile errand. The men apprehended in a swoop on a dubious area of the docks did not include Smight after all. The one thought to be the doctor had been identified – definitely identified – as a ne'er-do-well called Evans. It was unfortunate that the officer who arrested Evans was new to the force and had jumped to conclusions based on a slight physical similarity to Anthony Smight before he fired off the telegram to Durham.

When he heard the facts Traynor was immediately fearful of what might be happening back in the city and, remembering the assurances which he had given to Mr and Mrs Ansell, insisted they take the next train to Durham. Now he and Harcourt were returning to the police-house close by.

Tom breathlessly said that he very much feared that his wife had fallen into the hands of Anthony Smight. Major Marmont explained about the fake letter and his belief that Mrs Ansell and the murderous doctor might be together in the Palace of Varieties.

A force of half a dozen constables was speedily assembled and the bare circumstances outlined to them by Harcourt. They made an approach on foot to the variety hall. Tom was for running ahead and bursting into the place, but Inspector Traynor told him that this might cause the very thing they were desperate to avoid, a panicked or vindictive reaction by Smight. Sebastian Marmont held a set of keys to the theatre. He unlocked the double doors of the main entrance and a handful of men slipped into the lobby, where they were told to keep an absolute silence and not to enter the main auditorium until called for. Marmont himself, together with Dilip Gopal, Harcourt, Traynor, Tom and a couple more of the constables, crept down the alley that ran beside the wooden building. The side door, the performers' entrance, was unlocked.

The Superintendent and the Inspector went first down a short gaslit passage until they came to the flight of steps leading to the backstage area. The group paused, hardly daring to breathe. All of them could hear the sound of a man's voice. The words were indistinguishable but the low monotone carried from the stage. 'It's Smight,' mouthed Harcourt.

Tom pushed forward. His heart was beating hard and his mouth was dry. He felt a surge of hope. If Smight was there and if he was talking that could only mean that Helen was listening to him and that she was not . . . He didn't finish the thought.

William Traynor tapped his chest to indicate he would lead the way. The party crept up the stairs and clustered in the cramped area at the top. They were surrounded by boxes and scenery flats and hanging drapes. A subdued light filtered from the stage, together with the droning tones. Tom thought he recognized the voice as that of the man who had accosted them on the river-bank several days earlier, trying to hand Helen her dropped hand-kerchief.

Then there was the most extraordinary sound, the sound of cheerful laughter. And Tom knew it was Helen. The laughter was followed by footsteps crossing the stage and then an odd metallic grinding. Tom could not be held back any longer and he pushed at the heavy curtains which formed the wings of the theatre. At his heels were the others.

Tom saw Helen tied down to a kind of platform which appeared to be floating unsupported several feet above the floor. On the far side of the stage, next to a piece of apparatus equipped with gears and handles was Anthony Smight. He had been bending over the machine but at the sound of stamping feet he straight-ened up. Tom darted towards Helen, only to hear a shout of 'Don't, Mr Ansell!'

With a thrill of horror, Tom realized that not only was Helen secured by her arms and feet but that there was a thin wire pressing into her neck. Her eyes were tight shut and her face was suffused with red. If the platform shifted upwards by only an inch more she would be throttled. He seized the platform to try and push it down but it remained firmly fixed in space, held by dozens of fine wires. Off to the side he was aware of shouts and curses and the thud of police boots. There was a flash and a violent bang which left him deafened.

A body was lying in the wings next to the winding apparatus and he hoped it was Smight but, no, the doctor was still standing, waving a revolver in the air. Smight took aim at another figure, possibly Sebastian Marmont, but simultaneously with his straight-ening his arm to loose off a second shot, half a dozen individuals smothered him and brought him to the ground. The gun flew up in the air.

Tom stood by, still trying to push the floating platform down. Then he attempted to loosen the wire about Helen's neck but it was secured to a block underneath and he was terrified of increasing the pressure. He spoke to her, said her name, but did not know whether she heard. He grasped her hand and she opened her eyes, saw him and smiled. Then she closed her eyes again and seemed to lose consciousness.

Major Marmont took control of the winding mechanism and lowered the levitating platform so that the wire about Helen's neck slackened. Others freed her from the bonds about her hands and feet. Anthony Smight stood to one side, his hands already cuffed behind his back and with two of the constables gripping him tightly by either shoulder.

William Traynor went up to Smight. By now Tom's ears had stopped ringing. He heard the detective say to the doctor in a low but emphatic voice, 'You'll swing for this.'

At some point later Tom asked Helen if she remembered laughing out loud. At first she didn't wish to dwell on her captivity at the hands of Doctor Smight but, by degrees, Tom heard most of the story; Smight's explanation for his motives and actions, his desire to hurt Tom by taking her first. The crazily elaborate plan for murdering Helen.

'I wondered why he did not use the gun,' she said. 'He must have had it in his pocket and when you and the police burst in, he was quick enough to shoot poor Superintendent Harcourt. But I believe that he wanted me to suffer a little of what his brother Ernest had suffered as he drowned in the Thames. To be deprived of air, to be gasping for life. Like the Seldons, only with them he employed gas.'

Tom could say nothing. In his mind's eye, he saw Helen strapped to the levitation platform, the thin wire fastened tight about her white neck. The mark of that wire took more than two weeks to fade. Helen wore high-collared dresses to hide it. Tom turned cold at the memory as he did a dozen times a day. But now Helen was cheerful and wanted to talk.

'I saw myself as Smight must have seen me, a woman, a young woman tied to a platform on stage, for whom a tortuous death had been conceived. I was in a theatre, Tom! Even though there was no audience to see us. But it was like a scene from a melodrama where the villain has his hands on the heroine and is about to despatch her in a very lurid manner. If you are watching you may be thrilled but you also know that it is not real, it is almost absurd. You have faith too that at the last moment, the very last moment, rescue will come. The hero will burst through the window or break down the door of the cellar. He will strike out at the villain with a manly blow from his fist. He will sweep the heroine into his arms. If I was laughing it was because it was like such a scene.'

'But you did not know that rescue would come.'

'I did not know but I hoped.'

Execution

Tom and Helen Ansell had left Durham by the time sentence was carried out on Doctor Anthony Smight. The execution was fixed for three weeks after the end of the trial. There was no attempt at an appeal, no petition for clemency. Few new facts had been discovered about Smight and the story of the Demon Doctor faded from the front pages. The Durham superintendent who had been assigned by Chief Constable Huggins with the investigation of the murder of Eustace Flask, following Harcourt's own death, quietly closed the file since it was obvious that the doctor had killed the medium. No one greatly regretted Flask's demise apart, perhaps, from Julia Howlett – and she had been so absorbed in her niece's fate that she had little time to spare for 'poor Eustace'.

Smight had been an exemplary prisoner, in that he caused no trouble and made no requests. One day the governor of the gaol brought him a letter. It was an ill-written missive from George Forester, the man who had spied on the houses belonging to the Seldons and the Ansells in London. Forester, as Inspector Traynor had explained, could not square his conscience with his suspicions about the Seldons' deaths and so had informed on Smight. Naturally Forester said nothing of this in the letter but he expressed his regret that the good Doctor Tony was in gaol ('goal' as he wrote it) and his hope that he would find comfort ('cumfert') in the Lord. Oh, and Annie and the kids, specially ('spesherly') Mike, sent their loves.

Smight glanced at the letter, then screwed it up and tossed it into a corner of the cell. He was sent no other communication apart from two proposals of marriage which he never read because the governor intercepted and destroyed them. If his sister Ethel knew of his fate, she did not get in touch. He had no visitors other than, early on, his counsel wanting to discuss an appeal. Smight rejected the proposal.

If Smight was an exemplary prisoner he wasn't a popular one, in the way that some condemned men and women became popular by striking up a weird sort of friendship with the warders. Those assigned to guard Smight reminisced fondly about the recent occupants of the condemned quarter of the gaol, honest men brought down by drink or temper, everyday individuals who'd tumbled into murder by accident. They even had a good word for Mary Ann Cotton, who had been executed the previous year after an extensive poisoning spree. Mary was a dangerous bird all right, but she'd crack a joke with her keepers and pass the time of day with them, unlike the yellow-faced sour-guts presently sitting in the condemned cell. They said he was lucky. A few years earlier and the doctor would have been topped outside the gaol – or outside the new courthouse more precisely – for all the world to see. There'd have been a good turnout for a public turning-off, one to rival old Mary Cotton's.

Did Anthony Smight care about any of this? He did not appear to. He read poetry! He took his twice-daily exercise in the condemned yard which, with its high walls giving a view of nothing but sky and neighbouring chimney stacks, was like a prison within a prison. If he was pining for an opium-pipe, he did not indicate it by a single gesture or word. In fact, he continued to say almost nothing.

On the afternoon before the day of Smight's execution, the hangman William Marcraft arrived from London. He booked into one of the city's cheaper hotels and reported to the prison shortly before four o'clock, the hour stipulated in his memorandum of conditions. There he examined the scaffold and the pit in the yard, even though he was already familiar with these items. He tested the lever and trapdoors, he peered into the brick-lined pit below. He obtained details of the condemned man's weight and height from the prison doctor and snatched a look at Anthony Smight through a peephole in the cell door. He saw an individual stretched out on his bed, hands behind his head. He could not tell whether Smight was asleep.

Marcraft then returned to his inexpensive hotel and made a few calculations in a black-bound notebook which he kept for this purpose. He compared Smight's physical details with those of a couple of other individuals listed in the book. Marcraft went downstairs and had a supper of steak-and-kidney pie in the hotel dining room. He drank half a pint of porter. He was a naturally abstemious man whether in his regular trade as a barber or his occasional work as a hangman. The landlord knew the reason for Marcraft's presence in Durham as, most likely, did all of the staff, but no one said a word about it to the hangman's face. Nor did he mention it, again a condition that was laid down in his memorandum.

While William Marcraft was eating his pie, Anthony Smight was taking his last supper. He turned in at ten o'clock and, to those who inspected him throughout the night, he appeared to sleep soundly. So soundly that he had to be roused the next morning when the chaplain slipped into the cell, together with two warders. Smight had already rejected the chaplain's overtures on earlier visits and he proceeded to ignore the man as he tried a mixture of prayer, consolation and conversation while the doctor ate his breakfast. Smight did not eat much but he chewed and swallowed composedly.

Shortly before eight William Marcraft entered the cell, with the governor and another pair of warders. The hangman shook Smight's hand, a gesture that wasn't entirely courteous since it enabled him to half immobilize the condemned man as well as to gauge his nervousness by feeling him, palm to palm. But Anthony Smight's hand was dry as dust and he offered no struggle as his arms and hands were pinioned by two of the warders.

Then, with the neatness of a long-practised military drill, Smight was half-marched, half-escorted out of the cell and into the yard. It was already a fine morning, just past midsummer though no sun had yet reached the yard. Smight was placed between the posts of the scaffold and over the trapdoors which opened into the pit. He was permitted one final glimpse around, at the high walls, at the half dozen warders, the doleful-looking chaplain, the brisk-faced governor, the prison doctor, and William Marcraft himself.

Then the hangman drew the hood of coarse cloth over the doctor's face and adjusted the rope about his neck. Smight was left standing alone. There was the grating sound of a lever and the abrupt swing of the trapdoors. Smight dropped soundlessly. The rope jerked to a halt after what seemed an eternity but was scarcely a second. It quivered. What happened next was the real test of the hangman's skill. It might take minutes, even a whole quarter of an hour, for a man to die if the executioner had botched his job, signified by the continued shivering of the rope. But Marcraft was as careful in his preparations as he was restrained in his drinking habits. The rope trembled for a few instants only, and then fell still.

The witnesses crowded to the edge of the pit. Doctor Anthony Smight was dead, no question. He had died as silently as he had lived his last weeks in the condemned cell.

By half past eight the black flag had been raised above the gaol and a notice testifying to Smight's lawful execution posted on the main gate. A crowd of people quickly gathered to read it to each other and to conclude that justice had been done.

What About the Others?

And what about the other participants in this story – or some of them at any rate? None met so grisly a fate as Doctor Smight, who after being hanged was buried by the wall of the hospital prison, to join the rest of the executed men and women. If you go to search, you will find no name to mark his grave, only the date of his execution (27th July, 1874) inscribed over a down-ward-pointing arrow.

Eustace Flask fared rather better, one might say. After the arrest of Smight but before his trial, the medium was interred at a quiet ceremony in a quiet church on the fringe of the city. There were several mourners, including Julia Howlett and Septimus Sheridan, with Tom and Helen Ansell to keep them company. In addition there was a small turnout of constables and Inspector Traynor. Also present was Frank Harcourt's widow, Rhoda, who had prevailed on Traynor to escort her. She had fond memories of the deceased – all those little gifts! – and was willing to overlook the normal conventions of being in mourning for her husband to pay her respects to Flask. Then there were a few curious passers-by and droppers-in. Someone quietly but irreverently enquired, as the coffin was being borne in, whether Eustace was flinging around handfuls of flour and tambourines on the inside.

Aunt Julia had to use her influence to find a clergyman to officiate at the funeral and a cemetery willing to take Eustace's remains. His spiritualism was not approved of by the ecclesias-tical authorities in Durham and the first three clergy Julia approached had, politely, declined. But Julia was persistent, even relentless, and she eventually found a broad-minded cleric who would send Eustace packing in plain, low-church style. The oddest feature of the ceremony was the presence of a batch of paid mourners, with their professional long faces and black crêpe accessories. Aunt Julia denied that she had paid for them but no one else owned up.

Kitty Partout and Ambrose Barker did not attend Eustace's funeral. They were afraid of provoking more interest from the police. They did not stay in Durham to read about the execution of Anthony Smight in the *Advertiser*. They did not even wait for the outcome of the trial. Some instinct warned them to put a distance between themselves and this city. Besides, the rent on their house in Old Elvet had run out and so they decided to try their luck elsewhere. Not in the desperate business of enticement and robbery but by using the skills which they had acquired from Eustace Flask. Kitty had enjoyed playing the part of the Indian maid, Running Brook, and believed it would be no great step to turn herself into a fully-fledged medium. She had, almost unawares, absorbed plenty of Uncle Eustace's patter and knew the workings of the props such as the writing slate. Ambrose, glad to be reconciled with Kitty, was willing to take the more menial role of protector, carpenter and general handyman.

So Kitty and Ambrose took the train across the Pennines with their spirit cabinet and other gear stowed in the guard's van. They arrived in Carlisle. There Kitty developed her French strain. She became *Mademoiselle* Kitty Partout (always pronounced Partoo) and, once she had done a little research and felt confident enough, she claimed to be in touch with the spirit of Mary Queen of Scots who was Carlisle's most famous prisoner as well as being a French speaker. There are not many mediums who can claim to be inspired by a dead queen and she has met with some success.

Julia Howlett did not spend long in regret for the violent death of Eustace Flask but swiftly turned her attention to another object of interest. She and Septimus Sheridan were sitting quietly in the drawing-room of Colt House. Septimus was reading *The Durham Advertiser* while Julia Howlett was turning the pages of a quarterly called *The Spiritualist Adviser*.

'Septimus, I have been thinking.'

Septimus put down his paper and looked benignly at his landlady.

'Yes, Miss Howlett?'

'We have known each other these many years now.'

'Indeed we have.'

'There was a time when our friendship – I hope I may call it a friendship – threatened to turn into something different.'

Septimus noted her use of 'threatened'. But this was the first time she had raised the subject of their engagement since his arrival in Colt House as her lodger. His heart beating fast, he wondered whether he had the nerve to say what he wanted to say.

'Miss Howlett, all that is so long ago I can scarcely remember the reasons why it did not, in your apt expression, "turn into something different". But I do know that, whatever happened, it was my own fault.'

And I have regretted it ever since, he might have added.

'Let us not talk of faults or blame, Septimus,' she said. 'I think the time has come to turn over a new leaf.'

Septimus Sheridan's mouth was suddenly dry. His hands tightened on the newspaper. He could say no more than, 'It has?'

'Yes. I think it absurd that we should go on as we have been going on.'

Septimus made no reply. He was half afraid of what she might say next.

Was she about to ask him to leave Colt House? Was she about to make some roundabout suggestion of marriage? He could not decide which would be worse.

'Absurd, as I say. I have been calling you Septimus for years now while you, most politely, have always referred to me as Miss Howlett. But the time has surely come when you must – when you should – call me Julia.'

Septimus realized that he had been holding his breath. He let out a slow sigh. He rubbed at his straggly white hair. He almost smiled.

'Of course . . . Julia.'

'You see how easy it is. Do not let me interrupt your reading.'

'You are not interrupting anything. But I have just noticed an item about Major Marmont and his troupe. He is booked for a season in the Egyptian Hall.'

'Good Heavens, he is more intrepid than I thought if he is performing in Cairo.'

'The Egyptian Hall is in Piccadilly, Miss – Julia. It is a small theatre and it has a reputation for staging new magic tricks. At least that is what it says here in the paper. It also says: *Our Durham readers will no doubt be interested to hear of the progress of Major Sebastian Marmont and his Hindoo troupe after their recent and highly successful run at the Assembly Rooms. The magical Major has now repaired to the capital and two nights ago he unveiled one of his most extraordinary feats at Piccadilly's Egyptian Hall, a fashionable though not capacious venue for the latest acts from the conjuring world. We have heard of but never yet seen the famous rope trick, supposedly deriving from those fabulous lands in the Far East, and this is a deficiency that Major Marmont is determined to remedy, at least for the fortunate denizens of the metropolis. A correspondent tells us that any of our readers visiting London should be warned that the show is not for the faint-hearted but they may be assured, if they venture among the papyrus-leaf columns of the Egyptian Hall, of suspense and thrills a-plenty. It is to be hoped that if the miracle-working Major chooses to grace the north-east with his presence again he will deign to demonstrate the rope trick.'*

'Not for the faint-hearted. It sounds rather alarming to me, Septimus. I think we have had enough excitement here in Durham to last us for a year or two.'

'I agree with you, Julia.'

Septimus had recovered from the business of Eustace Flask's death. He had told no one apart from Julia and Superintendent Harcourt that he had been near the scene of the murder and, in any case, nothing had come of that since, with the arrest of Smight, the investigation came to an end. Septimus returned to his work in the cathedral library, the slow-developing study of the patristic fathers, and did his best to forget about the last few weeks. He was pleased that she was encouraging him to call her Julia. Now he had no other ambition than to be allowed to remain in Colt House as Miss Howlett's – Julia's – lodger or, perhaps more accurately, her companion.

'I'm sorry, Julia, were you saying something?'

'I too have been reading,' said Julia, indicating her copy of *The Spiritualist Adviser*. 'Although poor Eustace Flask has crossed over to the other side, the cause continues. It grows, it strengthens.'

'Of course it does, Miss – Julia.'

'I know that I am talking to a sceptic, Septimus. But even sceptics may be won round. I read in *The Adviser* of a new move-ment which is beginning in America, in New York. A woman called Madame Blavatsky has established a 'miracle club' there. It will provide clear proof that miracles can happen. The article says too that Madame Blavatsky is a Russian. She is investigating the secret lore of the Hindus, the Buddhists and the ancient Greeks, and will shortly announce the formation of a new religion.'

'A new religion? But I cannot see what is wrong with the old one.'

'Oh Septimus, you are such a stick-in-the-mud.'

Inspector William Traynor remained in Durham until a couple of days after the conclusion of Smight's trial. He did not wait for the execution. His presence wasn't necessary and he was no ghoul. He had moved out of Inspector Harcourt's house in Hallgarth Street since it would have been improper to continue to lodge with a fresh – and not unattractive – widow. Rhoda Harcourt was adequately distressed by her husband's death and, for months afterwards, she pored over the album of newspaper cuttings which she had compiled, cuttings describing the true-life drama in the Palace of Varieties. Rhoda became both tearful and proud at the references to her late husband as 'selfless' and 'heroic'. But she was not, potentially, inconsolable. For example, she was drawn, quite drawn, by the detective from Great Scotland Yard. She was aware of his bachelor status. She had even ventured to ask, in a slightly flirtatious way over the supper table, whether he was a bachelor by – how could she put this? – by conviction, or a bachelor by circumstance. Frank looked sharply at her but the Inspector did not seem put out by the question. In fact he hinted that, yes, although he might once have been disappointed in love he was now perfectly happy with his single existence.

Then the dreadful thing happened and Rhoda donned her widow's weeds, and Inspector Traynor moved into a hotel. But the Inspector uttered many kind and appropriate words after Harcourt's death. She prevailed on him to escort her to the funeral of Eustace Flask since, she said, the medium had been a good friend to both of them (Traynor was surprised to hear this).

At some point Rhoda mentioned having a sister in London, one to whom a visit was long overdue. As soon as a decent period of mourning had elapsed she might consider such a visit. William Traynor, quick to take a hint, said that if she did come to London, he could offer her a most satisfying afternoon. He explained that there was an area where prisoners' confiscated property was stored near the Yard in Whitehall Place. These were notorious prisoners, convicted of the worst or most curious crimes, and in this museum – he might go so far as to call it a museum – was a display of poisoners' phials, the spades and picks belonging to various resurrection men, the death masks of the more famous customers of the hangman, and so on. As a policeman's widow, she would surely be interested in a private tour of these criminal effects. This might not have been Rhoda Harcourt's idea of an enjoyable excursion but she put a good face on it. She promised to write to William Traynor as soon as she was free to visit London. Perhaps she was thinking of her promotion too, from a Durham Superintendent to a Great Scotland Yard Inspector.

Act Five

It is stifling in the theatre. The audience is tired but expectant. They have sat through some indifferent acts. Now they are waiting for the appearance of Major Sebastian Marmont and his travelling Hindoos. They want to see something remarkable, or at least something which will keep them in a state of happy bemusement as they make their way home. Why are the curtains staying closed for so long?

A quiet suddenly falls over the audience although it does not seem that any signal has been given. The house lights begin to dim and the stage foot-lamps too lose something of their demonic glow. There comes a queer fluting noise from the pit and the curtains part to reveal a set piece. A backdrop depicts a sandy plain with a river running through it – in India perhaps? – the whole scene surmounted by distant, snow-capped peaks. There are rocks, rocks which are artful fakery, in the fore-ground but they are interspersed with trees which look real, if unfamiliar, even foreign. Their thick drooping foliage quivers in the draughts of air from the wings. Now the light takes on a reddish tinge and through some effect, or perhaps because the audience wishes to believe it, it seems that the sun is beginning to set over an arid plain.

The silence which falls as the audience strains their eyes to take in this new setting through the thick air lasts perhaps half a minute. Then, when nothing occurs and nobody appears to break the tension, the whispers and rustlings become audible once again. Eventually, just when their patience is at breaking point, there wanders on to the stage a slight, dark-coloured individual, nonchalant as you please. Scarcely more than a boy, and a servant to judge by his simple white clothing and headgear. He is stagger-ing under the weight of a large basket chair which he places centre-stage before thinking better of it and shoving it into the shade of one of the drooping trees. The chair is a handsome object, almost a throne, with its padded arms and high back. The boy stands for a moment to admire the chair. Then there is a thunk as some object lands on the ground next to him and he jumps and looks up at the tree. Another thunk. The second object rolls across the stage. What is it? A coconut? Some other exotic fruit? Hard to see because although the light is bright it is also curiously opaque.

A kind of gibbering sound emerges from the depths of the tree and a hairy arm protrudes from the foliage. The boy shakes his fist in the direction of the arm. The members of the audience have gasped at seeing the arm. Now they laugh at the boy's anger and wonder when they will see the monkey. A sudden bark, a human bark, from the side of the stage causes the servant to jump again.

This time a man strides on in a solar topi and a white suit. He is short and spruce and has a military manner. He has a complexion the colour of teak and a fine pair of moustaches which he tugs and twirls. The boy becomes all deference, smiling and bowing him to his chair. The Major settles himself down. Another boy, as slight as the first one, enters, carrying a great palmyra leaf with which he proceeds to fan the seated white man to keep him cool under the heat of what, to judge by the glare of light on stage, is the sun as it begins its decline. A few of the people in the audience who know a bit about India nod to themselves. They've heard of these servant fellows they call 'punkah-wallahs'.

The first boy, the one who brought in the basket chair, reappears with a tray on which is a glass of amber liquid that seems to gather to itself the rays of the setting sun. The same heads in the audience nod again. The famous chota peg, to be taken in liberal quantities at the end of the day, and a very necessary help to the British in India as they bear the burden of rule.

But things go wrong before the boy even reaches the seated Major. Another coconut (or whatever it is!) falls (or is thrown!) from the tree, causing the hapless boy to stumble. The glass spills from the tray, almost sending its contents over the Major's suit. The Major rises in fury, his complexion turning even darker, the colour of the spilled whisky. The punkah-wallah backs away in alarm.

The first servant indicates the overhanging tree and makes monkey gestures as if to explain the accident but Major Marmont is having none of it, thank you very much. In fact, he seems to think he is being mocked. He shakes his head. He stamps his foot. He tugs his moustaches. He signals to the punkah-wallah, who scampers off stage with his great leaf and returns a few seconds later tugging a circular wicker basket. It is large enough to contain a small human being as is demonstrated almost straightaway when the Major lifts the lid and invites – no, orders – the first boy to climb inside. The boy does so, folding himself up like a discarded piece of clothing.

The audience is uneasy but curious. Presumably this is some kind of punishment but what is to follow? The punkah-wallah has again been sent on an errand and reappears bearing – a sword in its scabbard. It is Major Marmont's, a thing reserved for ceremonial purposes surely. But no, because now the Major impatiently takes the scabbard from the boy and withdraws the sword. He examines the thin blade, which gleams in the light. Then, without warning, he turns and plunges it into the wicker basket. From within there comes a shriek which echoes round the audience. Again and again, like a man possessed, he plunges the sword into the basket, darting round to jab the point in from every side. All this while, the noises from inside diminish, turning from shrieks to cries to whimpers . . . to silence. Even worse than this, perhaps, blood starts to seep from the basket, dripping from between the wickerwork and gathering in a pool about the base. At last the Major's fury is sated. He stops. His bloody sword droops in his hand.

It is too much for several of the women in the audience who shriek themselves hoarse and too much for at least one man, who gets up from his seat in the stalls and starts to clamber over his neighbours although whether he means to leave the theatre and summon help or to intervene himself, who knows?

But Major Marmont turns a stern eye on the audience and shakes his head. He waves the sword in the air once more. He gestures to the punkah-wallah who has been standing by all this time, horror-struck. The second boy walks warily towards the basket which stands centre stage. He lifts the lid. He peers into the interior. He looks up, horror turning to puzzlement. The Major himself peers inside. Together they tilt and angle the basket so that its interior is visible to all points of the house.

The basket is empty. No horrific corpse, no lacerated remains. Thank God for that! Then a stir from the back of the auditorium and a boy in white clothing is running down the aisle and scrambling across the pit. He leaps nimbly on to the stage. It is the boy from the basket, unharmed. Such a relief! Even the Major seems pleased. A smile splits his stern features. He pats the boy on the head. The punkah-wallah claps his hands in delight. The audience applauds.

The trio on stage turn their attention to the basket once more. There is no sign of blood, no pool of red on the boards. But the basket is no longer empty for from within its depths Major Marmont now plucks a coiled rope. He takes one end and throws it up into the air. The rope seems to hover for a moment of its own accord before beginning a sinuous ascent to the renewed sound of flute music from the pit. It stretches in a quivering line from the ground to a point below the top of the proscenium arch, seemingly held aloft by nothing at all. The music stops. By now a gentle dusk is descending on the scene. The snow-capped mountains of the backdrop are bathed in a golden light.

Suddenly from out of the tree there leaps a monkey. The audience gapes. The creature bounces up and down, it howls and it gibbers. It bares its teeth. It bounces on all fours to the footlights and stares beyond them, as if trying to pierce the darkness of the house. It capers round the Major and his boys before seizing the sword which the Major is still grasping. This wretched monkey handles the sword with the dexterity of a fencer, darting in the direction of the others, daring them to come near. Then it makes a jump for the rope. The rope sways under the monkey's impact as, grasping the sword with one paw, it scrambles up the cord, a tangle of black fur and long limbs.

Major Marmont snaps his fingers at the punkah-wallah. His meaning is obvious. Follow that monkey! The boy does not hesitate but seizes the bottom of the rope and proceeds to climb hand over hand, fast enough but with less nimbleness than the monkey. The creature meantime has reached the point where the rope appears to terminate. And then an extraordinary thing occurs. The monkey continues its climb through the empty air until it vanishes into the shadows, its long prehensile feet waving in mockery below the proscenium arch. Urged on by the Major, the punkah-wallah follows until he seems to be climbing through nothing, and his bare feet too are the last sight the audience have of him.

There is a momentary pause in the action. A silence. Then the rope stretching up from the stage and into the shadows slackens and falls down in a coiled clatter. How is the boy (and the monkey) to get back down to the ground again? Without the rope it is a dangerous even fatal drop, at least twenty feet. But there are greater dangers. The monkey has the Major's sword while the punkah-wallah is unarmed. Grunting sounds and gasps come from the area out of sight above the arch. Swishing noises, as of a blade slicing through the air. Gibbering and howling too.

The audience fear the worst. They hope for the worst. They are not to be disappointed. A pale object falls from the skies and lands with a terrible soft thump on the stage. The Major and the remaining boy, who have been gazing up with fixed expressions, start back. It is — it looks like — yes, a limb. A leg severed above the knee, all gouty with blood. Not a monkey's leg but a delicate brown one. The punkah-wallah's. This *is followed by a positive shower of limbs and parts. A foot, a pair of hands, an arm, something dreadful which might have been a torso. That monkey is as keen as a surgeon. The audience shriek as one. If they'd had time to think, they would have been worried for their own safety. What would happen if this dreadful monkey escaped from the stage and ran amok through the house? They have never seen anything so shocking. They are thoroughly enjoying themselves. It is ghastly. It is delightful.*

Another Disappearance

Tom and Helen Ansell were sitting with Major Marmont in his dressing room at the Egyptian Hall in Piccadilly. He had sent them free tickets for the show, the wicker basket trick and the Indian rope trick. He insisted they join him afterwards, claiming that he wanted to speak to them. When the Ansells arrived after the show in the dressing room backstage, they saw an object they had not yet seen. It was, explained Marmont, the new disappearing cabinet he had been working on, a device even better than the Perseus. He called it the Goldoni.

'Named after the famous Venetian magician of the eighteenth century. You've heard of him? No? Well, some say that he never existed.'

Tom and Helen were alone with the military magician. He had told Dilip Gopal to take himself and the boys to the nearest chop-house and to treat themselves to a slap-up supper to celebrate the end of the run. The Major lit a cigarette and poured a generous brandy for himself. He offered some to Tom and Helen but they refused, wanting to keep clear heads.

Like the rest of the audience, the Ansells were relieved to see the safe return of the punkah-wallah who'd ascended the rope. He appeared from the side of the stage, complete with all four limbs and quite unharmed. Tom recognized Alfred as the punkah-wallah (or perhaps Arthur) just as he thought it was probably Albert concealed inside the monkey costume. The monkey appeared from the opposite wing and he too took a bow.

The Ansells had been back in London for some weeks. Helen had horrified her mother all over again with a heavily edited account of what had happened up north, while Mrs Scott repeatedly blamed herself for despatching her daughter to persuade Aunt Julia against Eustace Flask. Tom gave a rather more detailed story to David Mackenzie and was pleased to see that even the sedate senior partner allowed his pipe to go out as he listened to the twists and turns of their adventures in Durham.

Events had brought about a kind of resolution to the double mission that Tom and Helen had been carrying out in the north. Sebastian Marmont never did complete the affidavit business since there was no chance of his recovering the Lucknow Dagger, the murder weapon used on Eustace Flask. The Dagger had been given by the Durham police for safe-keeping to Inspector Traynor (who brought it back to the Yard with the intention of donating it to the museum, whose delights he had promised to show to Rhoda Harcourt). And Aunt Julia's infatuation with the medium was over – although no one apart from Septimus Sheridan was aware of her new interest in Madame Blavatsky.

Now, in company with Sebastian Marmont, they surveyed the whole business of the Durham Deception. The Major, however, seemed uneasy. After they had complimented him on the Indian rope trick, Helen said, 'But it seems a rather ruthless departure for you, Major, that pretended killing in the basket, the limbs falling from the sky. My flesh crept.'

'It was meant to, my dear,' said the magician. But he spoke without his usual relish. 'You would prefer me to do disappearances and read minds? You don't like to think of me killing people?'

'But that is what you did, isn't it, Major?' said Tom, sensing the time had come for a final explanation. Helen and he had talked about this moment before they arrived at the theatre, wondering how to get round to the subject. Now Marmont was giving them an opening, perhaps deliberately, by his talk of killing people.

'It was you and not Anthony Smight who killed Eustace Flask.' Marmont nodded.

'I was present when he was killed. It was an accident, if you can believe me. On that morning after I'd called at his house I did indeed go in pursuit of him, though I didn't intend to. By chance I glimpsed his bright green coat as I was crossing the Elvet Bridge. He was walking down below on the river path. He saw me coming and turned aside. I confronted him in a kind of clearing in the woods and demanded he return to me the cursed Dagger. I was not frightened of Flask but I believe he was frightened of me. He drew out the Dagger and brandished it before my face. I moved to defend myself. It is many years since I was in the army, many years since my life has been in danger, but there are things which you learn and never forget. We tussled. Somehow in the struggle he was slashed across the throat. I have mentioned the dark history of the Lucknow Dagger. Lal had killed his own brother with it. It was why he fled his home. I have described before how the implement seemed to have a malign life of its own. And so it seemed in my struggle with Eustace Flask. I did not mean to kill him but he died nonetheless. I leaped back, horrified, as he tumbled to the ground with his fatal wound. I am afraid to confess that, in the heat and confusion of the moment, I did not do the honourable thing . . .'

'Which was . . .?'

'I should have stood my ground and waited for the arrival of the law. Instead I seized the Dagger and wiped at it with a handkerchief which Flask had dropped. Then I ran, taking both Dagger and handkerchief. I made some feeble amends to Flask later by paying for the mourners at his funeral. But I had no idea you were anywhere near the scene of his death, Helen.'

'Smight was also nearby,' said Helen. 'He knew or suspected you had done it. He was going to meet Eustace Flask. He told me so when he was keeping me prisoner in the Palace of Varieties.'

'Anthony Smight was a rival of mine from the Lucknow days. He maintained I had stolen his girl from him. That girl, Padma, became my beloved wife and mother to my boys. Smight had always nursed a grudge against me. If he was having a rendezvous with Flask it was no doubt to help the medium in his strategy of revenge. But he arrived too late. Although he did steal Flask's cravat-pin, perhaps thinking to use it in an attempt to blackmail me.'

'I understand now why you sent the box with the Dagger to the police station,' said Tom.

'I was appalled when I heard that you, Helen, had been apprehended,' said the Major.

'Though you pretended not to know about it.'

'There was a good deal I pretended not to know. I sent the Dagger and the bloodstained handkerchief to Harcourt together with the note proclaiming your innocence. I thought it would be sufficient to exonerate you without incriminating myself. I resorted to the childish trick of penning a nearly illiterate note—'

'Which you knew was anonymous,' said Tom. 'I remember you told us it was anonymous yet neither of us had said it was.'

'Not very conclusive, I should think,' said the Major. 'Most notes of that style sent to the police are likely to be anonymous.'

'But the box smelt of those cigarettes which you are smoking at the moment,' said Helen. 'It made me think of you at once.'

'Ah, the Luxor. Produced by the Alexandria Company of Artillery Lane, you know. Well, it was decent of you not to pass on your suspicions to Harcourt.'

'And then the hunt switched to Smight,' said Tom. 'Because he had carried out several murders already and intended to do more, it was natural that he should be thought responsible for Flask's. Whether you intended it or not, it was a piece of distraction like a conjuring trick. People stopped looking in the right direction.'

'I admit that Smight's arrest sat on my conscience,' said the Major. 'If he had been tried for the murder of Eustace Flask, I am not sure what I would have done. But he was sentenced for quite a different offence. And so everyone assumes that he did for Flask too. Except you, my dear friends.'

'Yes,' said Tom.

'Are you going to inform on me?'

'You are a client of Scott, Lye & Mackenzie. I suppose this counts as a privileged communication. As you say, a man has already been executed. It is difficult to mourn for Flask. He was an unscrupulous man.'

'That is hardly cause for a death sentence. But I thank you for . . . for a kind of absolution. In any case, I and my troupe are not intending to remain in England. This was our last, positively our last, performance. We are returning to India. My brother-in-law Mr Gopal will be happy to see his homeland once more. And I cannot tell you how much I long to go back to the country of my earlier days. I have been considering exploring further. They say that in Tibet there is a sect whose members live until they are two hundred years old. That would be some trick, eh?'

Their conversation was interrupted by the return of Dilip Gopal and Alfred, Albert and Arthur from their supper in the chop-house. The immaculately suited Indian shook hands with Tom and Helen and the boys stood in a dutiful line.

'Now, how should we end the story?' said the Major.

He glanced towards the Goldoni Cabinet. It was rather larger than the Perseus Cabinet, and decorated in black and gold. It was surmounted with a kind of prow which suggested a Venetian gondola.

'I would appreciate it very much if you were to be the first witnesses to my latest creation. Please . . . examine it.'

He opened the double doors. Tom and Helen together inspected the interior of the Goldoni Cabinet. There was a gas lantern burning in the interior but there were no mirrors as far as they could see. The walls were lined in rich paper but there was a lack of hidden compartments, of secret doors. They walked round it and, again, it seemed to be a solid construction.

When they had finished their inspection, the Major said, 'It's a piece of work. I tell you, this will set the world of magic by the ears. People will talk about this trick for years to come. Now, boys, I think that there is room for all of you to fit in together.'

And, obediently, Alfred and Arthur and Albert filed into the Goldoni Cabinet, and Marmont closed the doors upon them.

'Usually, of course, you would be hearing some distracting music at this point to mask . . . well, whatever it is that needs masking. But there are no distractions here.'

He waved his arms in the direction of the cabinet. Mr Gopal opened the double doors to reveal the interior, empty. The boys were nowhere in sight. Tom and Helen were stuck between bewilderment and admiration. They had been standing only about a dozen feet away. How had the trick been accomplished?

'Now, Mr Gopal, if you please.'

The Indian stepped into the cabinet and shut the doors upon himself. The Major allowed a few moments to pass before opening them again. Mr Gopal too had vanished. Helen gasped. Tom rubbed his eyes. He wondered if they were the subjects of some mesmeric process.

As if he could read their minds – which perhaps he could – Marmont said, 'There is no mental manipulation here, Mr and Mrs Ansell. No hypnotism or forced hallucination. What you are seeing is real. Real but a trick. Like all the best tricks it is clever and simple at the same time. Now it is my turn.'

He put on his solar topi to signal his departure.

'Wait a moment, Major,' said Helen.

'At least call me Sebastian once, my dear.'

'Are we going to see you again, Sebastian?'

'You might if you visit India. But I don't think you'll see me again in the Egyptian Hall or in Piccadilly – or Regent's Street or Lambeth, for that matter.'

'You sound as if you are going off on an expedition,' said Tom. 'A voyage.'

'The voyage of illusion,' said Sebastian Marmont. Then he laughed. 'There, isn't that the kind of thing you would expect a stage magician to say? A good example of professional patter. Now –'

He bent forward and gave Helen a peck on the cheek. He stuck out a manly hand for Tom to grasp. Then he stepped up into the empty Goldoni Cabinet. 'I shall close the doors. Allow me, oh, say five seconds to make my dispensations. Then you may have a look.'

The doors clicked to. The lights in the preparation room flickered, as if blown by a draught. Aloud, Helen and Tom counted to five. As one they moved towards the cabinet. They opened the double doors. They peered inside.

The gaslight within burned as bright as ever.

But the Major had gone.